THE

W
I
N
D
O
W

AMELIA BRUNSKILL

Delacorte Press

Text copyright © 2018 by Amelia Brunskill
Jacket art copyright © 2018 by Trevillion Images/Mark Owen

All rights reserved. Published in the United States by Delacorte Press, an imprint of Random House Children's Books, a division of Penguin Random House LLC, New York.

Delacorte Press is a registered trademark and the colophon is a trademark of Penguin Random House LLC.

GetUnderlined.com

Educators and librarians, for a variety of teaching tools, visit us at RHTeachersLibrarians.com

Library of Congress Cataloging-in-Publication Data
Names: Brunskill, Amelia, author.
Title: The window / Amelia Brunskill.
Description: First edition. | New York : Delacorte Press, [2018] |
Summary: After her twin sister Anna falls to her death while sneaking out her bedroom window, high school sophomore Jess tries to learn everything she can about the sister she thought she knew and soon discovers that her twin kept many dark secrets.
Identifiers: LCCN 2017013534 | ISBN 978-1-5247-2029-2 (hc) |
ISBN 978-1-5247-2031-5 (ebook)
Subjects: | CYAC: Sisters—Fiction. | Twins—Fiction. | Grief—Fiction. | Secrets—Fiction. | Mystery and detective stories.
Classification: LCC PZ7.1.B8124 Wi 2018 | DDC [Fic]—dc23

The text of this book is set in 11.5-point Adobe Caslon.
Jacket design by Regina Flath
Interior design by Jaclyn Whalen

Printed in the United States of America
10 9 8 7 6 5 4 3 2 1
First Edition

To Kevin, the heart of my heart

Sometimes I worry that I'm not a good person.
I think I used to be.
But I haven't been good lately.

ONE

I WAS INSPECTING MY SOCKS when they called my name.

It was first-period gym class, and I'd just realized that my socks were entirely wrong. They were long and pulled up straight to midcalf, while those of every other girl in the room were short, barely visible above their sneakers.

There were obviously unwritten sock protocols. They probably weren't even new—most likely I was only catching up three months into my sophomore year. Good at school, bad at life. That could be my slogan. Anna might get a kick out of that, even if she'd pretend to disagree.

"Jess?"

Mrs. Hayes, the school counselor, was standing inside the door of the gym, her hands locked in front of her, her back rigid. The gym teacher, Ms. Turner, stood beside her. Ms. Turner looked strange. It took a second before I realized why— her face lacked its trademark scowl. Its absence worried me, but what worried me more was that she appeared to be indicating that I should leave class and go with Mrs. Hayes.

"Jess, please come with me," Mrs. Hayes said.

I got up slowly, to see if Ms. Turner would object. She did not.

MRS. HAYES AND I LEFT the gym together and walked through the long, cool hallways. The pea-green lockers and yellow linoleum floors contributed to the schoolwide symphony of poor color choices. I felt a little nauseous.

Mrs. Hayes kept glancing at me as we walked, as though she suspected I might suddenly make a break for it.

It seemed like she should say something to me, something reassuring, but she said nothing, not even where we were going. I tried to think what this might be about, tried to remember if my parents had mentioned any recent health problems in either set of my grandparents. I didn't think they had, not beyond the usual. Anna would know, though; Anna paid attention.

We turned a corner and I saw Principal Stevens standing outside her office, looking toward us. As usual, everything about her seemed intentional: her fitted gray blazer, her crisp white shirt, her dark hair, which fell in a straight, glossy bob. She motioned us inside.

My dad sat in her office, slumped in a chair. When he saw me, he jerked upright, as if he'd been pulled by invisible strings. His face was taut and his mouth vibrated at the edges.

"What's going on?" I asked. "What happened?"

"Jess," he said, staring at me. "You should sit down."

I shook my head. "No," I said. "I want to stand."

He closed his eyes. "Jess. Please sit."

There was a gravity to what he said, a gravity that pulled me into a chair.

"There was an accident, we think, and . . ." His voice faltered and then he started again.

"I'm so sorry. . . ."

More words followed, a stream of them. They didn't make any sense.

I heard his words individually. *Anna. Fell. Bad. Sorry.* They didn't—couldn't—connect with each other. It was as if they were part of a riddle I couldn't decipher. *Fell, bad, Anna, sorry. Sorry, Anna, fell, bad.*

Anna.

Bad.

Fell.

Sorry.

Eventually, they slotted together. And I knew he was wrong. He was wrong because it couldn't be true. I would have known. I would have known from the moment I woke up, from the second it happened.

"You're wrong," I said, rising from my chair.

He began to stand up. "Jess . . ."

"No," I said, as calmly as I could. "You're wrong. I'd know if anything happened to her. She'll be in class right now. You'll see."

He opened his mouth again, but I didn't wait to hear what he had to say.

THE COOL AIR OF THE hallway felt good on my skin. The office had been way too warm. The thermostat must have been broken or set incorrectly. Such overheating was careless, environmentally irresponsible. It couldn't be good for the principal either, or for the crispness of her shirts.

A hum started in my brain: *Anna, bad, fell—*

No, everything was fine. We would laugh about this later, and everything would be fine. Completely fine.

Anna would be in history right now. I'd go there and she'd be at her desk. I walked faster, trying to outpace the hum in my brain.

I was almost running by the time I reached the classroom. I looked through the window in the door, knowing it had all been some bizarre mistake, knowing I'd see her there, sitting with one hand cupped under her chin, staring at the trees outside.

I searched for her among the sea of faces in the room.

I went through them all. Once, twice. Three times.

She wasn't there.

There was only an empty desk.

Oh.

There had been no mistake. It was true, true after all.

Anna, my sister, my twin, was dead.

Oh.

I've been thinking about how to tell you what
I've done. I've been rehearsing it.
This time I'm going to pretend you can hear me.
Maybe this time it will work.

TWO

THE STRANGE THING ABOUT THE worst day of your life, the day that changes everything, is you have to live through all of it moment by moment. You have to keep breathing and walking and acting like you're still a whole person.

And that was what I'd done. Gone with my dad through the doors of the school, out to the car. Sat upright in the passenger seat as he'd driven us to the hospital. *Hospital.* I'd felt a brief flicker of hope when he'd said that word, but he'd seen it in my face and responded with a shake of his head. "No," he'd said gently. "She's not— She wasn't . . . They just had to move her. I told Mom we'd meet her there."

And now I found myself on a hospital bench with a policewoman leaning toward me, her eyebrows drawn together, her face serious. It seemed like she might have something important to tell me, so I concentrated hard in order not to miss it.

"Would you like some hot chocolate?" she asked.

"I'm sorry?"

"Hot chocolate. I could get you some. It's a bit chilly in here."

Did I want hot chocolate? Was hot chocolate something I should want right now? I looked at my dad, who sat beside me on the bench, his back upright against the wall, his gaze unfocused.

I looked back at her, still unsure of how to respond.

She patted the arm of the bench. "You know what, I'll get you a cup. That way you'll have it if you want it."

By the time I managed to nod, she'd already left.

I took a breath, inhaling the faint scent of hand sanitizer.

The policewoman returned several minutes later, cradling a large paper cup. The heat of the cup against my hands made me realize that I was cold, that I was still wearing gym shorts.

Back when we'd first arrived, we'd been met not by doctors, but by the policewoman and another police officer, a man. She'd remained quiet as he expressed his condolences and then explained that Mom had found Anna lying outside, underneath her window: eyes closed, not moving. Officers were at our house now, looking through her room, examining the backyard. The police chief was at a conference in Boise, but they'd contacted him and he was on his way back. The officer mentioned that twice, as though it should provide reassurance that this matter was being taken seriously—their fearless leader abandoning the delights of Boise.

I'd stared at him, trying to remain calm, collected. It felt important to be seen as taking the news well somehow, as if this might in some way affect the outcome. As if the outcome were still a work in progress.

He asked us some questions and we answered them mechanically, with short, clean sentences. It was hard not to feel that our responses disappointed him.

No, Anna did not have a boyfriend.

No, she had not seemed upset recently.

No, nothing noteworthy had happened last night.

After the officer stopped speaking, he'd stood, feet apart, arms folded. He bowed his head for a moment and then abruptly turned and left. The policewoman had followed close behind.

HOLDING THE CUP, I THOUGHT about what he hadn't asked—perhaps because he was being kind or because he simply hadn't thought to—which was why we hadn't noticed she was missing that morning. Because we hadn't. At breakfast, I hadn't even been worried that she wasn't there. None of us had. She was on cross-country, and even in the cold, dark mornings of late autumn, she'd often get up early to run with some of the other girls on the team, catching a ride to school with them afterward.

So she'd been gone and none of us had thought twice about it. Mom had talked about how she was going to assist with three root canals later that day, and what she wouldn't give for people to stop lying already about how much they flossed. Dad had read the paper and made cryptic comments about the news. I'd eaten toast and ignored both of them as best I could as I read my book.

I tried again to think back to the night before, to see if there was anything strange about it that hadn't occurred to me. Had Anna seemed upset? I didn't think so. If anything, she'd seemed calmer than she'd been in a while, more peaceful. Happy, almost shining with it, like she had a secret. A good one.

MY HOT CHOCOLATE WAS COLD by the time Mom joined us in the waiting room, her eyes red and wild. She didn't sit. Instead, she paced in front of us, and soon she was crying so hard that she began to hyperventilate. The policewoman re-appeared and led Mom away again, murmuring to her about taking deep breaths.

Dad had also cried—briefly, silently—but my own eyes remained dry. It was like a nerve had been severed, the wound too deep to process how badly it was going to hurt.

Dad walked to the window, which overlooked the hospital's parking lot. He leaned his forehead against the glass.

A few minutes later, a man in a long white coat came and stood by his elbow.

"Your wife's ID is all we officially need," he told my dad, his voice deep and rough. "But if you'd like to view the body, I can show it to you."

"Show my daughter to me, you mean." Dad didn't look at the man as he said it.

The man flushed and then nodded. "Sorry, yes. Show your daughter to you. Did you want to see her?"

Dad blinked fast. Then he moved his shoulders back and straightened his spine.

"Yes, I'd like to see her." As he turned, he saw me and paused, as if he'd forgotten I was there. "Stay here, Jess," he said. "I'll be back soon."

"No," I said. "I'm coming with you."

The man in the white coat shook his head. "I don't think that's a good idea."

"I'm coming with you," I repeated.

THE ELEVATOR DOORS SHUDDERED SLIGHTLY when they opened, revealing the harshly lit halls of the hospital basement.

The path to Anna was long, taking the three of us past many open doors and little side hallways.

The room we eventually entered contained several long gurneys. Only one was occupied, the body covered with a pale blue sheet.

The man walked in and stood by the gurney.

Dad took the first step forward and I followed. Every step was harder than the last.

When we stopped, the man pulled back the sheet.

And there she was.

Very still.

The man's gaze flickered between me and her, matching our faces, comparing features. Dad crossed his arms tightly around himself. I stood quietly, even as the room began gently swaying around me and the edges started to blur.

"It's her," Dad said quietly.

She was wearing a dress, one she'd bought a few months back but had never worn before. It was dark purple, her favorite color, with little pearl buttons running down the front. She had a thick cardigan on over it, and one of her hands extended from underneath the long wool sleeve, fingers bent toward her palms. It was twisted, though, at a strange angle from the rest of her body.

It was easier to look at her body, or at least the part revealed from beneath the sheet, than her face. Her face, my face—her skin pale, with a hint of blue around her mouth. I felt myself reaching up to touch my own mouth, not sure whether my skin was still warm, not sure how it could be that she was on the table and I was still upright.

I dropped my hand and took another step toward her. Then it hit me. *Lavender,* I thought. *You smell like lavender. You're wearing a dress and you smell like lavender. That's not how it's supposed to be,* I thought. *This is all wrong.*

Dad took a deep breath. "Come on," he said. "Let's go check on Mom."

"No. She shouldn't be alone," I said.

"Jess . . ."

She'll wake up, I wanted to tell him. *If I stay, I'll find a way to wake her up. If you give me a minute, I'll figure something out.* But even as I opened my mouth, the words stuck in my throat, no match for her bluing skin, for the stiffness of her twisted limbs.

WE WERE ALMOST BACK TO the elevator when something broke inside me, slamming against my organs with the force of a fist. I swerved off course, staggering away from my dad and toward the closest bathroom. Inside, I lurched to the sink and grasped it with both hands to avoid sliding down to the tiled floor. I dry-heaved into the basin as my body tried to exorcise the image of Anna's too-pale face, the knowledge that she was gone.

But it was buried deep within me and could not be extracted.

*I don't know exactly when it started, when I
decided to diverge from who I was before.
It seems like there should have been one big
moment when it happened, when it all began
spiraling down.
Doesn't it?*

THREE

MY PARENTS USED TO THINK there was something wrong with me. They never said as much, but I clearly remember long drives to meet with doctors who asked me a lot of strange questions and spent no time checking my physical health. Anna came along on those visits, but she didn't get asked those questions—she was allowed to play with toys in the corner, to write and draw on sheets of construction paper. It'd be her turn next time, our parents said when we asked about this disparity. It never was.

I knew, of course, that people found Anna easier to get along with than me. I saw how their shoulders relaxed when they interacted with her, how those same shoulders tensed when they talked to me. How she somehow knew what to do, what to say. Sometimes I'd watch her and try to mimic her, but her words and gestures felt wooden, unnatural when I performed them.

Not that it really mattered. In Birdton, Montana—population 4,258—once people decide who you are, there's little you can do to change their minds. Everything about you could change, but they'd always remember the time when someone bumped against you in the grocery store and you screamed and screamed, or how, back in kindergarten, the teacher's aide had to come with you to the bathroom so you didn't spend thirty minutes washing your hands.

Anna knew those things were only small parts of my history, not the whole of who I was. She had been the only one who'd understood that. Who had understood me.

And I thought I'd understood her too. Thought I'd known everything about her. But I kept going back to the policeman's questions: if she'd seemed upset recently, if she'd had a boyfriend. I'd said no to both, without even thinking I could be wrong.

Yet looking back, things had been different for the past few months. We'd talked less, and she'd been tired, distracted, and forgetful. She'd even snapped at me a couple of times, which she'd never done before. I'd been so sure of what we were to each other that it hadn't occurred to me that these changes were a pattern, that they might indicate some larger problem beneath the surface.

I'd been so confident when I'd said there was no boyfriend. Anna used to talk to me about boys sometimes, starting back when we'd still shared a room, her words floating down to me from the top bunk, but it had been months since she'd commented on any boy in particular. And I hadn't asked, hadn't brought anyone up. Because boys remained a question mark for me. While it had been a long time since I'd screamed at an accidental touch, wanting to touch someone or to be touched weren't feelings I understood.

Once, Anna had told me how she imagined she'd get ready for a date. "I'd want to wear a dress," she'd said, her voice dreamy. "A pretty one. And perfume. I'd want to smell like lavender."

———

CASSEROLES WERE THE STANDARD TOKENS of condolence in Birdton, and within three days of Anna's death, we received eleven of them. The only one we ate was the one from the Andersons. The Andersons were notable for being the only black family in Birdton, and their casserole was notable for being the only one without cream of mushroom soup.

I assumed when the bell rang, on the fourth day, that we were about to receive our twelfth casserole. Instead, when Dad opened the door, the policeman from the hospital was on our front porch, holding not a casserole, but a notepad.

After an awkward pause, Dad ushered him in, told him to sit anywhere he wanted. Mom asked him if he wanted coffee, or if perhaps he'd prefer tea.

"No thank you," he said politely as he sat down on the edge of a chair, notebook in hand. Unlike some of the other people who'd dropped by—neighbors and family friends who seemed ready to camp out in our living room for as long as necessary—he appeared to have an efficient visit in mind.

"I'm sorry for the delay," he began. "We've been a bit short-staffed, and there was some confusion at the beginning, so it took longer than we thought to get to this point. But I wanted to let you know that the police chief himself has been very involved in this case, and we now have some information."

He paused and looked at me and my parents, all seated on the couch across from him, as if waiting for a sign that he should continue.

I glanced at my dad. He in turn looked at my mom. Tiny as she was, all small bones and narrow shoulders, she managed to look more solid than he did at that moment. "All right," she said to the policeman. "Tell us."

The policeman nodded. "Well, we've been talking to kids

at the high school. Anna's friends and classmates. Trying to figure out if there was anything we should know about what happened."

"Anything like what?" Mom asked.

"Just standard questions. Seeing if anyone had any information that might be useful. There was a big party that night down in the quarry, and most of the kids we talked to were down there. Anyway, we managed to find someone who knew what happened."

"Who?" I asked.

"Lily Stevens."

Lily. It made sense that it would be her. She and Anna had been partnered for a history project last spring and they'd become friends—and then in the fall they'd joined cross-country together. For a long time, Lily's claim to fame had been her parents' dramatic breakup, which involved her dad hightailing to Florida with his secretary, leaving behind only a sticky note on the kitchen table. Then, over the summer she'd suddenly gotten very pretty—in a cat-eyed, witchy kind of way—gotten a boyfriend, and become completely insufferable. Pretty or not, I was fairly sure she was, and had always been, a moron, although Anna had tried to combat this idea by saying that surely Lily's being in calculus with me was solid evidence to the contrary.

"Lily's mom was out of town," the officer continued. "Some seminar on"—he blinked at his notes—"spiritual healing. Lily said that she and Anna were going to hang out at her place—have some 'girl time.' When Anna didn't show up, Lily figured she'd been caught sneaking out. So it looks like it's what we thought—that she lost her footing climbing out her window. There'll be an autopsy with a toxicology screening, but we expect that to simply confirm that's what happened." He stopped and nodded, as if to punctuate his sentence.

"'Girl time'?" I repeated, incredulous. The phrase seemed plucked from another era, conjuring images of paper dolls and lemonade, pastel-colored magazines and curling irons. "Girl time" was not what Anna had in mind for that night. "Girl time" did not involve a change of clothes or perfume. "That's what Lily said?"

He consulted his notebook, scanning the page with a quick glance, and then nodded. "Yes. Something about movies and wine coolers."

"Movies and wine coolers? Just the two of them?"

"Yes," the officer said.

"At the station, they asked if Anna had a boyfriend."

"Yes, and you said she didn't," he said. "That's what all her classmates said as well."

"I know I said that. But she was wearing a dress. She was wearing perfume—lavender."

He shrugged. "Girls do that, right?"

"Anna didn't. She and Lily weren't planning to hang out by themselves. Lily's lying."

"Jess—" Mom's voice was quiet, measured, and I turned to her, hopeful that she'd back me up on this. Instead, she shook her head. "I know this wasn't typical for Anna, but that doesn't mean Lily's lying. Isn't Lily dating some boy at school?"

I nodded. "Charlie. Charlie Strumm."

"Okay, so maybe Lily and Anna thought he and a friend of his *might* come over, but there weren't any concrete plans. Or maybe Anna just wanted to get dressed up."

I stared at her. "Since when did Anna do that? Get dressed up just to get dressed up? Put on perfume?"

"People do that sometimes, sweetheart. People change, try new things—"

"No. That doesn't make any sense. Anna was going to see someone. She was going to see a boy." I was positive. Because of the dress. Because of the perfume. Because of something even less tangible that I couldn't explain.

Mom's eyes blurred. "Please don't yell. I know you and Anna had been fighting more recently, and that must make this even harder, but—"

I shook my head, frustrated and confused. "No. We weren't *fighting*. I'm not *yelling*—" Except now I could hear it myself—how my voice had become too loud, too fast—and I could see they'd all stopped listening to what I was saying, only registering the volume and my rising panic.

"Jess . . ." Mom closed her eyes for a second. "Okay, Jess. What do you think happened? Who do you think she was meeting?"

I took a deep breath, then another. Slowing myself, trying to make it so that they could hear me again. "I don't know," I said. "I didn't— She didn't say anything to me." I paused, then turned to the policeman. "Maybe we could check her contacts on her phone? She'd have had that with her."

"I'm sorry," the officer said. "Her phone was in her pocket. It's . . ."

He spread out his hands in front of him, palms up, as if waiting for a delicate way to explain what had happened to a phone that had fallen two stories. We all waited. But there was no delicate way, and so he remained silent, his hands out, unsure of how to finish.

"Maybe you're right, Jess," Mom said quietly. The ache in her voice nestled under my skin like barbed wire. "Maybe there was a boy. Maybe there wasn't. It doesn't really change any-thing. It doesn't matter."

Dad and the police officer both nodded, as if what she'd said was both hard-won wisdom and a self-evident truth.

But I didn't nod along. Because I didn't agree.

Because to me, it *did* matter.

Because I should have known. Because we were best friends. Because we were twins.

Because I couldn't shake the idea that she'd tried to tell me and I hadn't heard her.

That somehow I'd let her slip away.

FOUR

I STOOD IN THE DOORWAY of the church. The whole space stretched out before me, rows and rows of pews with tall stained-glass windows all around, yet all I could see was the mountain of daisies overflowing the casket, obscene in their brightness. It took all I had not to picture Anna inside the casket, dressed by strangers in the clothes Mom and I had picked out for her: her favorite jeans, her favorite cable-knit sweater.

The church was empty when we arrived, but soon, people began to filter in. Some of them, when they saw me and my parents standing together, maintained a careful distance. Others beelined right for us, eyes wide, hands clasped.

A group of cross-country girls came in, with Lily hanging toward the back. They hovered nearby as my parents spoke to some people from Dad's work. Mom gave me a meaningful look, nodding in the direction of the group of girls as if I might have missed them. I ignored her—I wanted to talk to Lily alone, to find out what Anna's real plans had been for that night. When I made the mistake of glancing over at the group a second time, though, they saw me do it and took it as a signal to walk over en masse.

There was a long pause as they stared at me. Then Rachel, a brunette with rabbity teeth and a nervous smile, spoke up. "We're so sorry. Anna was . . ." She faltered and looked down at the floor.

"Great," another girl supplied, triggering a wave of nodding. "Really great."

"Thanks," I said. I wasn't sure if that was the right response, but they began nodding again, and then we all just stood there.

Rachel started to cry, a soft, hiccupping cry. No one seemed to know whether they should comfort her, so we stood silently as the tears ran down her face, leaving tracks of mascara down her cheeks.

"I think I need to go sit down," I finally said.

"Of course," someone said. I wasn't sure who said it, only that it wasn't Lily, who stayed silent in the back of the group.

My parents tried to steer me toward the front, but I shook my head. I did not want to be that close to her casket.

The three of us ended up sitting near the back, one parent on either side of me. My mom sat bolt upright, her eyes fixed ahead; my dad's posture mimicked hers, but his hands lay limp and helpless in his lap.

When the pastor came to the altar, the room went so quiet I could hear the rustle of fabric when the woman in front of me adjusted her skirt.

Then someone behind me let out a muffled sob, which was quickly echoed by someone else. I closed my eyes and hoped they'd stop—the sound was contagious, but I couldn't let myself cry. If I started, I wouldn't be able to stop. I would dissolve, leaving only a ring of salt behind. I bit my tongue until it bled and my mouth tasted like rust.

When the pastor began to speak, I tried to focus on him and blur out the sound of the people crying around me, yet his words stirred up another unwanted emotion: anger. Because he was talking about angels being returned to heaven, about lambs and shepherds, about things that had nothing to do with Anna. Nothing to do with the person who'd made terrible jokes under her breath, who'd tried to nurse injured birds back to health, who'd been the only person who ever really made me feel like I fit into the world.

To distract myself—from the sobs, from the nasal, anger-inducing voice of the pastor—I stared out at the sea of heads in front of me, trying to identify people from school.

Some teachers had come. Anna's biology teacher, Ms. Brown, sat with Mr. Tutterline, her social studies teacher. Two pews up sat Mr. Matthews, who taught English and coached cross-country, his head bent forward as if in silent prayer.

On the other side of the church, the police chief sat up so straight that his spine could have been a steel rod. His wife sat on one side of him and on the other sat John Grahn, the head of the fire department.

Behind them sat their sons, Charlie Strumm and Brian Grahn, along with Nick Anderson. All three were juniors, basketball players.

I tried to think of what connections they had to Anna. Charlie was Lily's boyfriend, so he and Anna had probably spent time around each other because of that. Brian, I remembered, had been Anna's lab partner in bio that fall. I wasn't sure about Nick. His family had moved here six years ago, which meant, by Birdton standards, he'd practically just arrived.

Perhaps, though, one of them had a much greater connection to Anna than I'd realized. Maybe one of them was even the guy Anna had planned to see that night.

Or perhaps they were all simply vultures, drawn to the spectacle of it all, feeding on the collective grief.

Maybe the guy she was going to meet hadn't even bothered to come.

I wondered if she'd thought of him when she fell.

If she'd thought of me.

AFTER THE SERVICE ENDED, WE drove behind the hearse to the cemetery, the long blackness of it stretching out in front of us, filling our windshield.

Once we arrived, the pallbearers—my dad, his two brothers, and his best friend—removed the casket from the hearse. We followed them as they slowly walked through the cemetery, each of them matching the others' tempo, as if this was something they'd practiced.

They stopped at a hole in the ground, a spot near a group of old trees.

I stared up at the trees. Almost all their leaves were gone; only a few dry ones stubbornly remained, refusing to leave the branches behind.

More words were spoken. I didn't even try to listen.

I was still staring at the trees when I heard Dad's voice close to my ear.

"It's your turn, Jess," he whispered.

I looked down and found a flower grasped between my fingers. I didn't remember someone handing it to me, didn't remember accepting it. I stared at it for another moment; then I took a step forward and tossed it onto the casket, which had been lowered into the hole. The grave. Anna's grave. The flower bounced softly against the wood before settling.

More flowers followed, until I could no longer make mine out.

Finally, Mom took a deep breath. "It's done. Let's go to the car, sweetheart."

We started to make our way back to the car. Halfway there, my parents were waylaid by friends, so I turned away and watched as people continued toward their cars.

Watched Ms. Brown pause at another grave on the way and lightly touch the stone.

Watched one of my uncles pause at the edge of the grass and hug his wife, my aunt, close.

Watched Charlie take a discreet look around before pulling a flask out of his car. He took a drink, then offered it to Brian and Nick. Nick shook his head, but Brian took a long swig before handing it back. I looked for Lily, expecting to see her there with them. Usually she gravitated to wherever Charlie was, leaning into him as if having any air between the two of them was too much for her to bear.

Lily wasn't there, though. I searched for her among the remaining crowd, wondering if she was still with the cluster of cross-country girls. Instead, I found her lingering back by Anna's grave, finally by herself. Her hair fell around her face and her eyes were red. She was still holding a flower.

I started to walk across the grass toward her, and she

lifted her head, looking me right in the eyes. It seemed that she paused for a second, like she was waiting for me, like she wanted to tell me something I needed to know. But then she tossed her flower onto the casket and turned away, vanishing into the crowd again.

*Part of me would like to blame Lily for how it
    started, unfair as that may be.
It would be so easy to tell you that she pulled me
    in, set me on the path.
I think you'd believe me if I told you that.*

FIVE

THAT NIGHT, AFTER MY PARENTS went to bed, I went into Anna's room.

I curled up on top of her quilt, my thoughts snaking around in my mind. I tried to straighten them out, to separate them into orderly piles, but they kept wrapping around each other, slithering out of my grasp.

Anna had stopped by my room before I'd gone to sleep that night. I couldn't remember exactly what we'd said to each other. I couldn't remember waking up during the night either. I was a heavy sleeper, but surely I should've been jerked awake when Anna fell—if not by the noise, then by the sharp sensation of the cord between us being cut. It felt impossible that I'd slept through the night wrapped in blankets and the delusion that nothing had changed—that Anna was still alive, that I was still a twin.

The weight of what had happened began to press down on my lungs like a physical force, so I sat up and got out of her bed. I walked over to Anna's window, pulled open the curtains, and looked out at the ground underneath. I imagined opening the window and letting the cold air spill into the room. Imagined climbing out, carefully stretching my leg until my foot reached the very upper edge of the window below. *Who were you going to see?* I thought. *Where were you going? And why didn't you tell me?*

I put my hands on the windowsill. For a moment, I pretended my hands were her hands, that I was her and she was returning to her room, quietly closing the window again after a long night out. When my hands started to shake, I moved them back to my sides. *Stop it,* I told myself. *Go back to bed. Tomorrow you can start. Tomorrow you can see what answers you can find.*

THE WEAK WINTER SUN STRETCHED over the bed, signaling a new day. I sat up and surveyed Anna's room, trying to figure out where to start.

The police had searched her room, it was true, but they had no idea what was normal and what wasn't. I couldn't rely on them.

I decided to start with the obvious. I looked under the pillow I'd just slept on, felt underneath the mattress, still warm from my body. Nothing.

I lay down on the floor to look under her bed. It was too dark to see much, so I stuck my arm underneath and swept a cascade of clutter into the center of the room.

All told, it was pretty disgusting. Unwashed socks; dusty, dog-eared books; pens and pencils. Some of the pens had bite marks from her habit of chewing on them.

After saving a couple of the nicer, unchewed pens—most of which I was pretty sure had been mine to begin with—I pushed everything else back under the bed.

On her end table was a lamp and a framed picture of us. I was trying to be efficient, clinical, about this process, but I couldn't help picking up the picture.

It was one of my favorites of us, taken back when we were eight. We lay in the backyard grass, our heads touching, our hair swirled together, and our eyes closed, the light around us the perfect hazy gold of perfume commercials. Mom had taken it, thinking she'd captured us napping in the afternoon sun. We'd never told her that she was wrong, that we'd actually been wide-awake, trying to communicate without words, to project our thoughts to each other, concentrating so intently that we hadn't noticed her walk up and take the photograph.

In the photo, Anna's lips were curled up slightly, and mine were curled down. She looked like she knew exactly what I was thinking, and I looked like I was trying to translate a foreign language.

A tearing sensation started inside me, so I put the photograph back down, carefully placing it at the same angle to the lamp as it had been before, and opened the drawer. More pens. Several tins of breath mints. A couple of cardboard coasters with bright patterns, which was ironic considering that she— like our dad—never remembered to actually use a coaster. And that was it.

In her closet, I didn't find anything remarkable other than a rumpled hooded sweater with blue stripes that at first I couldn't place. It looked familiar, but it wasn't mine and it wasn't hers either. I looked at it more closely. Then I remembered Anna coming back from cross-country a few weeks earlier, soaking wet from an unexpected rainstorm, and Lily careening in be-hind her, laughing. Lily'd been wearing this sweater. Anna must have hung it up to dry and then forgotten about it. I made a mental note to give it back to Lily.

Next, I sat cross-legged on the floor with Anna's back-pack and pulled everything out, starting with her notebooks, looking for anything that might be useful. The first three contained only notes for school and the occasional abstract doodle.

The fourth, her English notebook, was more promising. In the back were pages of notes between her and Lily. One page started off with Lily writing a paean to her boyfriend, Charlie (*I mean, those eyelashes of his—they go on for miles! SO CUTE!! And he brought me flowers on Friday! FLOWERS!*). I tried not to imagine Anna smiling as she read it, laughing.

Farther down on the page, Lily wrote: *You like anyone? It'd be so fun for us to all go out.*

Unfortunately, Anna's response was vague: *I'll think about it.*

Fine, Lily wrote. *Better do it soon or I'll come up with a list. Make you pick one.*

I flipped to the next page, but it was blank.

Two sheets later, the notes started again.

Lily: *Oh my God, half the class is asleep, but you're so into this. You and Mr. M should just get a room already.*

Anna: *Not funny.*

Lily: *Tell me about all the great books, you bespectacled man hunk. Tell me about them slow.*

Anna: *You're an idiot.*

Lily *was* an idiot, I thought.

The rest of the notes weren't anything special, mostly complaints about it getting cold, having too much homework, and being sore from cross-country. So I set the notebooks aside and I moved on to Anna's bookshelf. My books were organized by genre, and then alphabetically by the author's last name. Anna's didn't seem to follow any system.

On the lowest shelf, there were some sheets of paper, folded small. I gently unfolded them, and on the open pages I recognized Anna's handwriting.

It was poetry. I hadn't known she wrote poetry.

I'd seen her sitting in the bleachers, waiting for cross-country to start, a notebook in her lap and a pen in her hand. She'd write and then pause, considering her next word. I'd assumed she was doing work for class, or maybe writing a story.

The poems were all about nature. The changing colors of the leaves and the promise of snow, the sound of dry grass, the feel of damp earth.

At least until I got to the last one. The last one was different.

It wasn't about nature—it was about a person.

It was a love poem.

It lacked any concrete details, such as names or physical descriptions, but it was obviously about someone she knew well. About a relationship that had been going on for some time.

I'd missed even more than I'd realized.

SIX

THERE WERE DECISIONS TO MAKE.

Green sweater? No, she'd worn that for her school picture.

Gray turtleneck? No, she'd borrowed it all the time. It probably even smelled like those mints she'd been obsessed with. I picked up the turtleneck and breathed in. Yes, mint. It was hard to put it down.

Today was going to be my first day back at school after four weeks away, and it was important, I thought, not to wear anything people might associate too closely with Anna. I'd made that mistake a few days after the funeral, when I'd worn a red sweater of hers and Mom immediately started crying when she saw it. I'd forgotten she'd knitted it for Anna—that they'd picked out the pattern and the wool together. There were land mines, I was discovering; land mines everywhere.

I ended up deciding on jeans, a black, long-sleeved T-shirt, and a navy hoodie. As far as I could remember, Anna had never borrowed them. They were absent of memories.

Which was good. Because today I didn't want memories. Today I was going to talk to Lily. I was going to make her tell me what really happened. I had waited long enough.

ANNA AND I HAD BEEN packing our own lunches since we were nine, but this morning Mom insisted on packing one for me. She offered me a ride to school too, although I'd always taken the bus.

"It might be easier that way," she said, her eyes searching mine. "And I can pick you up if you want? Leave work early?"

While I knew the offer was sincere, I couldn't help feeling that it also served as a probe of my emotional state, like her and Dad's suggestion that maybe I should speak with a counselor— an offer I'd politely and firmly declined. So I shook my head and told her I'd be fine.

I EXPERIENCED A PANG OF regret over my decision after climbing the steps of the bus. Standing beside the driver, I felt the weight of people looking at me, the weight of people *not* looking at me, pretending to be fascinated by something out their window or in their lap. I'd been naïve to think that what I wore might provide some shield, to think that my having the same face wouldn't trump all other details.

I sank into the nearest empty seat I could find.

AT SCHOOL I KEPT MY head down as I navigated through the mass of bodies in the hallway. I'd almost reached my first class when I saw Anna's locker.

Or, at least, the small amount of it visible behind a mountain of painted crosses, carnations, and stuffed animals in various shades of Pepto-Bismol piled in front of it.

I stopped and stared.

A sound rose from deep within my throat. A sound that was half sadness and half rage.

I reversed course.

ALL THINGS CONSIDERED, THE BATHROOM wasn't a terrible place to spend the morning. The sterile white tile, the strong smell of cleaning products, the relative lack of people were all reassuring. It felt safe.

When lunchtime rolled around, I considered and then rejected heading to the cafeteria, largely because I had no idea where I'd sit once I got there. Anna and I had always eaten together—always had all our classes together too, until they'd enacted that moronic school policy last summer about siblings not being in the same classes together. I had always resented that policy, and now I truly hated it.

My hands began trembling at the thought of all the time we'd been forced apart. It took a while for my hands to steady enough to unwrap my sandwich and take a bite.

When I did, I almost spit it right back out again.

It had the right kind of bread, the right kind of mustard, and yet something was wrong. I tasted bread, mustard, lettuce, and . . . I peeled back the slices to check. Yes, bread, mustard, and lettuce. That was it. Mom had officially made me a mustard and lettuce sandwich.

If I hadn't been so hungry, it might have been funny.

I DIDN'T LEAVE THE BATHROOM until calculus.

Just like last semester, Mr. Erickson had assigned seats,

posting the list by the door. This time, Lily was slated to sit right in front of me. Perfect.

Yet when Mr. Erickson started class, Lily's seat was still empty. For the entire period, I kept a steady eye on the door, expecting her to come in, mouthing a silent excuse to Mr. Erickson and flopping into her chair with a grand flourish. The door never opened. Lily never showed.

When the bell rang I slowly packed up my things, waiting for all the other kids to leave. Then I took a deep breath and went up to the front of the room, where Mr. Erickson was cleaning off the dry-erase board.

"Is Lily out sick?" I asked.

He turned, eraser in hand. His eyes went soft when he saw me. "Jess. I . . . I was so sorry to hear about—"

I cut him short. "Lily Stevens," I said. "Is she out sick? Or did she drop this class?"

He opened his mouth and searched my face, like he was figuring out how to get the conversation back on track. Then he shook his head. "Neither," he said. "I made the chart before I heard—Lily's gone to live with her dad in Florida."

"Florida?" I repeated, taken aback. Yet, Lily had always made a big deal out of her trips to Florida, like they were proof she was far more exotic and interesting than the rest of us. Given a chance to live there, it made sense that she'd jumped for it, even though it meant leaving her boyfriend and her friends behind.

"Yes," Mr. Erickson said. "I guess her parents decided it would be better for her to go live with him for a while."

I thought about Lily at the funeral, how she'd hung back in the group, how later she'd seen me coming and walked away. I'd thought she'd been overwhelmed, needed some time.

Apparently, I'd given her too much.

*No, I shouldn't blame anyone else. I should tell
   you the truth. I should always have told you
   the truth.*
So here it is:
*Somewhere along the line, I got tired of the
   constant comparisons.*
Tired of being the one who was nice, but boring.
The one always seen as normal, not special.
Always sitting beside you, getting Bs to your As.
*Well, except in English, of course. I was always
   better than you at making up stories.*

SEVEN

WHEN THE BUS ARRIVED THE following morning, I planned to do the same thing I had the day before—collapse into an empty seat near the front. That morning, though, the only empty seats were at the very back, which felt like miles away. Defeated, I took only a few steps in before turning to the seat closest to me.

"Do you mind if I sit here?" I asked, before I even saw who I was asking. Which turned out to be Sarah Hinter.

I knew Sarah only to the extent it's impossible not to know someone who has been in the same grade as you since kindergarten. I knew that she'd been on the cross-country team with Anna, that her personal style consisted of three constants: thick black eyeliner, black jeans, and large (black) headphones, and that her mom was widely considered the most beautiful woman in Birdton.

Sarah looked at me with a blank expression, her headphones still firmly secured to her ears. I pointed at the seat.

"Oh," she said loudly. "Sure."

She moved her coat, an enormous puffy thing that appeared fully capable of doubling as an airbag, into her lap to make room.

As I slid in next to her, the bus groaned and began moving with a jerk. I grabbed the edge of the seat to avoid pitching forward.

Sarah put her headphones around her neck, releasing the tinny sounds of a low repetitive beat. "You all right?" she asked, looking at my white knuckles still clutching the seat.

"I'm fine," I said, releasing my fingers. "I'm just concerned this bus is going to fall apart."

It wasn't really meant to be a joke, but she laughed. "What gave you that impression—the rattling noise or the lurching?"

"Both."

"Well, if it makes you feel any better, it's not just you. The driver claims he can't hear it, but I'm pretty sure he won't admit anything is wrong with this bus until it spontaneously bursts into flames."

"Thanks for that comforting image."

"Anytime," she said, flashing a quick grin as she pulled up her headphones again.

Okay, I thought as I closed my eyes, hoping to nap for the rest of the ride. *You found a seat, talked to another person. That's a good step. That's good practice for what you'll need to do next.* Which was getting Lily's phone number from the person I knew would have it: Charlie.

BY LUNCH, I STILL HADN'T managed to find Charlie. Or, rather, I'd found him—twice—but the first time he'd been surrounded by other basketball players, and the second, he'd been walking so fast that I'd have had to literally sprint down the hallway to catch up. And it's hard to casually ask for a phone number when you're struggling to breathe.

So instead, I was back in the bathroom stall, staring at my sandwich. This time when I gingerly peeled back the bread, I found that there wasn't even lettuce inside—nothing but a slick of yellow mustard against the white bread. Fortunately, I'd come prepared. Last night, I'd snuck into the kitchen after my parents went to bed and made my own sandwich as backup in case the mustard sandwich wasn't a fluke. Now it looked like that would need to be my official new system unless I wanted to either starve or inform my grieving mother that she'd been making me condiment sandwiches.

I set aside my mustard monstrosity and began unwrapping the sandwich I'd made.

When the main door swung open, I paused. While the bathroom was probably the cleanest place in this building, I didn't exactly want people knowing I was eating in here.

There was the sound of heavy backpacks landing on the tile floor in front of the sinks, and then zippers being undone. Apparently, it was primping time. I hoped they'd be quick about it. Yesterday afternoon, some girl had stayed in the bathroom for almost fifteen minutes, screaming into her phone at someone who was either her mother or her boyfriend (she hated them, they were too controlling, and she didn't appreciate their comments about her weight).

"God, I can't believe I got stuck with Mona as my lab partner in chem instead of Stephen," one girl said.

"Thanks, babe," someone, presumably Mona, replied. As far as I knew, there was only one Mona in the school: Mona Addle. She was a sophomore also, but we ran in very different crowds. She'd been a cheerleader freshman year.

"Okay, you know I love you, but I *love* love Stephen. Or I would if he'd let me. I sat right next to him so we'd get paired up, but Mr. Ryers is, like, against young love or something, I swear."

There was a snort of laughter from a third girl. "Whatever, he probably takes lousy notes. Paired with Mona, you'll actually pass. Besides, you're lucky you aren't taking bio. Ms. Tattin has gone completely insane. There are all these crazy labs—it's like it's never occurred to her that we might have other classes."

"They're all insane," Mona said. "Matthews is having us read practically a book a week. I couldn't believe it when I saw the syllabus. Then, when I asked him about it, he acted like I was being lazy."

"Yeah, I used to think he was kind of hot, but now he's all mopey and distracted," the first girl said. "He almost knocked into me in the hall yesterday."

"Well, we all know why he's acting like that," the third girl said, drawing her words out low and deliberate.

Intrigued in spite of myself, I leaned forward and peered through the small gap at the edge of the door. I saw the back of a glossy brown bob and skinny shoulders: Lauren Chambers, known for her big eyes and sharp tongue. Most of the unpleasant but accurate rumors at school could be traced back to her. Beth McConey and Mona, her inner circle, turned toward her in perfect sync, like trained dolphins performing for fish.

"No, I don't," said Beth. "Please tell me it's something good, like he got caught shooting up or something."

"No," Lauren said, shaking her head, a tiny smile on her mouth. "Nothing like that."

"What, then?"

"It's Anna."

Anna?

Beth frowned. "What about Anna? I mean, it's super sad and

all, but most people aren't trying to mow me down in the hall because of it."

Lauren leaned toward the mirror and slowly applied a light coat of foundation to her nose. "Mr. Matthews was weird about her," she said.

"Oh yeah?" Mona asked as she applied some mascara. "Weird how?"

"In cross-country he was always taking her aside, going on about how much potential she had, excusing any of her absences." She lowered her voice. "It was creepy. Like he had a thing for her."

She let that hang there for a second before she pulled her features into a pious expression. "I'm not saying he did, necessarily, just that that's what it looked like."

"Eww," Beth said. "That's revolting. The police interviewed everyone on cross-country, right? Did you say anything to them?"

Lauren glanced at Mona, who'd paused, mascara wand poised in the air. Then Lauren turned back to the mirror and rolled her eyes, the whites flashing. "Oh my God, Beth, it's not like I actually *saw* anything. Besides, I don't want to, like, shatter your faith in our police force, but they're incompetent assholes. No point in pouring grease on that fire." She stared at her reflection for a second, pursing her lips, and then she grabbed her bag and swept out of the bathroom. Beth and Mona followed close behind.

Only after the door banged shut did I let out my breath, the air escaping with a soft whine.

I want you to know that at first, he wasn't even part of the equation, wasn't why I started sliding out my window into the dark of night. At first it was just me and Lily, both of us bored with being ourselves, ready to test out who the world would let us be.

EIGHT

MR. MATTHEWS.

Mr. Matthews and Anna.

He had "a thing" for her.

Lily thought they "should get a room."

I took some long deep breaths and tried to dissect it all as logically as I could.

On the one hand, even if Anna had been interested in Mr. Matthews, even if Mr. Matthews had given her special attention, that didn't mean he was who she'd gone out to see that night. Having a crush on a teacher was one thing, but actually getting involved with one was totally different. And a teacher wasn't what I'd have expected for Anna at all. I'd have expected a guy at school, some guy with nice hair and a slow smile. Preferably one who read the occasional book. Not that a teacher was literally impossible—I'd seen the Lifetime movies—but I really struggled to see Anna going that route.

On the other hand, there were things it would explain, like why Lily refused to talk about what happened and why the guy hadn't come forward. And why Anna had snuck out in the middle of the night to see him.

That last one had seemed particularly strange to me. Because it would be one thing for her to sneak out and meet someone I'd already known she was seeing—I got that people did that—but I didn't understand the secrecy about the guy himself. Our parents weren't strict, had never laid down any rules about dating. At most, they might have teased her briefly if she'd told them she was going out with a guy at school, joked about making him come over for dinner so they could grill him about his intentions.

I did know that Anna had liked Mr. Matthews. As a teacher, as a coach. I remembered her telling me he asked students to call him by his first name (Ben), that he assigned good readings and thoughtful homework. She'd also mentioned that he took his role as the cross-country coach very seriously—unlike the volleyball coach, who was known for spending entire games playing Candy Crush.

And I'd been surprised when Anna had signed up for cross-country. While she'd always had an innate athleticism, always done well in gym, she'd never been particularly interested in sports. I'd assumed cross-country was Lily's idea, but now I wondered if Mr. Matthews had been part of it, even the main motivating factor.

I hated that idea. Hated the idea that Anna might have been involved with some creepy guy at least twice her age.

Still, I thought back to Mr. Matthews at the funeral, his head bowed, seated apart from the other teachers.

And I thought . . . maybe.

The first time we went to a bar, it was more of a dare than anything else—like kids taking two steps into a scary neighbor's yard. The outcome was the same too, in that less than nothing happened—we were turned away literally as soon as we walked in.

NINE

I STAYED IN THE BATHROOM for a long time, all through lunch and the next period. When I finally made my way out, there was Charlie walking by. Alone. Which was perfect, because now I needed to speak with Lily more than ever.

"Hey, Charlie," I said. "Can I talk to you for a minute?"

Charlie paused, his hands wrapped loosely around the straps of his backpack. "I'm running late for practice," he said. "So actually—"

"This is quick. I just need Lily's number."

"Lily's number?" He gave me an odd look. "I didn't realize you two were friends."

"We're not." He continued to look at me strangely, so I elaborated. "If we were friends, then I'd have her number."

"Well, sorry, but I don't have it," he said, starting to walk away.

I didn't understand. "You don't have your girlfriend's phone number?" I called after him.

He turned back around. "*Ex*-girlfriend. Lily and I aren't together anymore."

"Oh. Sorry."

He shrugged. "Well, she moved to Florida—I guess that's

how it works. Anyway, I got a new phone and I don't have her in my contacts."

"Okay, so who would have it, then? One of the girls from cross-country?"

His laughter surprised me.

"Oh, I don't think so. Lily wasn't exactly a girl's girl, if you know what I mean."

I had absolutely no idea what he meant, but I'd long learned to treat that statement as rhetorical.

"Okay, so who might, then?" I asked.

He looked at me, annoyed, like he really wanted to tell me to stop asking questions and get out of his way already. "You could try Brian," he said. "He'd probably have it."

I FOUND BRIAN SHOOTING HOOPS in the gym. He was dribbling back after making a basket when he saw me standing silently in the doorway. The ball bounced twice before he started dribbling again.

"Has nobody ever told you it's creepy to watch people like that?" he asked.

I shrugged. "You were concentrating. I didn't want to interrupt."

The ball hit the floor another two times as he stood there staring at me. "Is there something you want, Jess?"

"Do you have Lily's phone number?"

He palmed the ball. "Why do you want her number?"

"She left a sweater in Anna's room. I wanted to get her address and send it to her. Charlie said you might have it."

He didn't say anything. This, I felt, was harder than it should be.

"Do you have it or not?" I asked. "If you don't, I'll ask her mom." I didn't relish this idea, since Lily's mom was a new age hippie type, prone to trying to read my aura, but I'd do it if I needed to.

Brian deliberated for a moment, then shrugged. "Fine, I'll check." He walked over to his jacket, took out his phone, and made some quick flicks across the screen.

"I guess I do have it," he said, and held his phone out to me.

I took it and added Lily's number to my phone. Then I paused, curious, and scrolled from the *L*s to the *A*s. There was an entry for Anna.

"Were you and Anna friends?"

"Me and Anna?" He paused, as if surprised into considering this idea. "We were lab partners and our friends were together," he said eventually. "We weren't exactly close or anything."

"She said you were a good lab partner," I said. "Better than she'd expected, anyway."

His mouth twitched. "Funny, that first part sounds like her, and then that second part sounds a lot more like you." He stuck out his hand and motioned with his fingers. "Time to give back my phone, Jess."

TEN

WHEN I GOT BACK FROM school, I headed right to my bedroom. I braced myself against my bed and stared at Lily's number glowing on my phone screen. Then I hit the call button.

Lily answered on the second ring.

"Hello?" She sounded relaxed, bouncy—her normal, hair-tossing self.

"Hi, Lily," I said.

There was a long pause during which I realized she probably had no idea who I was.

"It's Jess," I said. "Jess Cutter." I wasn't sure why I felt the need to include my last name.

"Oh," she said. "Hi." Her voice lost its bounce, becoming guarded.

"How's Florida?" I asked. "I bet it's, uh, sunny down there."

"Yeah, it is." She paused. "Why are you calling me?"

I led with the easy part, hoping she'd relax again, let her guard down. "I found a sweater of yours," I said. "I was wondering if you wanted it."

"A sweater?"

"Yes. It has a hood and blue stripes. You must have left it

here." I looked at it on the bed where I'd laid it out. "It's . . . cute," I added.

"Oh—I know which one you mean," she said, her voice lightening. "I totally forgot about it. I really like that sweater. I mean, I don't really need sweaters outside much, but the air-conditioning down here can be brutal."

"Sure. Did you want me to send it to you?"

"Yeah, that would be great. I'll give you my address."

"Sure," I said. "Give me a minute—I need to find something to write with."

There was a pen right in front of me, but I wandered around my room, buying myself time.

"I actually wanted to talk to you about something," I said. "About how you said that Anna was supposed to meet you that night. That the two of you were going to hang out."

There was a pause on the line. "That's right," she said carefully. "She didn't show up. I already told the police that."

"Weren't you worried when she didn't show up?"

"No."

"No?"

"Why would I be? This is Birdton we're talking about—the place where nothing happens, not somewhere she's going to get jumped in the middle of the street. Besides, it's not like we hadn't done it before—"

She stopped abruptly.

"You'd done it before? A lot?"

"That's not what I meant."

"It's what you said." I doubled down. "So who was he? The guy? The one she was going to meet. Her boyfriend?"

I expected another pause, but this time her response came back right away. "She didn't have a boyfriend."

I flinched at the hardness in her voice. I hadn't expected her to lie. Maybe to deflect or avoid the question. Not to lie outright, though. Not to me.

"I don't want to get anyone in trouble. I just need to know."

"There was no boyfriend," she said.

"I know there was a guy. I'm sure of it."

"Look, I need to go."

"Why can't you tell me?"

"Jess . . ." Then she stopped.

I waited, thinking she might be wavering.

"She was coming to see me," she said eventually. "We were going to hang out. That's all."

I shook my head in frustration. I was done with waiting now, done with being patient.

"Was it Mr. Matthews?"

"Mr. Matthews?" Her voice came out strange, the syllables of his name elongated. Because I was wrong? Because I was right? I couldn't tell.

"Yes," I said. "Mr. Matthews. Was she seeing him? Were they . . . together?"

The line filled with another long pause, like she was weighing whether to say anything. I held my arm tight, making myself stay quiet, willing myself not to rush her.

"Look, I have to go," she said finally. "I'm sorry about Anna, Jess. I really am. I wish . . . I wish she was still here."

Her voice broke, and I believed her. Believed she hadn't just left Birdton for Florida for the sun, for bragging rights. Believed that she missed Anna, if only a fraction of how much I did.

"Maybe we can talk later—" I tried.

"No," she said, her voice suddenly firm. "I'm sorry, but don't call me again. I won't answer if you do."

Before I could say anything else, the dial tone sounded in my ear.

She hadn't even given me her address.

ELEVEN

I'D THOUGHT LILY MIGHT BE bluffing. After three calls that rang only once before going to voicemail, though, it was clear that she'd already blocked my number.

I was still mulling over what to do two days later when my mom summoned me to the living room, saying that she and my dad wanted to talk to me about something.

This was not promising.

Downstairs, my parents arranged themselves on the couch across from me. They looked nervous and full of resolve.

"We've been doing some reading," Mom started.

"A *lot* of reading," Dad added.

Mom nodded. "Yes, a lot of reading."

"Good for you," I said. "I always thought you should both read more."

They turned to each other for a moment, as if to regroup.

"Sorry," Mom said. "Let me start again. The counselor at your school, Mrs. Hayes, reached out to us, and she recommended a lot of books about loss. We've been reading through them, and a number of them have really stressed the importance of structure."

She paused and took a breath. When she breathed out again, the air came slow, like a sigh.

Dad took over. "Yes, they really emphasized structure. So, while we know you aren't a big fan of group activities, we've decided it would be really beneficial for you to be part of a structured activity."

"I'm in the chess club," I reminded them. "That's a structured activity."

"When's the last time you actually went?" Mom asked.

I shrugged. While I'd signed up at the beginning of freshman year and had continued to receive their emails and newsletter, I had yet to attend a meeting. Which was probably for the best, since I didn't, technically speaking, know how to play.

"You could do some community service," Dad suggested, moving his eyes up from his hands with some effort. "Or debate, maybe? I'm sure you'd be good at that. You're very—" He paused. I could see words spinning through his head like pictures of fruit in a slot machine. *Argumentative? Combative? Unyielding?* He settled on "Rational. You're very rational."

"Yes," Mom said, her voice filled with false cheer. "Debate could be good. Community service . . . The important thing is just that you pick something and really give it a chance. It could take a while, but in time you might find that you enjoy being part of a group."

"'Enjoy being part of a group'?" She couldn't possibly believe that. No one who knew me at all, let alone someone who'd lived with me for the past fifteen years, could believe that.

Her face reddened, but she nodded. "Yes. In time, I think you might."

It's hard to respond when people resort to blatant lying.

Then it occurred to me that this might in fact be an opportunity—a chance to do something that would usually seem suspiciously out of character.

So I looked at my parents, both so intent on turning me into a well-adjusted person by forcing me to engage with my peers.

"Okay," I said. "Fine."

Mom's shoulders dropped, as if she'd been relieved of some great burden. "Wonderful. You can take a while to think about what to join. Just let us know sometime in the next week or two—"

"Actually, I've already decided," I told her.

"Oh," she said. She sounded both pleased and surprised. "Great. What would you like to do?"

"Track," I said.

*When we tried again, at another bar farther
outside town, we expected the same thing to
happen as before. Expected them to take one
look at us and tell us to head right back out.
I don't know which of us was more surprised
when they let us stay and order a drink.*

TWELVE

ON THE BUS THE NEXT day, I stared at the seat in front of me, focusing on the spot where someone had carved their initials deep into the plastic. The lines were clean and sharp, and I wondered what they'd used to make them. Maybe an X-Acto knife? A switchblade? While I admired the neatness of their work, it was unnerving to consider how many people on the bus might have something on them that, in a pinch, could be used to kill someone.

There had again been no empty seats, so Sarah sat beside me, nodding in time to her music. *Boom, boom, boom.* Nod, nod, nod. As the nodding increased in intensity, I had a flashback to seeing her doing this before, at one of the cross-country meets my parents had dragged me to in the fall. She'd sat at the top of the bleachers, headphones on, her eyes trained on the field, her head mapping out a beat audible only to her. A thought occurred to me.

"Hey, do you do track?" I asked her.

"Sorry?" she said, lowering her headphones. "Did you say something?"

"Do you do track? Once it starts, I mean? I know you did cross-country."

"Yeah," she said. "Cross-country kind of blows, honestly—it's so boring—but track I actually like." She began to raise her headphones again and then stopped. "Wait—are you doing track? I don't remember you being on the list."

"I'm thinking of signing up late." I paused. "What's Mr. Matthews like?"

She shrugged. "He's fine."

I kept looking at her, hoping she'd elaborate.

She seemed to interpret my stare as disbelief. "No, honestly, he's okay. He and my dad are both big basketball fans, so they go out for beers occasionally and watch games, so he's maybe a bit nicer to me because of that, but he's really okay. I know some people get all bent out of shape because they think track is going to be an easy way to get out of gym and it's not, but that's on them." She said the last part with surprising forcefulness, as if their laziness were a personal affront.

"No, that's not it. I heard . . ."

That he's a pervert who had a thing for my sister. And I'm wondering if she was in love with him.

". . . that he's kind of a flirt."

She frowned. "Mr. Matthews? I don't know, I wouldn't say that. He's definitely not like Mr. Richards or anything."

Mr. Richards, the shop class teacher, was fifty if he was a day and had a huge potbelly and a receding hairline. "Who on earth would be flirting with Mr. Richards?"

"Oh, no one's flirting back, but trust me, you do not want to wear a low-cut shirt in his class. And if he asks if you want help using the circular saw, the answer is always, always no."

I shivered at the thought. "Good to know."

"Yeah. I recommend turtlenecks around that guy. Or chain

mail if you have any." She tucked her legs up against the seat and put her headphones back on.

I leaned back and tried to read my book, only to find myself rereading the same sentence over and over. I wondered if it had been a bad call to say I'd join track. Maybe Lauren didn't know what the hell she was talking about and I'd be stuck taking part in an exhausting, sweaty sport for absolutely no reason. It would be awkward, but I could still go for debate or something else less physically taxing instead. Before I signed up for track, I should see if there was any other reason to think something might have been going on between Mr. Matthews and Anna. Anything tangible.

WHEN I TRIED THE DOOR of Mr. Matthews's classroom, it eased right on open.

The walls were plastered with large posters of literary figures with inspirational quotes about the power of the written word, and the air smelled like dry-erase markers and peppermint, a strange but not entirely unpleasant combination. The whiteboard was covered with notes from his last class, his handwriting displaying the kind of perfectly formed letters typically associated with kindergarten teachers or amateur calligraphers.

The precision of his handwriting was in notable contrast to the complete shambles of his desk. His ancient PC monitor barely peered above the surrounding piles of paper, and his keyboard was swamped on all sides.

I carefully opened the shallow drawer underneath his keyboard, hoping there'd be something personal and enlightening inside, but there were only three pens, a mechanical pencil, and a pack of Mentos with the foil partially peeled back.

I shut the drawer and opened the deeper one underneath it. Here there were stapled papers sorted into hanging files. Not labeled, unfortunately. I took the papers out of the first file and began to look through them, curious to see if there was anything left from last quarter, anything from Anna. Flipping through them, I noticed that Mr. Matthews kept his comments brief, almost clipped:

> *Good job!*
> *Nice work—a real improvement from last year!*
> *Decent start, but needs a good edit.*

After looking through the stack, I returned the papers to the file. In the back of the drawer was a thin file. I pulled the whole file out this time. There were only four papers in it, all from the fall. Two of them were Anna's. One she'd only turned in the day before she died. It was unmarked. I held on to it briefly, wondering if he'd held it in his hands after learning what had happened to her. *Did you read it?* I wondered. *Did you want to? Or was it too hard to look at?* I slipped it back into the file and pulled out her second paper. This one had been graded; she'd received an A. That, in and of itself, was hardly suspicious—while her science grades had been mediocre, she'd typically done well in humanities.

I flipped the pages until I reached his comment at the back.

> *Beautiful work, Anna—you really captured the*
> *heart of the issues at play here. You are growing*

into a wonderful writer. I'm so very glad to have
a student like you in my class.

I stood there quietly, looking at his words.

> *So very glad.*
> *Student like you.*
> *Like you.*
> *You.*

I slipped the paper back into the folder, holding it by the cold metal of the staple, the paper itself feeling too personal all of a sudden, an object they'd both touched.

I don't want to believe, I thought. *But I do want to know.*

THIRTEEN

"I'M THINKING OF BUYING A new table," Mom announced at breakfast the next day, throwing the words down like a gauntlet.

Dad lowered his newspaper, and I tried to refocus my thoughts, which had been trained on planning when to ask Mr. Matthews about signing up for track. Lunch, I'd thought, might work best.

"A new table for the living room?" I asked.

"No," she said. "Although maybe we should replace that one too. I meant this one." She tapped her finger on the square kitchen table we were all sitting at. "A round one might be nice."

All three of us looked over at the empty fourth side of the table, where Anna had always sat. Where none of us had been able to bring ourselves to sit since.

"Right," Dad said. "Sure. A round one sounds good."

I'D PLANNED TO EAT MY sandwich quickly in the bathroom at lunch, as usual, and then try to find Mr. Matthews in his classroom. At 12:01, I was about to turn into the bathroom when I heard someone call out, "You heading to the cafeteria?"

I turned to see Sarah close behind me.

"Yes," I said, conscious of the weight of my lunch bag in my hand. "Just heading to the bathroom first."

"Okay," she said. "I need to grab my lunch from my locker, but could you save me a seat?"

"In the cafeteria?" I hoped there was some other interpretation for what she was saying. Not that one really sprang to mind.

"No, in the *bathroom*," she said, with a laugh. "I've been eating backstage so I can listen to my music in peace and not smell like the caf for the rest of the day, but now the drama kids are doing rehearsals there during lunch. Anyway, it feels like maybe I should just suck it up and eat at a table, you know?"

I thought about how I'd been eating, cross-legged on a closed toilet seat, balancing my lunch on my lap.

"Yes," I said. "I'll save you a seat."

IN MY HEAD, I'D BUILT up the cafeteria as this huge, imposing space, loud and intimidating. In reality, it really wasn't that big or that loud. I did wish Sarah hadn't mentioned the smell, though. I'd never noticed it before, but now the weird meaty smell assaulted my nose, leaving me a tad nauseated.

I claimed an empty table at the edge of the room and began to relax. This wasn't so terrible; plus, it was nice to be able to lay out my lunch in front of me on a flat surface, rather than crouching over it like a dog guarding a bone.

Sarah arrived a few minutes later. "God, it smells terrible in here," she said as she sat down. "I should bring an oxygen tank into this place so I don't have to actually breathe the air."

"You wouldn't be able to eat, though," I pointed out.

She gave me a quizzical look.

"With an oxygen tank," I added.

"Right," she said. "I suspected there might be some flaws with that plan."

With that, she unzipped her bag and pulled out a large paper bag, which held a seemingly endless number of small containers.

"What is all that stuff?" I asked.

"My mom's an amateur nutritionist," she said, with a roll of her eyes. "She goes on these kicks about different 'super-foods,' freaking out about how junk food—like anything with carbs or actual flavor—will rot my insides, and this is the result."

"Is any of it good?"

"*Good* is a strong word. I'd say that some of it's at least relatively normal, like blueberries and yogurt. But other stuff is vile—like wheat germ and cold, unseasoned tofu."

I looked at my apple and sandwiches.

"Guess I should be glad my mom doesn't take that active an interest in my diet."

"Yes," she said. "You should be very grateful." She opened one of the containers, which contained a substance that looked like seaweed. Then she looked over at my lunch.

"What's with the two sandwiches, though? You one of those people with the hummingbird-style metabolisms?"

"No, it's just that the one my mom made is less than appealing." I lifted one of the pieces of bread on the one Mom made, showing Sarah the slick coating of bright yellow against the white bread.

"Ugh," she said.

"Yeah. Though I should pack more food in anyway—halfway through the afternoon, I'm usually starving."

"Poor you," she said. She paused and looked down at her own lunch. "Well, could I interest you in some kale chips?"

"God, no," I said without thinking.

Her eyebrows shot up and I worried that I'd offended her. Then she broke out laughing.

SARAH PROVED TO BE A slow eater, so I ended up going to Mr. Matthews's class only after calculus ended, hoping that he hadn't headed right out as soon as his last student left. Luckily, he was still there, sitting at his desk, head down, straightening papers.

For a few moments, I stood watching him. Was he someone Anna had actually found attractive? I tried to see him through her eyes, tried to see him as a random guy rather than as a teacher. There was a certain wiry energy to him even as he sorted papers, and he had nice hair, I decided—dark brown and wavy—that was longer than you'd expect for a teacher, and it made him seem younger, more approachable. At the same time, his ears were on the large side, and while there was nothing wrong with his face, there wasn't anything terribly memorable about it either. Overall, he definitely wasn't ugly, but he was hardly a Greek god either.

I coughed to get his attention. "Mr. Matthews?"

He started and glanced up. When he saw me, he looked confused, even upset, before he managed to plaster on a more neutral expression.

"Jess. How can I help you?"

"I would like to join the track team," I said. "Please."

He looked at me blankly. "You want to join the track team?"

"Yes."

"Oh," he said. "Actually the sign-up time is over. . . ." He trailed off.

I kept standing there quietly. The sign-up period was indeed over, and yet here I was.

He straightened himself in his chair and rubbed his forehead. Stalling.

This was unusual. If anything, I'd found people had been more accommodating of me recently, more likely to bend the rules in my favor. I began to wonder if his apparent unease with my joining the team was an indication that something really had happened between him and Anna. Maybe he felt uncomfortable with me being around. Maybe I was an unpleasant reminder of what he'd done, what he'd lost.

Then again, maybe he just didn't want to deal with the logistics of a late sign-up.

Finally, he nodded. "Sorry, of course. I can make it work. We'd be happy to have you." He paused. "Uh, do you know what events you would be interested in?"

I did not. It hadn't occurred to me that I might need to feign some interest in and understanding of the whole thing.

"No," I said. "Maybe running?" Running and shot put were the only trackish things I could think of, and I couldn't even pretend to be interested in shot put.

"Five-hundred meter? Hundred meter?"

This time it was my turn to give him a blank look.

He backed off. "That's fine. We can see what suits once you get started."

I nodded.

"Well, practices start in two weeks." He furrowed his brow and fingered the worn fabric at the elbow of his sweater. "You can pick up the athletic forms from the main office. Once we get those back, we can order you a uniform—I guess you can wear your own stuff until it arrives."

I nodded again.

He attempted a smile. "Great. It'll be good to have you on the team, Anna—" He froze. His face turned white and then bright pink.

My eye twitched. Other than that, I remained perfectly still.

"Jess," he said carefully. "Good to have you on the team."

*It felt like we were in control, sneaking out and
    going to the bar—just far enough out of town
    where we wouldn't be recognized, but close
    enough that we could get back home before
    morning.
Usually we wouldn't even have more than a
    drink or two.
Sometimes I slipped coasters into my pockets,
    as proof to myself that it happened. That I
    wasn't as boring as everyone thought.*

FOURTEEN

OCCASIONALLY, I'D SEE IT COMING. The grief. Not the constant version, which always hummed in the background, like white noise, but the gut-pummeling, breath-stealing kind. Sometimes I could see it rolling in toward me, growing larger, feeding on itself, like a wave hurtling toward the shore.

Once the grief was on the horizon, all I could do was wait for the worst of it to pass, wondering all the while if maybe this time it would pull me under long enough that I wouldn't surface.

Today it happened in English class. A simple thing triggered it: the girl in front of me playing with her hair. She'd been twirling it around her hand and letting it fall back down to bounce over her shoulders. Finally, she'd picked up a pencil and twisted her hair with it, fixing it tidily into place with a last decisive thrust. Anna used to try to do that, biting her lip in concentration as she worked the pencil into her hair, only to have it all come tumbling back down. For one moment, the girl in front of me was Anna: Anna, who'd gotten the best of that stupid pencil. In the next moment, she wasn't anything like her.

Blood rushed in my ears and the space around me contracted. The wave was coming, so close I could touch it, hear its roar.

I stood up and left the classroom, ignoring the protest of Mrs. Wristel, ignoring everything between me and the door.

I was aiming for the bathroom, but I didn't make it that far down the hallway before I had to crumple down against one of the lockers. My head between my knees, I counted breaths, trying to force myself to calm down, to not let myself spiral out of control. I tried not to think about her, not to think of anything but the count of air going in and out of my lungs.

I was at over three hundred breaths when I heard footsteps coming in my direction. I kept my head down, hoping that whoever it was would ignore me and keep going. *Nothing to see here,* I thought. *Please keep right on moving along.* Instead, the footsteps slowed and then came to a stop.

Reluctantly, I looked up, expecting it to be one of the teachers, or maybe Mrs. Hayes—someone who felt morally obligated to intervene.

But it was Nick Anderson, towering above me.

"Hi," he said. Almost like he expected to see me here, like it was completely normal for me to be sitting in the empty hallway with my arms wrapped tight around my legs as though practicing for an earthquake drill. "Mind if I sit?"

I gave a stiff shrug. "It's not my hallway."

While my tone was hardly welcoming, he smiled and eased down beside me, stretching out his legs.

"Shouldn't you be in class?" I asked, irritated at how comfortable he was making himself. Which might have been hypocritical, given that I should have been in class myself. Then again, I had been crying; his excuse was less clear.

"Bathroom break," he said. "I guess that's what happens when you start off the day with a Big Gulp."

"I didn't think people actually bought those things."

"Sure they do," he said. "I mean—they're so big. And so cheap. They're like everything good about America."

I made a sound that could be charitably described as a laugh. Then I leaned my head back and stared at the wall across from me. There was a big banner posted across the top of the lockers for a dance that had been held the weekend before. The lettering was done in metallic gold, and there was liberal use of glitter glue. Subtle it was not.

"Did you go?" Nick asked, tilting his chin toward the poster.

"No," I said. "But not for lack of publicity—I have five flyers for it stuffed in my backpack."

"Five?"

I nodded. "I counted. I keep meaning to throw them out, but I only remember when I get home."

"Why don't you throw them out at home?"

I shrugged. "I worry my mom might find them and get all wistful and hint-y about how maybe I should've gone."

"Let me guess: was she the homecoming queen?" he asked with a laugh. "Trying to relive her glory days?"

That hadn't occurred to me, honestly. I realized I didn't actually know if my mom had been the homecoming queen—didn't really know anything about her life at that time, about what she'd been like. It was a jarring thought.

"Maybe." I paused. "I don't think that's most of it, though—it's more her wanting me to be okay and, you know, involved. Like if I'm around other people enough, I'll be all right, or at least I'll be someone else's problem for a while."

His smile flagged.

Maybe that was too much. Then again, too much or nothing at all was all I had. Whatever. It was his own fault. He

71

should have left me alone to begin with—just kept on walking. I didn't understand why he hadn't.

We sat there, staring at the poster's gold lettering.

"I liked Anna," Nick said quietly. "I always liked her."

I turned my head, surprised into looking at him directly for the first time since he'd sat down.

"I'd thought about asking her out before . . ." He faltered.

Before she died, I filled in. *You can say it,* I wanted to tell him. *It won't make it any more real than it already is, can't hurt me any more than it has.*

He shook his head and continued. "I didn't, though. I don't know why. Maybe I was waiting for something, but I can't remember what anymore."

He stared at the ground and then rubbed his neck and sighed.

"I'm sorry—I didn't mean to talk about that. It was stupid to bring it up."

I opened my mouth to respond, not knowing what I was going to say, except that what he'd said wasn't stupid. That it was, in a way, nice to hear someone talk about how they felt about her, instead of how sorry they were for my loss, instead of looking at me with big eyes as if waiting for me to come apart. That was too many words, though, and I didn't trust myself to say them. So we just continued to sit there, the only sound between us the muffled noise of distant classroom discussions.

After a few minutes, he stood up, stretching his arms above his head as if to break some tension there. "I should probably head back to class before someone puts out an APB," he said. "See you later, Jess."

"See you later," I echoed.

———

I WENT BACK TO ENGLISH a few minutes before the bell rang. I didn't explain myself, didn't mouth an apology to Ms. Wristel; I simply sat down at my desk and started taking notes. Not very good notes, not the kind of thorough, verbatim ones I used to take. Because in truth, I wasn't paying close attention. I was thinking about Nick, about him sitting with Brian and Charlie at the funeral. About how before, I hadn't understood why he'd come.

WHEN I GOT HOME, MOM was leaning against the kitchen wall, one hand holding her phone, the other gently pressed to her temple.

"Thank you," I heard her say into the phone. "I appreciate that."

She nodded and pressed her hand to her head a fraction harder, like she was trying to forestall a headache.

"Okay," she said. "Well, I guess that's what we expected. I guess it makes sense."

I dropped my backpack on the couch and headed into the kitchen to get some water. Mom started when I walked in. "Hi, sweetheart," she said, covering the receiver. "I'll take this upstairs. Back in a minute."

I shrugged and grabbed a glass from the cupboard.

"Yes, I'm still here," I heard her say as she headed up the stairs.

The water came out of the tap incredibly cold, just how I liked it—the cold giving it almost a mineral flavor, the way I imagined granite might taste. Anna once wrote a story after I told her that, a story about a girl who turned to rock and ice after drinking from a mysterious well. I'd asked her if the girl was supposed to be me. She'd said no. She'd paused first.

I was reading in the living room when Mom came back downstairs. "Sorry about that," she said.

"It's fine," I said as I flipped the page. "Who was it?"

"Hmmm?" she said, opening the fridge door and starting to poke around inside. "Oh, that was Stan's Furniture. There was an issue with the table I picked out, so it's going to take a bit longer than we expected."

"That's too bad," I said.

"Yes," she said. "It is." Her voice held more emotion than I'd expected, given that we were talking about a kitchen table. Maybe, I thought, I wasn't the only one who should be taking part in structured activities.

FIFTEEN

ON THE FIRST DAY OF track, I was horrified to discover there were a number of girls on the team who were *extremely* comfortable changing around other people. They were unselfconscious to a degree I simply could not understand—pausing, shirt off, bra off, to expound on nonurgent topics like their plans for the evening, or what fast-food places they were applying for work at. I held my bag of clothes tight to my chest and selected a locker as close as possible to the lone private changing room.

The curtain of the changing room was drawn, and a pair of bare feet was visible underneath, so I sat and waited on the bench in front of my locker. As I waited, I put my bag on my lap and pretended to search through it in order to avoid looking at my half-naked peers. My track uniform hadn't arrived yet, so my bag contained a pair of sweatpants and a loose T-shirt—a vastly superior outfit to the actual uniform, a sleeveless shirt and track shorts that ended a scant two inches below the crotch. Given how cold it still was outside, the tininess of the uniform seemed both indecent and inhumane.

I only looked up from my bag when I heard the clatter of the changing-room curtain being pulled back. Lauren stepped out and started when she saw me.

"What are you doing here?" she asked as I stood up. Her tone indicated that the surprise wasn't a pleasant one. Then she glanced down, took in my bag. Something shifted in her face. "Oh, are those Anna's things? I'd wondered when someone was going to come get them."

"No, these are my things," I told her. "I joined track." I paused. "Who would I ask about getting access to Anna's locker? Mr. Matthews?"

"No way, none of the male teachers are allowed in here—that'd be lawsuit city."

"Okay, who, then?"

"Find one of the female coaches—they'll be able to pull the locker codes and open it for you. If you want to do it after practice, then someone's usually still around doing grading in their office."

"Thanks," I said. "Do you know which locker was hers?"

Lauren sighed, as if she'd felt she'd already been more helpful than necessary. Then she relented and pointed. "That one," she said. I followed her finger, and there it was—the locker right next to the one I'd chosen.

OUTSIDE, THE WEATHER WAS OVERCAST and cold. It had rained earlier in the day, and the red track glistened against the wet grass, which was muddy and patchy as it began its gradual recovery from winter.

"Welcome back, you guys," Mr. Matthews said as everyone huddled together on the bleachers. "I know the weather isn't the best, but thank you for coming out. We're going to have a great season this year."

The words seemed like the right thing to say, the sort of cheery "we're all in this together" speech that coaches are supposed to give, but the tone was subdued and the smile on his face didn't reach his eyes. Of course, the damp cold meant no one exactly seemed enthusiastic. Well, no one except Sarah, who'd been weirdly bright-eyed from the moment she'd whipped her hair back into a ponytail in the locker room.

Mr. Matthews coaxed us onto the field, where he started us off with some laps. After that, we moved on to drills, which involved a lot of starting and stopping and changing of direction.

As I stumbled back and forth, my teammates running alongside me, a couple of things soon became clear:

- Running was harder than it looked;
- Sarah was by far the fastest person on the team;
- Sarah was *very* fast.

The first thing was concerning and the last two were surprising. Sarah had said that she liked track, but I'd had no sense of how good she was or how seriously she took it. It was like finding out that your lab partner who "enjoyed swimming" was going to the Olympics.

I'd somehow expected that by joining track, I would enjoy newfound proximity to Mr. Matthews and be able to spend plenty of time during practice observing him and gaining useful insights into his character. While the proximity part was true, as practice continued, I came to the disappointing realization that the latter part was pure delusion. Because at least so far, it looked like I'd be spending every minute of track either frantically trying to keep up or trying not to keel over from exhaustion.

After one particularly grueling series of sprints, Sarah came over and elbowed me roughly in the side. "Fun, right?"

I narrowed my eyes at her, noting that her eyeliner hadn't so much as smudged, while I had sweat pouring down every inch of my body.

"You may be the devil," I managed to get out.

"Aw," she said. "You'll learn to love it."

"I think I'm going to vomit. Or faint. My body can't decide which."

"All part of the process," she said.

"You should've warned me."

"Oh, don't be such a baby—you'll be totally fine. Anyway, this part isn't so bad—it's tomorrow that you'll really feel it." She flashed me an evil smile and elbowed me again.

I was about to object to all the elbowing when she called out, "Isn't that right, Mr. Matthews?"

I turned to see him passing close behind us.

He slowed down. "Isn't what right?"

"I was telling Jess that feeling rough the first day is normal."

He turned and faced me for a moment. "Completely normal. Don't worry about it."

"See?" Sarah said to me. "And besides, you have a good build for running. You'll probably turn out to be a natural."

"Like Anna," I said, carefully watching Mr. Matthews's face.

For a moment, his eyes flicked away, and he took a breath. I wondered if in that moment, he saw her, caught a glimpse of her face. If the sound of her name destabilized his heart.

"Yes," he said. "Like Anna."

And I thought I saw something in his eyes, thought there was something more he wanted to say. Then one of the other girls called out, yelling that she thought she'd pulled a muscle. He jogged off toward her, leaving me to wonder what he would've said, or if he'd even been planning to say anything at all.

WHEN PRACTICE ENDED, I LET Lauren use the changing room first. It was meant as a nice gesture, as thanks for her help before. It went utterly unacknowledged, of course.

After changing, I roamed the halls, searching for a lit classroom containing a female coach. The one I found was Ms. Turner, who also served as the school's algebra and geometry teacher.

The two of us hadn't interacted since I'd been called out of gym, since she'd stood beside Mrs. Hayes and watched as I'd left the room.

We didn't speak of that day now, when I entered the classroom and she looked up from grading papers. We barely spoke, yet soon we were trudging back to the locker room together, and then she was having me hold out the locker code book so she could squint between it and the lock as she twisted the knob to first one number, then the next. It took her two tries, with vigorous resetting in between, before the lock popped open.

"There you go," she said.

I nodded and she nodded back. She looked relieved, I thought, that I didn't need anything more from her.

I sat on the bench and waited until she and the last remaining stragglers from the track team had left before I started to go through Anna's locker.

The top shelf was relatively tidy. A stick of unscented deodorant stood on the left side, and beside it were a hairbrush and a pile of plain hairbands.

The bottom shelf was pure chaos. A pair of loose socks I

rolled together and tucked into her shoes, and then I gingerly removed and folded a T-shirt and a sports bra before packing them into the gym bag.

Toward the back of the locker, I found another, clean pair of socks that she'd already rolled together. When I picked them up, my fingertips encountered something hard underneath the cotton. Something solid and circular had been tucked up inside them. Slowly, I undid the roll and pulled out the object.

It looked like a makeup compact. When I opened it, though, I realized that it was something else entirely—something I'd seen before, in health class, but never held in my hand. A round, plastic dial of birth control pills, half empty.

I stared at it, the smooth plastic cool against the palm of my hand.

I had wanted something tangible, and here it was. Proof that she really was hiding something from me. From everyone.

We got attention, of course. Two girls in a bar,
    girls who obviously shouldn't be there. Got
    attention, especially when a song came on
    that we liked and we danced—arms up, hair
    flying.
It felt like a game, one that Lily and I were too
    smart to lose. Because two beers in, we were
    so very, very smart. Smart, and beautiful like
    diamonds that could cut right through the soft
    flesh of the men who watched us.
Their desire was a joke, because we didn't
    want them back. Even if we had, she had
    a boyfriend and I, I had common sense. I
    believed that back then.

SIXTEEN

SEX AND DEATH.

Before Anna died, I never really thought much about either of those things. Now it felt like those were the only two topics available.

Sex I'd always actively avoided thinking about. The whole thing seemed horrifying, frankly. Even leaving aside the specific mechanics of the act, that amount of touching, that amount of skin seemed utterly repellent.

I knew Anna didn't feel the same way. I'd accepted, on some level, that she probably had some kind of physical relationship with whoever she was meeting, but the pills . . . the pills felt like damning evidence of how far apart we'd drifted, of how many milestones I'd missed.

Dying, on the other hand, I hadn't avoided thinking about as such. I just hadn't spent any real time considering it. It had seemed like a pointless thing to spend any mental energy on. Where life was concerned, the options were binary: you were either alive or not.

Which had suited me fine, until now. Especially since in my experience, all dead people were old or strangers. Which didn't mean that death wasn't sad, didn't mean everyone got as many years as they wanted. It just was what it was.

Now I wanted there to be more options. I'd had no training wheels—while I'd once wound up at the hospital with a concussion and a broken arm after a rope swing accident, Anna had never had anything worse than a cold or a skinned knee.

So it simply had not occurred to me that Anna could be hurt in any serious way, let alone be suddenly gone entirely.

Of course, maybe not thinking about it was the only way to stay sane—anything else could drive a person crazy, knowing that at any moment they could lose everything.

I don't know. It's hard to say.

THE NEW TABLE ARRIVED THAT weekend.

"I really think this will be better," Mom said. "Don't you?"

"It's nice," I said. "The other one was ugly."

"I agree. Your dad bought it at a garage sale, and when he brought it home I didn't have the heart to tell him." She smiled and then shook her head. "The one nice thing about it being so ugly was that I never cared about water stains. Want to bet how long it will take before this one is marked with its first?"

I began to smile and then I paused. "Wait a minute." I jogged up to Anna's room and began to remove three of the coasters from her bedside table. Then, as I held them in my hand, I imagined these things of hers absorbing water from our glasses, the cardboard buckling over time, until one of my parents deemed them no longer usable and tossed them away. I slid them back into the drawer.

Not wanting to come back downstairs empty-handed, I walked to my room and grabbed some old paperback books I'd been planning to get rid of.

"Here you go," I said as I deposited the books on the new table. "We can use these until we get new coasters."

While I didn't expect her to give me the third degree, I did think she might at least pause, silently questioning why I thought books would make good coasters—or—even granting that—why *these* particular books, when the living room was full of contenders. But her expression didn't even flicker. "Okay," she said. "Thanks." Then she smiled at me and pulled a book over to her side of the table.

Sometimes I wondered if I should find it convenient or unnerving just how odd my parents apparently expected me to be.

Drinking in a bar, dancing. It felt like I was changing my story, rewriting my script, but it was rebellion lite—not really hurting anyone, not even myself.

The boundaries between him and me, those remained clear. I might have been pushing other lines, might have occasionally had a third beer—gotten a little blurry from it—but I didn't mess with that one. We stayed in our right roles.

SEVENTEEN

THERE HAD BEEN OCCASIONAL MOMENTS over the last week when I'd thought I might actually be getting better at this running thing. On Tuesday, my legs had hurt less, not more, than the day before, and I thought I'd turned a corner. Since then, I'd had a relapse, though, and now I was back to doing the sit-ups portion of the drills as slowly as possible to give myself a break from dashing around like a headless chicken.

Beside me, Sarah was doing her sit-ups so fast she reminded me of a rower heading right for the finish line. *I could probably bounce a quarter off her stomach*, I thought. *Not that I want to, but I bet I could. I bet it'd fly straight back up.*

Suddenly I found Mr. Matthews leaning over me. "You okay there?" he asked. "Did you get winded?"

I blinked and realized that I'd paused between sit-ups and was staring at Sarah's stomach.

"No, everything's fine," I said, and slid back down to complete another sit-up.

———

THROUGH THE SWEAT AND EXHAUSTION of my time in track, I'd learned the following about Mr. Matthews.

- He drove a green VW Beetle, but only if the weather was bad.
- He tapped the side of his leg when a race was close.
- He began to stammer when he got annoyed.

I had no idea if any of these things were relevant.

I suspected not.

Sometimes I found myself staring at him too hard in practice and had to force myself to look away. I couldn't help but wonder, if it was true about him and Anna, how it could've started. Would it have been a slow process, a gradual accumulation of a million small movements, impossible to pinpoint exactly when the line was crossed? Or was there no doubt about when they became something different to each other, when he was no longer her teacher, her coach, when she was no longer his student?

I didn't know that either. The only thing that was becoming increasingly clear was that to get any closer to the truth, I'd need to supplement track practice with observations of him in other settings.

Watching him when he wasn't expecting it. Possibly, for example, in the privacy of his home.

TWO DAYS LATER, I STRETCHED at the side of the school, attempting to look casual and sporty as I monitored the door, waiting for Mr. Matthews. Slowly, I rotated through all the stretches I knew. Once I'd exhausted those, I began making up others.

I was starting to worry he was staying late at his desk and I'd be forced to head home for dinner before he even emerged. Or that he'd used the back entrance and I was turning myself into a human pretzel for no reason.

Fortunately, not long after I'd begun to consider heading on home, he came out and started walking.

Through a combination of stretching and running in place, I maintained a reasonable distance between us, enough for plausible deniability. If he'd turned around and spotted me, then I'd decided that I'd either run right past him, with a quick, breezy wave, or go in a different direction and circle back around. He never looked back, though, just kept walking with his eyes fixed straight ahead. It was almost disappointing how little subterfuge was required.

We'd been going for about a mile when he left the sidewalk and proceeded up the walkway of a small yellow house with a neat square of grass in front and his green VW in the driveway. Along the side of the house was a narrow path to the backyard—my next logical destination.

Once he closed the door I started to jog in place, looking around to see if anyone might be watching. The street was empty and there were no faces pressed against the glass of the nearby windows, but I kept jogging in place, suddenly feeling self-conscious. Was I actually doing this? Was this actually a reasonable plan?

Then I thought of Anna. The notes between her and Lily, how Lily had lied about that night. Thought of how badly I needed to understand what had happened. To Anna, but also to us.

And I stopped jogging in place and darted down the path into his backyard.

I positioned myself beneath a large window and took some long, deep breaths to get my heartbeat back under control. It felt strange how easy it had been to do this, how no one had stopped me, how no sirens had gone off. The line between right and wrong was thinner than I'd expected.

The window had blinds, but there was a gap at the bottom that I could see through. Mr. Matthews was hanging up his coat by the door. He took off his shoes and dropped them on a shoe rack.

Then he disappeared from view. After a minute, I heard chopping sounds, from what I supposed was the kitchen.

In his absence, I inventoried the living room. It didn't take long. There were only a few pieces of furniture: a small, patterned green couch, two tall bookcases, a short-legged coffee table with two wineglasses on it, and a television mounted on the wall. There were no pictures on the walls or framed photographs on either of the bookcases. The room had a temporary feel to it, the feel of someone who hadn't really moved in yet, who was awaiting the arrival of the rest of their things. The only indication of stability, of a continuous existence, was how densely filled the bookshelves were. They were almost spilling over with books. And many, I noticed, appeared to be books of poetry.

A few minutes later, he reemerged with an oversized bowl of salad. He flopped onto the couch with it, put his feet up on the coffee table, and proceeded to flip channels, eventually settling on a documentary about insects. A cat entered the room, swaying nonchalantly, and curled up beside him. It stared intently at the television, flicking its tail with interest as an insect slowly made its way across the screen. Mr. Matthews put his hand on the cat's head and the cat permitted him to pet it for a while before it arched its back and stalked off to the far end of the couch.

During one of the commercial breaks, he picked up his phone—a clunky old one that was anything but smart. He stared at it for a long beat and then he put it back down.

I wondered who he'd been considering calling. I wondered if it was the person the second wineglass was for. If Anna had ever used that glass.

The cat began wandering around the room, eventually managing to get stuck on top of a tall bookcase. It mewed pathetically, seemingly unable to remember how it had gotten up there.

"We've done this before," Mr. Matthews said. I froze for a second before realizing he was addressing his cat. "You're perfectly capable of getting down by yourself."

The cat mewed again, and Mr. Matthews shook his head.

After that Mr. Matthews ignored the cat for a while, the cat mewing ever more sadly and loudly. During the next commercial break, he sighed and got up. He and the cat stared at each other. "You win," he said. He disappeared and then returned carrying a wooden chair.

Standing on the chair, he coaxed the cat gently to the edge of the shelf. When the cat got close, he moved his hands gently around its sides, holding it so carefully it was almost as though he weren't touching it at all.

Before I could stop myself, I wondered if he and Anna might have been like that sometimes. Like butterflies circling each other.

I backed away from the window, feeling suddenly that I'd seen enough for now. That it was time to head home.

As I walked, I told myself I might not return. That it was probably a waste of time, that even if he was the one Anna had been with, I was unlikely to learn anything from watching him like this.

But I was lying to myself. Because I knew I'd come back.

Until I knew the truth about him and Anna, I wouldn't be able to stay away.

EIGHTEEN

I'D NEVER SEEN SARAH SO happy. Her mom had the flu, so instead of her usual rabbit food, she had a tray full of Birdton High's finest cuisine in front of her.

"You wouldn't be this excited about it if you ate it every day," I said. "Maybe your mom's doing you a favor, teaching you to appreciate it properly."

"Ha," she said, not bothering to look up from her food. "You are hilariously, incredibly wrong. The only thing I appreciate is that now I don't have to try to smuggle my tray out of the cafeteria and into the theater. The lunch ladies have eagle eyes."

"Did you always eat in the theater before?"

Sarah briefly tore her gaze from her pair of English-muffin pizzas with their chunks of sausage and dollops of bright orange grease and shrugged. "Mostly. Occasionally, I'd sit with some of the other kids on track, but half the time one of the guys would try to talk to me about how hot my mom is, which was just so gross I couldn't take it."

"I always ate with Anna."

"I know," she said, wiping up some extra sauce with the edge of one of her pizzas. "I remember thinking it was funny how the two of you talked so much when you were together, yet on your own you were both pretty quiet—you in a kind of hostile way, her in more of a friendly way." She paused. "I'm sorry, is it weird to talk about her?"

"No, it's okay." I said.

"Cool," she said. "I mean—not *cool*, cool. . . . You know what I mean. I didn't want to upset you by bringing her up, but then I kinda worried I was being an asshole by not."

"Don't worry. I'll be sure to tell you if you're being an asshole."

"Thanks," she said. "I appreciate that. I think."

For a minute, we concentrated on our food, and then my curiosity got the better of me.

"So what else did you notice about us?"

"You and Anna?"

I nodded.

She stirred her chocolate pudding and considered.

"I don't know. It was like you both got lighter around each other, like you sped up. I swear, sometimes it was like you guys were talking in code or something—she'd say two words to you and you'd start cracking up. She was more self-conscious about the twin thing, though, I think."

"Self-conscious?"

"Not in a bad way, just less comfortable drawing attention to it."

"How so?" I asked.

Sarah raised a finger, closed her eyes, and ate a spoonful of pudding. Then she put down her spoon.

"Remember back in middle school when you guys both wore gold headbands one day?" she asked. "And how Chris Marset made fun of them, saying you guys were too old to do the matching thing anymore?"

I nodded.

"Well, Anna took hers off immediately, but you left yours on the whole day."

I loved that headband. I probably still had it somewhere.

But, thinking back, after that, Anna never again wanted us to get two of anything, had been sensitive about us wearing anything that matched, no matter how small it was. Sometimes she'd even change if we accidentally got dressed in clothes that were too similar. I'd assumed she just didn't want to deal with people teasing us. Maybe it wasn't that, though. Maybe she'd been embarrassed about being a twin. Or maybe, more specifically, she'd been embarrassed about being *my* twin. I pushed the thought away.

"Chris Marset was an idiot," I said.

"Correction, Chris *is* an idiot." She offered me part of her brownie, having polished off her pudding.

"I wouldn't have expected you to notice all that," I said as I accepted the piece of brownie.

"You were identical twins—everyone noticed you guys. Even if you pretty much ignored the rest of us."

"Anna didn't ignore people," I said.

"No, *she* didn't," Sarah said with a laugh. "I meant *you* as in *you*, Cutter."

"None of you liked me," I said. "I was just ignoring you all back."

"That's your version of it," she said. "I bet a lot of people would say you never gave them a chance."

Some nights after we left the bar, the road would
feel unsteady, the asphalt almost liquid
beneath the wheels of the car. I'd close my
eyes and pray that we'd make it back safely.
In those moments, all I wanted was to curl
up next to you, fall asleep listening to your
breath. Wake up centered again, on firm
ground.
Once I got home, though, I'd always go straight to
my own bed. Because I knew if you woke up
to the stink of smoke on my skin, alcohol on my
breath, you'd make me explain.
And if I did, you'd tell me to stop.

NINETEEN

MR. MATTHEWS AND I HAD settled into a rhythm.

Well, I had. He wasn't exactly aware of it.

Twice a week, I'd follow him home. I couldn't stay that long, usually only an hour. Occasionally, I'd do a weekend visit, but it was easier to go during the week. Plus, part of me felt like he should get the weekend off.

Most days followed a similar pattern: he made himself something to eat and then settled down to either read a book or watch some television. He also drank a lot of tea, always letting it steep for exactly five minutes. He set a timer. I approved.

One time, he ate quickly, took two aspirin, and then disappeared into a room I couldn't see into because the window had blinds that extended past the bottom of the pane. That day I left early. I wanted him to call someone, have someone over, go somewhere other than right home—anything that might yield something more conclusive. That hadn't happened. I'd only heard him talk to his cat, asking it if it was hungry (it always was) or if it wanted him to rub its stomach (its responses were more variable).

I wondered if this was what life was like for most people who lived alone. Quiet, contemplative, a little sad. I wondered if it was how it had always been for him. Wondered who that second wineglass had been intended for.

WHEN YOU START PAYING ATTENTION, start watching someone, it's hard to turn it off, even when they're not around. Particularly since until I could confirm something about Mr. Matthews, I wanted to be open to any stray scraps of information that might be useful, might set me on a different course.

It was exhausting, paying attention. I never used to, not really, and I missed floating through it all, oblivious.

Still, it was occasionally interesting what you could learn simply by watching people.

For example, Lauren pretends the reason she weighs nothing is because she has an amped-up metabolism. That's not true. In reality, she weighs nothing because she doesn't eat. At lunch, she moves her food around and then talks about how full she is. The rest of her friends joke about how they should watch what they eat, but they do eat, while she throws all her food away. I'd initially thought her insistence on using the changing room was about modesty, same as me, but now I thought it was more about concealing the razor sharpness of her collarbone, the starkness of her ribs.

Brian and Charlie are practically attached at the hip, although they don't seem to be able to decide whether they're best friends or worst enemies. Sometimes they seem relaxed around each other, joking and laughing—leaning against Charlie's car in the parking lot, passing a flask between them, hiding it when a teacher strolls by—other times they look like they're ready to fight to the death. When I mentioned this to Sarah, she said it made sense—that their dads were best friends from way back, so Charlie and Brian basically grew up together, were practically siblings. Which didn't follow for me, because Anna and I were never like that. Maybe brothers are different, though.

A kid in my English class, Tom, spends the whole period making elaborate and extremely violent drawings: samurai beheading each other, men with machine guns, guys being strangled with their own intestines—the last one seeming like overkill because once your intestines are outside your body, I'm pretty sure your time is limited. The drawings were pretty good, although his shading skills needed work. If I had to guess, he was on track to become either a video game designer or a serial killer. Every class, I debated whether I should sit close to him so I could watch him draw or stay as far away as possible.

Too close or too far. Maybe there was no middle distance, no safety zone. Once you begin watching people, you can end up seeing stuff you don't want to see, stuff you don't know how to handle.

TWENTY

AN UNEXPECTED BENEFIT OF BEING on the track team was that it gave me an easy excuse to get out of the house. All I had to do was put on my sweatpants and gym shoes and announce that I was going out for a run and I had a free pass. I didn't have to explain to my parents how hard it was to be at home sometimes, how without Anna it felt like the house had grown smaller and the walls were in danger of closing in.

Usually, the running ruse only lasted for a couple of blocks, until I was safely out of sight of the house. After that, I'd just walk around, carefully navigating Birdton's poorly maintained sidewalks, or sit in the park for a while, wishing I'd figured out a way to bring a book along with me without ruining the pretense. But on Sunday I found myself still running well past my usual stopping points. It was something about the weather, I thought, something about how it was bright and not too cold, with a slight breeze. It was the first day that really felt like spring was on the horizon, and instead of being simply a chore, an excuse, running felt like a reasonable thing to do. Something I might get good at. There was still a heaviness in my limbs, yet it felt more solid, more like strength than before.

I was on one of the few stretches of decent sidewalk when Nick rounded the corner and came running in my direction, head down, legs churning. I considered lowering my head as well and barreling on past. Then I thought of him in the hallway, talking about Anna.

I cleared my throat nosily.

He jerked his head up and came to a halt a few feet away.

"Hey," I said. I wasn't sure what to do with my hands suddenly, so I wrapped my arms tightly around my rib cage.

"Hey," he said. "So you're a runner, huh?"

"Technically, I suppose," I said. I was proud of how evenly my words came out. "You?"

He shrugged modestly. "I try to do a couple miles every day, more on the weekends. It helps for basketball—you know, conditioning."

"That makes sense," I said. Basketball wasn't exactly my thing—still, running seemed like a good preparation for most sports. Well, other than archery. Or golf.

We stood in silence, both shifting from leg to leg. The ease we'd briefly shared in the hallway was gone, and neither of us seemed to know what to say.

Then he smiled. "So, you want to race?"

Did I? I hadn't really thought about it.

"I guess," I said. "As long as you don't get upset if you lose."

He laughed. "Wow. Someone had their Wheaties this morning."

I shook my head. "No, raisin bran."

He opened his mouth and then closed it again.

I belatedly realized he'd been making a joke. And suddenly, all I wanted to do was get moving again. "Let's go,"

I said, and then I sprinted past him, hoping to get a good lead.

For a while, I wasn't even sure if he had followed me or if I was speeding through the park on my own. Then I glanced over my shoulder and found that he was close behind me.

Soon we ran out of the park, following an old trail that ran beside the river, snaking along a series of fields and pastures. In time, we stopped racing and instead ended up running side by side, one of us inching forward and then the other, neither of us getting too far ahead.

Running with Nick felt good—graceful, even. There was a rhythm to it, a pattern of movement between us. He had called me a runner, and I liked that. Liked the idea that maybe I was, or at least could be.

But eventually, my lungs, first politely and then insistently, indicated that a break was needed. I slowed to a jog and then stopped altogether, standing with my fists propped on my hips, trying to resist the urge to flop down onto the grass and heave in air like a drowning victim.

Nick stopped as well and stood with his head between his legs to catch his breath.

"You're good at this," he said between breaths.

"No, but I'm getting better," I said. "Slowly." Short sentences were all I could manage.

"Could've fooled me."

Our exhaustion saved us from talking more for a while, but then our breathing normalized and it felt like we should begin again. And I was so tired and loose that talking didn't feel as daunting as it usually might.

"We liked your mom's casserole," I said. "It was the best

one we got." It felt good to have gotten that out. A couple of months late, sure, but better late than never.

He looked puzzled for a second and then smiled. "Oh, that wasn't my mom's casserole. That was my dad's super-secret-recipe casserole. He takes it very seriously."

"Your dad cooks?" I knew, in theory, that men could cook, yet I'd seen little evidence in practice. Birdton was pretty far from progressive in that and many, many other ways.

"Only when he feels we've earned it," he said.

"Do you guys bring stuff to people a lot?"

"Not really. Mom does the occasional bake sale stuff for church, but that's it. And Dad's cooking is usually just for family."

"So how did we end up with the honor?"

He looked away from me, up toward the horizon. "Because I asked him to."

It was a simple, straightforward answer with infinite layers. Looking at his profile, I wondered what would've happened if he'd told Anna how he felt. Maybe it wouldn't have changed anything—maybe she'd already fallen for Mr. Matthews or whoever it was, and Nick never had a chance. Or maybe it would have changed everything.

I stood up carefully and started doing some stretching. After a moment, Nick followed suit.

We jogged back to the park. It hadn't felt that far on the way out, but now that we were tired and going slower, it seemed the route had stretched itself during our break. When we reached the park, we paused.

"Well, I'm that way," he said, pointing north.

"Yeah. And I'm that way." I pointed south.

"Okay. So . . . same time next week?"

"All right," I said, unsure whether it was a genuine suggestion or just an attempt to make our parting less awkward.

We stood there for a moment and then he jogged off.

Watching him grow smaller and smaller, I briefly found myself wanting to call out and ask him to come back, despite having no idea what I would say if he did.

*I was amazed that I got away with as much as I
did, disturbed by how easy it was to lie, to act
like nothing had changed.*

*Yet it took me by surprise when one morning
Mom said that I looked tired, asked if
anything was wrong.*

*I told her I hadn't slept well—that we'd had a
fight.*

*I told myself that was the only thing I could think
of, the only thing she'd believe.*

That's not true, though.

*There were a million other things I could've come
up with: a bad grade, a mean comment from
someone in cross-country, a snub from a boy I
liked.*

*I think what I was really doing was trying to
punish you a little, because you should have
noticed. You should have seen through the lies
about where I was, who I was with. About
all those runs I took.*

TWENTY-ONE

ON MONDAY, I WAS DISTRACTED, out of sync from the moment I woke up. Even the sound of my alarm clock seemed different—louder, more insistent than I remembered it—and when I got out of bed, I promptly smacked my shin against the bed frame, leaving a large welt that I could immediately feel hardening into a bruise.

So it was hardly surprising that as I hurried through the hall on the way to second period, my head down, I smashed into someone.

"Watch it!" an annoyed male voice said.

"Sorry," I mumbled, looking up to see who I'd bumped into. It turned out to be Charlie. His face was tense, and his hands were raised as if to either brace himself or steady me. A few steps behind me, Nick and Brian had paused and were looking back at us.

"Jess." Charlie blinked, and relaxed his face into a smile. "Well, I guess neither of us was paying attention."

"I guess not."

He nodded. I expected him to walk away at that point, to catch up with Nick and Brian. Instead, he remained standing there. "So did you end up getting ahold of Lily?" he asked. "Brian said something about you having a sweater of hers?"

"Yeah." I paused. "It turned out the sweater wasn't a priority for her."

"Makes sense," he said. "She's probably enjoying being by a beach. Probably getting a tan—happy to not be stuck in this dump anymore."

Brian took a step toward Charlie, looking impatient. "You coming?" he asked.

Charlie ignored him.

"She say anything else? Anything about me?" he asked.

"Of course she didn't say anything about you," Brian interjected. "Let's go."

Charlie frowned, and a note of anger entered his voice. "Look, just because you and your ex are a garbage fire doesn't mean I can't ask about mine."

Brian tensed. "Watch it," he said.

"No, you watch it. I'm tired of walking on damn eggshells. You're the one who needs to move on already. She was just a giant time suck for you anyway—I barely saw you when you guys were together. You're better off without her."

Brian's face went dark and he stepped forward. Nick shook his head and put his hand out to stop him. "Come on, guys," he said. "Don't do this."

Brian glared at Nick. "*I'm* not doing anything," he said.

I didn't really seem to have a role in the conversation anymore, so I started to leave them to it.

Charlie noticed me moving away. "Sorry. Anyway, I'm glad you got ahold of Lily—if you talk to her again, tell her I say hi."

"I don't think that's going to happen," I said. "She wasn't exactly happy to hear from me."

All three boys stared at me when I said that. So I shrugged, with an effort. "She was Anna's friend, not mine."

"Right," Charlie said. Then he paused, like people often did after I said her name—like I'd thrown it down like a gauntlet. "Hey, I'm sorry about Anna—she was a nice girl."

A nice girl. I tried to push down the flare of frustration the phrase provoked, the idea that others would remember her that way. That they thought it meant anything.

"Sure," I said stiffly. "Okay."

Brian had started to turn away, but he paused when I said that and looked at me more carefully, like he was recalibrating. "Look, you really shouldn't pay attention to that stuff that was written about her."

"What stuff?"

"Oh, never mind," Brian said. "Sorry. For a second, I thought you'd heard. . . . Never mind."

"What stuff?" I asked again.

"Nothing," he said. "Really. Forget I said anything."

I looked at Charlie and Nick. "What's he talking about?" I asked them.

It was several beats before either of them spoke. And then Charlie shook his head. "Nothing," he said. "He's probably thinking about someone else." I looked at him and then at Nick.

Nick nodded. "Yeah, he's just being an idiot. Ignore him. Anyway, we should get going. But I'll see you on Sunday, right? At the park?"

I nodded, watching his face, still trying to figure out if he actually meant it. Surely saying it twice had to mean something, though. Didn't it?

Charlie's sudden laugh jerked me back into the moment.

"Wow," he said to Nick. "You certainly have a type, don't you?"

Nick flushed, Brian shot Charlie another dark look, and then suddenly the three of them were headed down the hall again.

IT STARTED RAINING JUST BEFORE track practice. A pounding, ceaseless downpour that came down like the wrath of Norse gods. It was far too heavy for us to run in, yet it was so intense it seemed it might pass quickly, so Mr. Matthews made us all wait around in the gym to see if it would clear up.

I headed to the bleachers and pulled out my book. A few seconds later, I received a sharp smack in the arm. "Put that down," Sarah said.

"Ow," I said, rubbing the spot she'd hit.

Sarah pulled an apologetic face as she sprawled out beside me. "Sorry. Sometimes I don't know my own strength. Still, no reading for you. I'm bored and need someone to entertain me."

"And that's my problem?"

"Of course it is. That's the price of my friendship."

"Why can't you just play around on your phone? Quietly?"

"I'd love to, but it ran out of battery. It's been glitchy recently—not holding a charge as long as it should. I'm thinking about getting my phone guy to take a look at it."

"Fine," I said, setting my book down on my lap. "What would you like to converse about?"

"Well, I'm going to have some fun with the fact that you just used the phrase 'converse about.' I think that's going to keep me going for quite some time." Sarah waggled her eyebrows at me.

I sighed. She sighed back, longer and louder.

ELEVEN MINUTES LATER, MR. MATTHEWS finally called uncle in the standoff between him and the rain and told us we could all go home.

Sarah borrowed my phone to call her parents.

"You want a ride?" she asked, before she started to dial. "You don't want to walk back in this." I hesitated for a moment. "Don't worry," she said. "It's my dad's turn to pick up."

I'd gotten rides with Sarah a couple of times now. Usually her dad got us—but the last time it had been her mom, and the trip had been marked by long stretches of awkward silence, interrupted only by her mom's occasional comments, which were somehow directed at neither me nor Sarah but instead at some invisible third girl interested in fashion tips and DIY pedicures.

I nodded, embarrassed at Sarah's having understood the source of my hesitation.

"Cool," she said. "I'll let him know we'll be dropping you off."

WHEN SARAH'S DAD ARRIVED, HE honked twice and we sprinted from the door of the gym out through the rain and shoved ourselves breathlessly through the car doors.

Even with windshield wipers going double-time, the rain made it difficult to see, so he drove very slowly after giving Sarah an affectionate pat on the shoulder.

"So," he said, glancing at me in the car mirror and smiling. "Sarah tells me you're getting good at this whole running thing."

"I'm getting better," I said.

"That's great. It's about time someone started making Sarah

work for her wins. I'm pretty sure she's starting to think she's all that and a really fast bag of chips."

"Dad," Sarah said. "That doesn't even make sense."

"No, her head has been getting too big, I tell you. She needs to know she has some competition out there." He glanced back at me again. "So at your first meet, you need to crush her, okay? Put her in her place."

I felt myself turning pink.

Sarah laughed. "You're embarrassing her. Besides, I don't even remember talking to you about Jess's running—you must have gotten that from Mr. Matthews in one of your little huddle sessions. You really should spend less time analyzing my competition and more time explaining to Mom that teenagers can't survive on kale and crackers."

"C'mon, you know why your mom's like that," he said, a slight edge to his voice.

"Yeah, I know, I know. She was overweight for like two days while she was growing up and it was the worst thing ever, and she just wants to protect me from the trauma."

"Be nice, Sarah. People were horrible to her about it. Really cruel." Then he took a deep breath and lightened his tone. "Anyway, you were definitely the one who told me about Jess's running. I remember it distinctly."

Sarah rolled her eyes at me. I smiled and then looked out at the field through the rain-smeared window. Mr. Matthews stood at the edge of the track, his clothes heavy with water. And while the rain fell too fast for me to be sure, and he began moving almost immediately after I saw him, it looked like he was staring at the car, watching me go.

*He claims I was the one who started it. That
I began smiling at him in a different way,
moving closer and closer. That he tried to
resist, but I made it too difficult.
It could be he's right—that you can draw someone
to you without realizing you're doing it. I'm
not sure, though, because looking back, I don't
think it even occurred to me that he was an
option.
At least part of me was still good back then.*

TWENTY-TWO

IN THE FALL, THE LOCKDOWN drill had taken place in the middle of fifth period. We'd all been informed about it ahead of time, so it had been no surprise when the announcement had come over the loudspeaker. My history teacher had dutifully locked the door, turned off the lights, closed the blinds, and motioned to us all to huddle behind our desks. None of us had bothered moving all that fast, not even the teacher, and we'd spent less than ten minutes sitting on the floor before we'd gotten the all clear. There had been no urgency, no realism—it had simply been an exercise in following basic protocol.

Apparently, the administration wanted to shake things up, because this time there was no warning, and the intercom came on during lunch, right after I'd tossed the remains of my food into the trash and headed into the hallway.

"This is a lockdown drill," the principal said. "Please quickly proceed to the nearest location you can secure. This is a drill, but we ask that you take it very seriously."

I looked around for Sarah, before remembering she'd gone to fill up her water bottle, leaving from a different exit. I studied the cafeteria, unsure whether I should go back in. Could it be secured? Probably, but I couldn't tell if the doors locked. I swiveled around, searching for another location, even as other people swirled around me, making similar calculations. Then I spotted Brian and Charlie disappearing into the chemistry lab, so I started to make my way toward it, speeding up when Charlie began to pull the door shut behind him.

"Wait," I called. "I'm coming."

Charlie paused, leaving the door partway open. I ran the last few steps and slid inside the room.

"Thanks," I said.

"Not a problem," he said as he locked the door. "Get the lights."

I found the switch on the wall and flicked it off.

Charlie stared at the door. "Why doesn't this window have shades?" He turned and called out over his shoulder. "Brian, can you grab a couple of pieces of paper and some tape so we can cover the window? Right now, they could see right in."

Brian walked over to the teacher's desk, which was empty. Mr. Ryers must have still been at lunch.

There was a loud knock on the door. "Hey, open up."

"Are you the shooter?" Charlie said, craning his head to the window. "Because if so, I'm pretty sure I'm not supposed to let you in."

"You can see me, Charlie," the girl said. Her voice was familiar, but I couldn't quite place it. "You can see both of us. Let us in."

"One of you could have a gun in your backpack," he said. "Or a machete. I should probably leave you both out there. Better safe than sorry."

"I promise that neither of us has a damn machete, all right? Let us in." I placed the voice: Lauren. Lauren, in her natural state: pissed off.

"Let her in," Brian said, walking over with the paper and a roll of tape. "She's just going to keep knocking until you do."

Charlie shrugged. "I was only looking out for you." He unlocked the door and pulled it open.

Lauren threw Charlie an annoyed look as she walked into the dark room. Mona followed close behind her. She paused when she saw Brian, and for a second it looked like she might turn back. But Charlie was already locking the door again.

"You're welcome," Charlie called over his shoulder toward Lauren. "Please don't murder us all now."

Lauren rolled her eyes. "Whatever." Then she looked at Mona and followed her gaze to Brian. "Come on, Mona," she said. "Let's go to the back. This will be over in a couple of minutes."

Brian continued to hold the paper, unmoving, as Lauren steered Mona firmly toward the back of the room.

Charlie shook his head, annoyed. "Brian, forget about that mess and bring over the damn paper," he said. "I'm not interested in getting a lecture from my dad about how we screwed this up."

Brian tore his gaze away from Mona. "Okay, I'm coming," he said. He held the paper up against the glass with one hand and carefully taped it using the other. "There."

"You should use a second sheet," I said. "It's thin paper. You can practically see through it."

"One is fine," Charlie said. "All that matters is that we covered it."

Brian paused, the second sheet of paper in his hands, and that was when we all heard it. The sound of heavy footsteps coming down the empty hallway.

I crouched down against the wall, and Brian silently stepped away from the door, paper still in his hand, and crouched down beside me.

Walking, walking, stop. A pause, a sound of clicking, and then more walking. Doors: he was trying the doors. Last time, there had been yelling, the role of the active shooter played by a community theater volunteer relishing his moment in the spotlight, but this time there was only the footsteps and the turning of knobs. And the sound of Brian's slow breathing beside me.

I felt exposed sitting there, with nothing but Brian between me and the door. I should have gone to the back of the room. Or behind the teacher's desk. The footsteps were getting closer, though, so I stayed put. As they echoed down the hall, I couldn't help but remember the video they'd made us all watch freshman year. In it, the shooter had worn heavy army boots and fatigue pants, and in one chilling frame the shadow of him and the gun he carried had stretched out along the expanse of empty hall. His face registered only as a sketch in my mind, with the wide jaw and unsmiling eyes of an action figure.

It was easier that way, I thought, to think of the shooter as an anonymous outsider, to mute the reality that it was far more likely to be a fellow student. Maybe that was the thing no one really knew how to prepare for, that your life might ultimately depend on how quickly you could switch from seeing the shooter as the person who sat two seats away from you in history—the person who offered you a stick of gum—seeing them as the person who might kill you.

The footsteps grew closer and closer and then they stopped right outside the door. Through the thin sheet of paper covering the glass, I could make out the faint shape of a head. *This is not real,* I told myself, even as I stopped breathing and closed my eyes, waiting for the sound of them trying the doorknob.

Click, click. He paused and then tried again. *Click, click.*

It was locked. The room was dark. There was paper over the window.

Please keep walking, I thought. *We followed the rules.*

For another long, long second there was silence. And then the footsteps started again, this time walking away, toward the gym.

I wondered if they'd been able to secure the doors.

Brian shifted beside me, quietly stretching his legs.

"What were you talking about the other day?" I whispered. "About Anna?"

"I don't know what you mean," he said. "Keep quiet."

"I am being quiet," I said, still whispering, but pressing my advantage now that he couldn't just walk off. "You said there was some stuff written about her. What did someone write about her?"

Brian shook his head. "Nothing."

"It wasn't nothing. Tell me."

He looked toward the intercom, as if willing it to come on and release him from this room, this conversation. "Look, some idiot wrote some stuff about her in the bathroom," he said eventually. "That's all."

I took that in, processing it. "Which bathroom?" I asked.

"By the music room," he said. "But it's really no big deal. You should just forget about it."

"Sure," I said, having no intention whatsoever of doing that. Then I leaned back and listened to the sound of footsteps walking away from the cafeteria, away from the chem lab, heading down the hall to the next room.

It felt like it took a very long time before the intercom crackled on again, telling us all that it was over.

AFTER TRACK, I TOLD SARAH I'd walk home, that I'd forgotten something in my locker and didn't want to keep her. She offered to wait but I said no, that I could use the exercise. Which was, perhaps, an odd comment after running for over an hour, but she didn't ask any follow-up questions.

The hallway was deserted, but I still knocked before entering the bathroom. Two loud, sharp knocks. I waited for a few seconds, listening for a flush, an annoyed response. There was nothing, no sound of life, so I went in.

Inside, there was an old brick for when the door needed to be propped upon. I slid it against the door so that no one else could enter.

The air was stale, and the lone window looked like it hadn't been opened in a very long time. Each of the stalls featured a handful of scrawls—mostly a call-and-response of expletives with the occasional indecipherable drawing. None of them had anything to do with Anna.

It was only as I was leaving the second stall that I saw what I'd missed before on the opposite wall. There had been an attempt to cover the words with a layer of paint, and from a certain angle the effort had succeeded, but more paint was needed to truly obscure them from straight on.

The words were written in furious capital letters:

ANNA CUTTER IS A WHORE.

What I do know is that he was the first one
to initiate contact, to vault across that gulf
between us.
When he did, when he touched me in that
unmistakable way, I almost stopped breathing.
I want to tell you that I moved away
immediately. Instead, it took full, long
seconds—ones that stretched like caramel,
crackling at the edges like burnt sugar.

TWENTY-THREE

ANNA WAS THE GOOD ONE. People had always thought of her that way. The one who wouldn't cause problems, the one who was kind—considerate. The one who opened doors for people, who bought thoughtful birthday presents and volunteered for food drives.

If someone had told me before, back when she was alive, that someone had called her a whore, had scrawled it across the wall of the boys' bathroom, I'd have assumed they were making a terrible joke.

But someone had written that about her, had written it out in permanent black ink. Someone who'd seen her with someone? The person she'd been with? I didn't know.

I WAS STARING OUT THE window in class, still thinking about the graffiti, when I saw a girl sitting on the edge of the roof—legs dangling back and forth, dark hair blowing in the breeze.

I thought it was Anna. Which meant it had happened, that I'd finally, officially lost it—not just momentarily seeing her in someone else, but seeing her in a place where there wasn't anyone at all.

I closed my eyes tight and then reopened them.

The girl was still there. She wasn't Anna, but she wasn't a figment of my imagination either. It was a real girl up there, leaning forward at a dangerous angle.

I got up and ran out of the classroom. The hallway was longer than it had ever been. When I finally reached the stairs that led to the roof, I took them two at a time. I slowed down only right before I reached the door out to the roof, as my only working brain cell warned me against startling the girl perched on the ledge.

As the door closed quietly behind me, I stood and looked for the girl, afraid I might already be too late. I wasn't. She was still there, her darks curls moving in the wind.

It was Mona, Lauren's friend. She sat with her back to me, arms at her sides, holding on to the ledge with a troubling lightness.

I walked toward her cautiously, at an angle, so that she could see me before I reached her. She turned as my shadow fell along her back.

"Hey, Mona," I said.

"Jess?" Her eyes were red, her skin pink and blotchy.

"That's right," I said as I kept walking toward her.

With a few more steps, I reached the ledge. I carefully lifted one leg over and then the other, sitting back as far as possible.

Don't look down, I thought. *Don't look down and don't think about Anna.*

First, my eyes disobeyed me, training themselves on the pavement below, and then my brain disobeyed me, and I thought of Anna. Anna underneath the blue sheet. I clutched the ledge hard, the rough concrete grinding into my palms.

"This isn't what it looks like," Mona said.

"Okay." I didn't believe her. I thought it was probably exactly what it looked like. I looked down at her hand resting on the ledge. I wondered if I'd be able to grab her in time if I needed to. I moved my hand closer to hers to improve my odds.

"It's quiet up here," she said quietly. "It's a good place to think."

So is the library, I thought. *So is the base of one of the many trees surrounding the school.* There were many, many places that were good places to think—good places to cry, even—that were on ground level.

"It's a nice view," I said instead, making myself stare out in the distance. *Keep talking,* I thought. *Something neutral, something mundane.* "I can almost see my house." I pointed with my free hand, leaving my other one near hers, tightly grasping the ledge. "I think it's behind those trees. Where's yours?"

She skimmed the horizon and then pointed to a spot close to the park. "Over there," she said. "The one with the reddish roof and the blue siding."

"I run through that park. There's a path at the edge that goes out through the fields."

She nodded. "Yeah, my mom used to go jogging on it—I'd go with her sometimes."

"She stopped?"

She smiled for the first time since she'd seen me. "Oh yeah—she *hates* exercise. She just wanted to lose weight—she was always in a terrible mood when she got back. My dad and I practically begged her to stop." She paused. "I've seen you running on the track—it looks like you actually enjoy it."

I thought about how it felt when I was running. The quiet satisfaction of my body doing what I asked it to. The relief of not being so much in my own head for a while, the tension inside me temporarily loosening its hold. "I do like running," I said. "I didn't think I would, but I do. It feels like it makes me . . . clean, somehow."

I didn't know quite what I meant by that, only that it felt right.

Mona nodded like she understood. "That's how I used to feel about cheerleading," she said. "I knew exactly what I was supposed to be doing, exactly where I was supposed to be. I had this complete faith in my body that it could do whatever it needed to do, to flip through the air."

I imagined Mona hurtling through the air, doing a high flip, knowing that she would land perfectly on her feet—and that being all that mattered in that particular moment. I could remember her last year, leaning against her locker, laughing, wearing her cheerleader outfit. She'd looked confident, happy—so sure in her skin that it almost hurt to look at her, even as you couldn't quite bring yourself to look away.

"What happened?" I asked.

"It didn't feel the same anymore. I lost that feeling, that sense of ownership over my body. Plus, I couldn't cheer anymore, not for—" She paused and shook her head. "I don't know. It's different. I'm different."

"Maybe you'll get that feeling back," I said.

"Maybe," she said. "Sometimes I come out on game nights, just sit outside in the parking lot and listen to the music, try to imagine myself doing it again. I can't, though. I think that version of me, of my life, is gone."

She sounded so tired, so lost. And I knew it too well, what it felt like to lose a version of yourself. I closed my eyes, overwhelmed. It was all too close to the bone. The sadness. Girls on roofs, girls and windows. Losing their balance. Falling. Jumping.

"You don't need to stay," she said. "Really. I promise I'm not going to do anything."

I wanted to believe her. I wasn't sure I did. Promises could be so easily broken.

"It really is peaceful up here," I said. "I think I'll stay for a while. Until you're ready to go back inside."

"Okay," she said.

And so we sat there together, not speaking.

And I couldn't help but wonder if I'd prevented something from happening or only delayed it.

TWENTY-FOUR

ON SUNDAY MORNING, I TOLD myself I wasn't necessarily expecting Nick to show up at the park again, despite his having mentioned it twice. But there he was, stretching against a tree, right on time. He'd been serious after all. And so had I. Of course, I was always serious.

"I've decided not to take it easy on you this time," he said. "I've been practicing."

"Me too," I said.

"Good. I like a worthy competitor." Then he grinned at me and took off.

I managed to keep going until he finally slowed and then flopped down unceremoniously beneath a tall tree with thick branches. I planted myself on a stretch of grass nearby, my lungs burning.

"Running around on the court is going to be nothing after all this," he said, shaking his head in mock wonderment. "At this rate, I'll never sit on the bench again."

I took in a deep breath. "You sit on the bench often?"

"Not really. But it's awful when I do—not only because I'm not playing, but also because that's where the coach hangs out for most of the game."

"That's a bad thing?"

"It's definitely not a *good* thing. The guy yells himself hoarse, and he has one of the worst cases of body odor ever."

I wasn't sure I smelled exactly amazing myself, so I clamped my arms tightly to my sides and made a mental note to put on extra deodorant next time. *Next time.* Funny how I was already assuming (hoping?) there would be a next time. "That's too bad," I said.

"Oh, it could be worse," he said. "He's all bark and no bite, really. Also, while I could do without all the yelling, it's hard not to kind of like the guy after you've heard him on the phone with his four-year-old daughter. He once read her a bedtime story on the bus when we were coming back late from an away game—did all the voices and everything. Plus, he wears a bracelet she gave him at all the big games—it's his lucky thing."

"Lucky thing?"

"Oh yeah, most of the guys on the team have something like that. Eric wears the same bandanna every game and doesn't wash it all season. Brian, he eats like fifty red hots because one time last year he did that and it was our best game ever. And Charlie won't drink a thing for forty-eight hours before a game."

"He doesn't drink anything? Isn't that dangerous?"

He laughed. "Oh, I mean he won't *drink* drink. He'll have nonalcoholic stuff. But for a guy who's always got not one but two flasks in his car, that's a big deal."

"Two flasks? Seems like he should just get one big one," I said. "More efficient. Unless he has different kinds of liquor in each?"

He shrugged. "Maybe. Maybe he has the super-good stuff in one. Or maybe it's just easier to be discreet if you have two small ones."

"So what's your thing?" I asked. "What weird thing do you do before a game?"

"Me?" He shrugged again. "I don't believe in that stuff. I believe whatever's going to happen will happen, that there isn't any point in trying to shape the future."

I looked out at the fields and wondered about what I believed. I wasn't sure what I thought about shaping the future, yet perhaps I did believe, deep down, that there was a chance I could reshape the past. That if I found out what, or even who, had come between me and Anna so I could fix it. Reset time.

I rolled onto my side and looked at Nick.

"What did you like about her?"

He blinked. "About who?"

"About Anna." *Please tell me something good*, I thought. *Something that mattered.*

The pause stretched out until I thought he wasn't going to answer.

Then he did. Slowly, thoughtfully.

"I liked a lot of things about her," he said. "I liked how kind she was to people. I liked how I'd see her chewing on her pen all secretive-like when she thought no one was looking. I liked how she once tried to save a crow that was hit by one of the buses— even though it was scared and kept trying to peck at her."

Then his tone changed, going lower and deeper. "But honestly, I only noticed those things after I already knew I liked her." He closed his eyes. "She held my hand once, did you know that? Just saw I looked upset about something and came up beside me and held my hand. That was years ago, and I don't even remember what I was upset about anymore, but I liked her from then on. It just built. More and more reasons to like her, and no reasons not to."

His eyes were still closed, but around the edges there was a thin line of moisture. The sun was bright, I thought; that was all. Incredibly bright.

So I closed my eyes as well. He'd risen to the challenge, remembered things that mattered. Yet there was also a weird feeling in my chest. A feeling someone who didn't know better might have labeled jealousy.

*After I moved away, leaving his fingers flexed
in midair, neither of us said anything. We
brushed it off as if it were an accident,
something that would never happen again.
Yet I felt branded by it—like the weight of his
fingers on my thigh had turned me into
a different person.*

TWENTY-FIVE

ALL THE TIMES THAT I'D followed Mr. Matthews home, watched him from his window, I'd never gotten caught. Hadn't even come close.

Which meant I started to get sloppy. Didn't leave as much room between us as I had at first. Didn't bother stretching as much as I used to. In a way, I'd come to feel that we were simply spending time together, getting to know each other. The fact that it wasn't actually a mutual relationship was something I mostly skimmed over in my mind.

And one day, it seemed like he was walking more slowly than usual. As there's a limit to how slowly you can jog, I kept getting closer and closer to him.

Less than a block away from his house, there was the sharp cracking sound of a car backfiring behind us. He swiveled around and there I was, less than fifteen feet behind him, smack in the middle of open, empty pavement.

"Jess?" He cocked his head, staring at me like he barely recognized me out of context.

I froze. *Act natural*, my brain commanded. *Act natural*. Unfortunately, I could not remember what on earth that might look like.

He started to walk toward me.

I opened my mouth. No words came out, just an odd, scratchy noise from the back of my throat. I feigned a coughing fit to cover it up.

"Are you okay?" he asked.

I nodded as I continued to cough, trying to extend it as long as I could. Once I'd bought as much time as I could without permanently damaging my throat, I made my eyes go wide. "You surprised me," I said.

He furrowed his eyebrows. "How did I surprise you? You were running right behind me."

I edited myself. "I meant that the noise surprised me."

"Oh, sure," he said. "It was pretty loud."

"Yes, it was."

He continued to look at me strangely, so I seized on the first thing that seemed faintly plausible.

"I was actually trying to catch up with you. I was about to call out to get your attention when the car backfired."

"Okay," he said. "What did you want to tell me?"

Oh. Right. I hadn't gotten that far. I considered faking another coughing fit, but that seemed a bit much. I looked down at my gym shoes and then back up.

"Track," I said. "I wanted to tell you that I appreciate you letting me on the team even though the sign-up period was over. I'm enjoying it."

I prayed he wouldn't ask why I suddenly wanted to talk to him about that now. Because I had no answer.

Fortunately, he seemed to accept the comment at face value. "That's great," he said. "It seems like you're really taking to it."

"Thanks."

I wondered if we could leave it at that, but I wasn't sure how to make an easy retreat, so I decided to keep talking—bury the awkwardness of it all with more inane chatter.

"I've heard good things about your English class," I offered. *Lay it on thick,* I thought. *Compliment him into a stupor and then head for the hills.*

"I'm glad," he said. "You should sign up for it next year." He said it more like he thought he should say it rather than like he genuinely meant it. Still, I was surprised that he was tactless enough to say it at all.

"Yeah, I guess I could do that, now."

"Now?"

I flushed, annoyed that he was making me spell it out. "Anna was in your class before. So I had to go in another section. Because of the policy."

"I don't know what you mean," he said.

"The policy about siblings. About them not being in the same class."

He shook his head slowly. "There isn't a policy about that."

"Yes, there is."

"No, there isn't. There are two brothers in one of my AP classes right now."

"That's against the rules, then. Because there's a policy. It's new—they rolled it out last summer. That's why Anna and I didn't take classes together this year. I distinctly remember her telling me. . . ."

His face fell, taking on a look of sad embarrassment. I recognized that look, had seen many variations of it over the years. It meant I hadn't understood something someone had said and they weren't sure how to explain it to me.

I traced back. He'd said there was no policy. That he currently had siblings in one of his classes. Anna had been so clear on that point, telling me that if we didn't pick different classes one of us would be forced to select again later.

Had she been lying?

I looked at Mr. Matthews's face, his eyes filled with pity.

She had been lying.

He started to backtrack. "I mean, I could be wrong—maybe they made an exception for the kids in my class. . . ."

He fell silent again. Because he wasn't wrong. We both knew that.

I tried to make my voice even; instead, it crackled with hysteria. "Sure. I really should get going."

"Jess—"

I shook my head. Hard and fast. Hard and fast. "No, I should head home."

He reached out toward my arm. I jerked away. No touching. No, no, *no* touching. Especially not by him. Especially not like this.

I turned and started to run, to put as much space as possible between us.

Because I needed to process this alone.

Alone.

Apparently, that was what I had been for a long time. Had been even before Anna fell.

TWENTY-SIX

MRS. HAYES LOOKED AT ME steadily, her fingers loosely laced together on her desk. I stared back, trying to keep my face as neutral as possible.

We had been sitting in silence for over five minutes and she'd only blinked a handful of times. If this had been a staring content, she'd have won it. Under normal circumstances, I might have been impressed. But she was a counselor, and I did not wish to be counseled.

"I don't understand why I'm here," I said eventually. "I told you I'm fine."

"Your teachers are worried about you."

"I don't know why."

"Okay," she said. Then she flipped through a small notebook and consulted one of the pages. "So you don't understand why they might be worried about you repeatedly running out of class with no explanation? About you handing in a blank sheet of paper for your English exam?"

It felt unfair to have the running-out-of-class part flung in my face, particularly since most recently I'd done that to check on Mona—a perfectly reasonable thing to do that should not have been counted against me. A reasonable thing that I didn't feel like was mine to talk about.

"I was getting up to use the restroom," I said. "And the English exam was a mistake."

"Mistake" felt like a justifiable description of it. Because I had studied for that exam, had studied for it for weeks—stockpiling a rich supply of examples and opinions to use to answer questions posed in the exam. Sitting at my desk, though, my thoughts had left their tracks. Because Anna had lied to me. Not just not told me things, actively lied. Lied to get away from me.

"What do you mean, it was a mistake?"

"I wasn't feeling well. I'm going to ask to retake it. My other grades are fine—it's not like I'm failing any of my classes."

She leaned forward. "This isn't really about your academic performance. It's about checking in with you, seeing if there's anything we can do to make things easier. Everyone understands how hard this must be for you."

"I'm doing fine. I just didn't feel well yesterday. I should have gone home instead of trying to make it through the day." I paused. "I've had a fragile stomach recently. That's why I left abruptly for the bathroom too. I thought I was going to be sick." I was proud of myself for thinking of that.

Mrs. Hayes looked at me for a long moment. And then she nodded to herself and wrote something in her notebook. Something quite long.

"What did you just write?"

"I wrote that you said you weren't feeling well."

"And that's it?"

"What else do you think I wrote?"

"I don't know, that's why I asked."

Her smile wavered. "Jess, did something happen? It makes sense that you'll have ups and downs, but it had really seemed like you were finding a good path forward—joining track, hanging out with Sarah. Turning in a blank test—that's so unlike you."

Joining track, hanging out with Sarah. Finding a path. It hadn't occurred to me that my behavior was being judged and monitored, that my teachers and Mrs. Hayes were grading my progress, even as they watched for cracks to form underneath the surface. I wondered if Mr. Matthews was part of this, if he'd told them about our encounter. Maybe that was what this was really about, not the English exam, not leaving class at all. Maybe that was what Mrs. Hayes was trying to get me to tell her, how my own sister hadn't liked me, hadn't wanted me around. If so, too bad. She could try all she liked, but I was never going to talk to her about that.

I tried to calm myself down, yet my hands itched to snatch the notebook from her hands so I could see what she'd written, see if Mr. Matthews was the one who had thrown me into this mess.

"Nothing happened," I said.

"Nothing?"

"Nothing."

She continued to stare at me. It was unnerving how good she was at it. Most people weren't. She was good enough to unsettle me. Make me want to tell her something, anything to get her to stop staring.

Then I remembered it. The completely reasonable thing that I could tell her—that she might even already know about. Something that *had* upset me, quite deeply.

"There was some graffiti," I said. "In the boys' bathroom.

About Anna. Someone mentioned it to me recently. I didn't know about it before. It was . . ." I closed my eyes and saw it again, the faint image of it on the wall. "It threw me off. That someone would write something like that about her."

Her stare softened, like it had done its job, forcing me to finally admit to a feeling she could cleanly parse and address. "I'm so sorry. Of course that upset you. Boys can be so . . . Well, that definitely shouldn't have happened."

"I don't understand why someone would write that about her."

"It's hard to say. Boys' minds can be an ugly place. There may well not be a reason. People are just cruel sometimes—lash out because they're frustrated or jealous or because things ended badly. I wouldn't put any stock in it." She sighed. "I really wish no one had told you about it."

"They didn't mean to," I said.

"Well, good. Some things only hurt to learn about, and they don't change anything."

Her phone buzzed on her desk, vibrating harshly against the wooden surface.

She glanced at it and her eyebrows went up. "I'm sorry, it's my son's school. Just a second."

She picked up her phone and walked over to the window, turning her back to me. Her notebook lay on the desk, only a few feet away.

"Hello," she said into her phone. "Is everything okay?"

I laid my hands on the desk. I wanted to know what she'd written about me. I wanted to know if Mr. Matthews had said anything about me.

"What? Peanuts? No, I don't think . . . Oh, I'm so sorry."

I slid my arms forward on the desk, as if I were stretching.

My fingertips brushed against the notebook. I paused and then looked over at Mrs. Hayes. She was braced against the window, her fingers against her forehead.

"Yes," she said, "his grandmother brought some cookies over and I didn't think to ask. I thought they were chocolate chip."

I leaned farther forward and I pulled her notebook back toward me, flipping it around so I could read it more easily.

Her handwriting was neat, precise.

> *Jess claims to have been sick. Obviously not*
> *true—already talked to parents. Denial?*
> *Depression? Compulsive lying? Recommend that*
> *she be referred to a psychologist? Psychiatrist?*

Psychiatrist. Parents. I didn't know she'd talked to them. I wondered for the first time if they hadn't stopped believing that there was something wrong with me, if they'd just given up figuring out what. The thought stung. *No*, I thought, *that's not right. They know me. They know there's nothing wrong with me.* Then I thought about the coasters, about how nervous I seemed to make Mom and Dad sometimes now that Anna wasn't there as a buffer between us.

I leafed through the previous pages, looking to see who else she'd been talking to, if Mr. Matthews had mentioned our encounter to her. She'd seemed to buy that the graffiti was the main issue, but perhaps she was socking away additional intel.

I couldn't find anything, though. Everything else appeared to be about other students.

Then, from the corner of my eye, I saw Mrs. Hayes turning away from the window.

"Thanks," she said, still talking into the phone. "I appreciate that. I'll definitely be more careful in the future. I'm so glad no one got hurt."

I thumbed back to the page she'd left off on, the page about me, and slid the notebook back across the table, retracting my hands to my lap right as she ended the call.

"I'm so sorry about that," she said as she sat back down. "It seems I accidentally almost killed half of my son's kindergarten class."

"Not a problem," I said. "I'm glad everyone is okay."

"Me too," she said. Then she reached for her notebook. As she did so, I realized that I'd left it oriented facing me. I watched her notice it, saw her eyes flick back to me. She opened her mouth, as if to ask me about it. I kept my face as blank as possible. Then she shook herself a little, like a dog coming in from the rain, and closed her mouth again.

"Is there anything else you'd like to tell me about, Jess?"

"No," I said. "That's the only thing that comes to mind."

That first time, we'd been alone, inside—
  contained by walls.
The second time, it was out in the open. His
  hands on me on the bleachers as I waited for
  Lily to come out of the locker room. The risk
  of it, the audacity, made it seem like he'd lost
  control, like we'd both lost control.
Lost control. It feels good to phrase it like that.
  Like control is something that fell through my
  fingers, leaving me blameless.

TWENTY-SEVEN

THE NEXT DAY, I SAT on the bleachers with a book perched in front of me, doing my best impression of reading. I wasn't, though. Nor, for once, was I focused on Mr. Matthews, who sat a few rows down from me, waiting for the basketball team to finish doing laps. I wasn't even thinking about the graffiti, Anna, or Mrs. Hayes.

Instead, I was watching Nick run.

Watching how the thin layer of sweat on his arms and neck made him look like he was made of liquid glass, and thinking about how, depending on the light, his eyes ranged from the color of root beer to the color of bark after a rain.

These were unusual thoughts for me.

Highly unusual.

Still, I wasn't sure I wanted anything to happen between us. Anything physical. I honestly didn't know if I wanted him to touch me at all. At the same time, I was . . . curious about touching him. His arm, his shoulder, the knob of bone on his wrist. Something. To touch him and not immediately move away.

The bleachers began to vibrate under the weight of someone's footsteps. I turned to see Sarah banging her way up toward me. She sank down beside me, giving me a funny side-ways grin.

"So who is it?" she asked as she flipped her head over to put her hair into that perfect ponytail of hers. She could do it almost in a single motion, but when I tried to replicate it once it did not end well.

"Who's what?"

She flipped her head right-side up again, ponytail complete. "Who are you staring at?"

"I don't know what you're talking about," I said, making a production of closing my book. "I've been reading."

"Ha. I'm pretty sure reading involves you actually looking at the pages, not just having the thing propped in front of you while you drool over someone."

My fingers moved toward my mouth.

"*Figurative* drooling," she said. "Not literal. Oh God, you are so busted."

At that moment, Nick turned onto the stretch of track closest to where I was sitting. He looked up and waved. Without even thinking, I waved back.

I expected that exchange to elicit further teasing from Sarah. Instead, she looked thoughtful. "Oh," she said. "I was just teasing. I didn't know you and Nick were actually a thing."

"We're not. We're just friends."

She raised one of her eyebrows. "Friends?"

"Friends. Really."

"Okay," she said. "Good."

"Okay." I paused and mulled it over. "Wait, why is that good?"

"I don't know," she said awkwardly. "It's just, you hear stuff sometimes."

"About Nick?"

"Not specifically. But he's on the basketball team. And I've heard . . ." She shook her head. "I don't know. I go to games sometimes, and they're kind of vicious. Plus, they party pretty hard. Doesn't seem like your scene."

"Okay," I said. "Nick's not like that, though."

"You sure about that?"

I thought of Nick, of how he'd shaken his head when Charlie offered him the flask at Anna's funeral. Thought of his smile. Thought of his face when he talked about Anna.

"Yeah, I'm sure."

"All right." She looked at me closely, closely enough that I started to blush. "You're starting to fall for him, aren't you?" It was as gentle as anything I'd ever heard from her.

"It doesn't feel like falling," I said slowly.

"What does it feel like?"

I watched Nick slow down to a jog as the basketball coach began to usher everyone off the track. "It feels more like I'm starting to wake up."

TWENTY-EIGHT

A FEW DAYS LATER, I lay on my stomach in the grass and stared at Nick as he idly picked at a small batch of flowers by his side, rolling one of the buds around between his fingers. I wondered what I'd do if he let it go and moved closer, if he reached toward me. Would I remain still? Or would that familiar feeling of panic rise in my chest, leading me to flinch and move away? I wondered if it even had occurred to him to try, or if I was only his weekend running partner, the awkward twin of the girl he'd liked—someone too messed up to seriously consider.

"It's just a flower, Jess."

I started. "What?"

"You're looking at this"—he lightly tapped the flower with his index finger—"like it's a Magic Eight Ball about to reveal your future. What are you thinking about?"

Whether you want to touch me, I thought. *How it might feel if you did.*

"Nothing, really. It's just been a weird week," I said. And I thought back to sitting in Mrs. Hayes's office, hearing her talk about my finding a path. Thought about how strange, how uncomfortable it had felt. "I used to be able to coast along without people paying too much attention, or at least I didn't notice if they did. And now it's like there's a spotlight on me and there's no rest from it. It's like they're waiting for me to fall apart." I shrugged. "I don't know, maybe that doesn't make sense."

Nick made an odd sound.

"What?"

He waved his hand. "Sorry, I didn't mean to laugh."

I was annoyed that my opening up had amused him. "Why is that funny to you?"

"It's not funny. Really, it's not. It's just that I think you're forgetting who you're talking to. Because I'm literally the only black guy in the whole school. I've had a spotlight on me from the day we moved here. People watch me like a hawk, and most of them don't even know they're doing it. So believe me, I totally get it." He sighed. "I mean, before I got here, I was this really mellow person. My cousins used to call me Yoda because I didn't get all worked up about things. And I liked that about myself, I did. But here it's like this constant buzz of disapproval, where all my movements are second-guessed. Like when I take one sip of a beer, I'm an alcoholic, but when I pass, I'm a straight-edge asshole. It's like sandpaper on my nerves. I worry people will just keep working away at me until all the good parts are gone."

"They can't do that," I said. "People can't change who you are."

He shook his head. "You're wrong about that," he said. "How people treat you can absolutely change who you are. And around here, half the people act like they're scared of me, like I'm a time bomb waiting to go off, and the other half are trying to light the damn fuse. I worry one day someone will shoulder-check me in the hall or whisper something as I go by and I'll lose it. And it'll just confirm everything they thought all along."

I wanted to believe I wasn't part of the "they" he referred to. Wanted to feel confident that I was different, that I'd always seen him as more than the color of his skin, that I hadn't let that define him for me. But I wasn't sure that was true, that I'd really treated him, thought about him, like everyone else.

I pushed that tangle of thoughts down, unwilling to pull apart the threads.

"You have friends on the basketball team, though, right?"

He flicked the flower away.

"I'm friends with Brian, and Charlie mostly tolerates me by proxy, but that's about it. The minute the game is over, the rest of them are all gone. Sometimes they leave in a big pack and I just head on home." His mouth stretched in a half smile. "Once, I asked one of them about it, and he said they assumed I had other plans. Who knows—maybe they really thought that. Maybe they think I get flown out by helicopter every evening to some big city where I go clubbing with my twenty best black friends."

While it was utterly beside the point, I was temporarily distracted by the thought of him dancing underneath flashing lights, moving to a deep bass that reverberated through the floor.

He shook his head again. "Half the time I don't even turn my phone on—I get sick of seeing pictures of parties I didn't even know were happening, or the great time everyone else had at the few I actually hear about." Then he laughed, dry and bitter. "The one thing I do get is the ball during games. When I got to this place I wasn't even all that great at basketball, but everyone was so sure the black guy was going to be amazing that I got more court time than anyone else. Now I'm one of the best players on the team."

Then he rolled onto his back, done with this line of conversation.

I leaned back on my forearms and stared at the sky, which was streaked with clouds.

Once upon a time, I'd studied clouds, learned the names of all the different types. The only one I could bring to mind now was "nimbus" and I had no idea what those looked like or what weather conditions they signified.

I thought about clouds and rain.

I thought about time.

About Nick. About Anna.

About whether things would be different between Nick and me if I could turn back time and be the one who'd gone up to him when he'd been upset, be the one who'd held his hand. Except, if I could turn back time, then I'd have kept Anna from leaving that night and I'd be with her now instead of lying here with Nick in the grass.

Time only moves in one direction, though, so I just kept looking up at the sky and watching the unnamed clouds go by.

We were more discreet after that. More secretive.
Still, there were times when I wanted to tell
    you so much it was like pressure on a bruise,
    growing ever darker and more sensitive to the
    touch. I wanted to try to explain it to you.
But I didn't think there was a way to make
    you—you, who could barely stand to be
    near anyone other than me—understand
    how it felt to be touched like that. Make you
    understand how I thought feeling like that
    must mean I was falling in love.

TWENTY-NINE

THE DOORBELL RANG SOON AFTER I got back to the house after my run, catching me while I was getting ready to shower. My parents were out grocery shopping, according to the note they'd left on the table, so I pulled my sweatpants back on, tossed on a clean shirt, and headed downstairs to answer the door. The doorbell rang again right as I opened the door to reveal a police officer standing on our porch, his finger still on the bell.

It was the same one who'd come to our house before, except this time he was holding a medium-sized cardboard box. When he saw me, he took a half step back and tightened his grip on it.

"Hello. Are your parents home?" he asked.

"No, they're out."

"Oh." He looked down at the box and then up at me. "I'm here to give this to them."

"What is it?"

"It's her things, your sister's things," he said. He flushed, his pink skin turning a deep shade of salmon. "They should have been returned earlier but they got misfiled."

I wondered if *misfiled* was simply a polite term for their

having gotten left in some random room or shoved under someone's desk, slowly getting buried beneath a layer of papers and miscellaneous office supplies.

"Fine," I said. "I can take it." I reached for the box.

He seemed unclear as to whether this was an acceptable option and continued to hold the box close to his body.

"Give it to me," I said.

He didn't so much hand it over as reluctantly allow me to free it from his grasp. I gave him a few extra seconds in case there was something he needed to add. He said nothing, just continued standing there with an uncertain look on his face. I gave him a small wave, for politeness's sake, and then closed the door.

I took the box up to my room. I sat on my bed and held the box tight to my chest. I thought about Anna, about how wrong I'd been about what we were to each other, about how little she'd wanted me to know about her life.

I wondered if I had any right to look at what was inside.

I sat for a long time before I opened it. I felt guilty, like a thief, as I took out each item and laid it on my bed.

First, her phone, the screen smashed. I tried turning it on. Nothing. I put it aside.

After her phone came her shoes, tights, dress, cardigan, underwear, and hair clip. Everything she had been wearing that night, neatly folded. The idea of a policeman, or even policewoman, touching her socks, her underwear, made my stomach clench. It was difficult to accept how after her death nothing had been private anymore.

I ran my hands over her cardigan. I remembered her wearing it after she first got it, just months earlier, how I'd been envious of how warm it looked. In my arms, it was heavy and soft, but when I raised it to my face it didn't smell like Anna; it smelled like detergent. Not even the detergent we used. They must have washed it. I didn't want to think about why they'd have done that.

I left the cardigan draped over my lap as I unfolded the dress. It was a deep, dark purple—eggplant, I guess it would be called. Toward the bottom edge a button was missing, only a scrap of thread left behind. I searched the box to see if it had fallen off inside, but it wasn't there. It must have fallen off that night. When she fell.

I laid the dress on my bed and then I went outside, to the back of our house, to the stretch of grass beneath Anna's window. I got down on my knees and searched the grass, the dirt and stones beneath it, looking for the white button, for that glint of pearl, planning to sew it back onto the dress. I wanted to make one small thing of hers whole again, the way it should be.

I couldn't find it, not even after I expanded the area I searched, trying to account for its being moved around under layers of snow and ice. I kept searching, though, until I heard my parents' car coming up the drive. Only then did I dive back into the house and run upstairs to the bathroom, where I scrubbed my hands so they wouldn't question me about the layer of dirt under my nails.

And before I went downstairs for dinner, I refolded the dress and cardigan and tucked them back in the box. I was about to add her phone as well, but I hesitated. I ultimately set it aside, and then gently slid the box, with the rest of Anna's things, under my bed, out of sight.

I didn't want anyone else touching her things. They'd been touched too much already.

THIRTY

USUALLY WHEN I SAT DOWN on the bus, I got a nod from Sarah and not much more. Sarah was not exactly a morning person. But the very moment I sat down the next day, Sarah whipped off her headphones and treated me to a long rant about driver's ed. It seemed she'd been storing up all her feelings and frustrations about it, and I was, apparently, the lucky recipient. I waited it out as best I could.

"Are you done now?" I asked, after she'd finally paused for longer than a brief second to draw another breath.

"For the moment," she said. "But if I fail the test, there'll be a whole other round, I promise you. And if the instructor tells me again that it's 'cute' how nervous I am, then you'll need to bring me a cake with a saw in it while I'm in jail."

"Noted," I said. "Anyway, I wanted to ask—do you really have a 'phone guy'?"

"Yep. Phone girl, actually." Then she paused and considered. "Or maybe as a feminist I should say phone woman?"

"Is she good?"

"Yeah. I used to take it to the place where I bought it, but they'd usually try to get me to buy a new one rather than repairing it—somehow none of the stuff I do is ever covered under warranty. Mona's managed to keep it limping along for years."

"Mona? Mona Addle is your phone woman?"

"Yep."

"How did that happen?"

Sarah raised her eyebrows at me. "You see, I'm not one hundred percent sure whether you're surprised because you don't think she's capable of fixing people's phones, or because you don't understand what a girl like Mona would have to do with the humble likes of me."

I considered these two choices. Honestly, I was a bit surprised by both.

Sarah laughed. "Wow, you need to work on your poker face. Mona is a secret nerd. It's not even like it's a real secret—it's just, between all the curls and the cheerleading, people manage to forget about all her science fair trophies and think that maybe she just wandered into AP Bio by mistake or something."

"What's in it for her?"

"The two of us used to be friends. Then she got popular in middle school and dropped me," Sarah said. "Later she felt bad and tried to reconnect, but I was over it. Now I just reach out when I need some troubleshooting, and she helps me. I think it makes her feel good—like she's doing community service."

"Do you think she might look at something for me?"

Sarah shrugged. "Maybe. Honestly, though, she gets a bit grumpy when I bring her small stuff, so if it's something pretty basic you might want to first search the interwebs for an answer yourself. What she likes best is when I bring her the hard stuff."

"Mine's pretty hard. I don't think she'll even be able to do anything with it."

Sarah smiled. "Say it exactly like that. That will drive her crazy. I'll ask her about my phone too while we're at it—it's still not back to its old self." Then she paused. "Oh, and this really wouldn't be like you anyway, but just a word to the wise—do not bring up Brian with her."

"Why would I do that?"

"Because they broke up last spring. It's still a super-touchy subject. And I say this as someone who teases her about a lot—do not bring up Brian. I made that mistake already, and she'll assume I'm behind it if it happens again."

"Okay," I said.

And I meant it. But I couldn't help thinking back to Mona rushing past him during the lockdown drill, and to that day on the roof. Couldn't help wondering what exactly had happened between the two of them.

*Or maybe it's not fair to say I didn't tell you
    because I was afraid you wouldn't understand.
Maybe it was more that I was afraid that if I
    talked about it, I'd find how little there was
    to say, the words crumbling in my mouth.
    How impossible it was to explain why I
    couldn't stop.
Because obviously, I needed to stop.
Yet I couldn't. It was inevitable, like magnets.
That's an excuse. That's the truth.
I still can't explain how both of those things can be
    true at the same time.*

THIRTY-ONE

SARAH TEXTED ME LATER THAT morning to let me know that Mona would meet us in the computer lab at lunch. When we arrived, she was already there.

Waiting for her to finish up something she was doing on the computer, I found myself mesmerized by her hair. I wasn't a hair person, but I had to admit that Mona's hair was a work of art. Each curl appeared to have a full and complete life of its own.

"She won't let you boing them, if that's what you're wondering. I tried once and she wasn't having it."

Sarah was grinning at me from her seat on one of the computer lab tables, her feet pushing a chair onto its back legs until it almost tipped over.

I flushed. "I wasn't wondering that. I would never—"

Mona shook her head. "It's okay, I know." She shot Sarah an unimpressed look. "Sarah is just winding you up. She's a big fan of doing that to people."

Sarah tilted her head and looked dismayed. "Oh no—was that a dig at my social skills, perchance? Should I reform my ways so I can be part of your idiotic girl gang?"

Mona rolled her eyes, then typed a few more words. "Okay,

I'm done," she said. "And it's a squad, not a gang. And dialing back the sarcasm wouldn't be a terrible idea, if you're planning on asking me for a favor."

I started to relax. I'd been worried about this meeting, about how awkward it might be between me and Mona. But this Mona was an entirely different creature from the Mona on the roof, or even the Mona with Lauren and Beth. She seemed confident, at ease. Like she was slipping right back into a conversation she'd been having with Sarah forever.

"Favor?" Sarah asked, eyes wide and innocent. "I don't know about that. Of course, if you're bored, then I might have something you could take a look at. Jess might have something too, if you can handle it."

"Thanks oh so much. What do you have for me this time?"

"Well, since you insist—my phone is being kind of weird."

"Weird? Did you try turning it off and then on again?"

"Yeah, like ten times. You've drilled that into me. I even do that with my damn toaster now when it starts burning the bread. Off, wait ten seconds, and then on again. I'm a goddamn off-and-then-on-again robot."

"Does it help with the toaster?"

"Sometimes."

"Well, there you go. Have you been making all the updates to your phone, like I told you to?"

"Yes." Sarah paused. "Like, most of them, anyway."

Mona sighed. "So what's it doing?"

"It will barely hold a charge. It's completely drained after two hours. I've started carrying my charger around everywhere I go, but competition for the outlets is fierce."

Mona made a beckoning gesture. "Give." Sarah pulled it

from her pocket and Mona frowned as she reached over to take it. Then Mona turned to me. "So what did you bring me? I'm hoping something more exciting than this piece of junk."

I unzipped my bag and gently pulled out the Ziploc bag containing Anna's phone and handed it over.

"Whoa," she said, eyebrows shooting up. She turned it over with a reverent expression. "Now, that's what I'd call broken."

Sarah smiled. "Glad we could bring you something worth your while."

Mona opened the bag, slid out the phone, and examined it more closely.

"So what did you do to it?"

"Nothing," I said. "I mean, it's not . . . it's not really my phone."

Sarah frowned. "Wait, then whose . . ." She trailed off.

Mona looked at Sarah and then back at me. "Anna?" she asked gently.

I nodded.

Mona started to put Anna's phone down. "I'm sorry, but I don't know if this is a good idea. Besides, this is just a hobby for me, and this phone—I don't know if anyone could do anything with this phone."

"Couldn't you try?"

"I could, but . . ." She shook her head. "Look, I know she was your sister—"

"She wasn't just my *sister;* she was my twin." I closed my eyes tight, embarrassed at how suddenly they'd begun to flood. *Don't cry,* I thought. *Just take the phone and get out of here. This was a bad idea. The phone is obviously ruined; it was only going to be a dead end anyway.*

"Okay," Mona said quietly. "I'm sorry. I— Phones are just really personal things. But I get that this is different, especially since—"

Especially since Anna's never coming back.

"—you guys were twins," she finished awkwardly.

"Thanks," I said, pinching my arm hard to keep the tears from spilling out.

"Do you think there's any way you might be able to fix it?" Sarah asked.

"I don't know," Mona said. "I'd like to try. I've never seen a phone this messed up before, though. Not in person." She stared at the phone. What she said next was so quiet I barely heard her, so quiet I wasn't even sure she knew she asking it aloud. "Two stories, right?"

I nodded. "Two stories." Two stories and the weight of my twin sister. *This is what your phone would look like, Mona,* I thought, *if you had jumped.* And when I looked up at her again, as she moved her fingers softly over the shattered screen, it seemed like she was thinking that same thing.

The three of us were silent for a minute. Then Mona closed her fingers around the phone and gave me a single decisive nod.

"I can't make any promises, but I'll do my best." She stood up, tucked Anna's phone back into the bag, and placed it in the front pocket of her backpack. Sarah's phone she left on the table.

"Hey, what about mine?" Sarah asked.

"I changed my mind," Mona said. "It's time for you to get a new one."

THIRTY-TWO

LATER THAT WEEK, I SAT outside Mr. Matthews's house, looking into his living room. He'd been quieter than usual at track practice, distracted. He'd claimed to have a cold, but when one of the girls told him he should take vitamin C, he'd given her a blank look before smiling weakly and promising to stock up on orange juice.

After he arrived home, he'd hung up his coat slowly. I waited for him to go to the kitchen as he usually did. Instead, he stood in the middle of the room, staring at the window. I worried that he'd seen me, careful though I was, and then I noticed that his gaze was unfocused. He walked over to the couch, his gait unsteady, and lowered himself onto it. There, he crumpled in on himself and started to cry.

The only grown man I'd ever seen cry before was Dad, the day Anna died. Dad's tears had seemed almost painted on his rigid face, like rain on a statue. This was something altogether different. Mr. Matthews gave himself over to it completely, crying the way you cry when no one is watching, when there's no reason to try to keep it together. Ugly, heartbroken crying. His whole body curled up and he shook.

It was hard to watch, yet I was mesmerized, unable to look away.

I didn't know that he was crying about Anna. He could have been crying for any number of reasons—a sick family member, a bad teaching review, anything. The weird thing was, at that moment, I wanted it to be about Anna. I wanted him to be crying for her. I wanted someone to have been so in love with her that it broke their damn heart she was gone, that pressure built up inside them every day she wasn't there. I wanted her to have had that. Not some guy who'd already forgotten about her, who never realized how special she was.

Also, more selfishly, I wanted there to be someone else who knew the specific grief that was no longer having her in their life. Who wasn't sure how they were supposed to make it through the rest of their days without her. Because the thought of there being someone else like that made me feel, for a brief moment, less alone.

I thought I'd never be the kind of girl who changed because of a guy. Yet I did. When he said he liked my hair down, I started wearing it down more. When he said the perfume I was wearing was too strong— even though I wasn't even wearing any— I switched to an unscented deodorant. When he told me not to think too much, to cancel plans, I did that too.

I made those changes.

But then, after a month, I decided it had to end. Whatever it was. Whatever he and I were.

THIRTY-THREE

UP TO MY ELBOWS IN warm, soapy water and worn-out from a particularly grueling track practice, I felt relaxed. Very relaxed. So relaxed that I pondered aloud about the theoretical appropriateness of relationships with older men, right as I was handing my mom a sharp knife to rinse off and place on the drying rack.

The knife slipped in her hand and the tip grazed her palm. "Excuse me?" she asked.

"I think the knife got you," I said as I watched a dot of blood blossom on her hand.

"I'm fine," she said, not looking at it. "Did you just ask me whether I thought a relationship between a teenager and an adult could work out?"

"I don't think that's exactly what I said. And you really should put a Band-Aid on that," I told her as the dot grew larger. "If you don't, you'll get blood on the dishes and I'll have to redo them."

"I'm fine," she repeated. "I'd really like you to tell me why you brought that up just now. Why you think that kind of relationship might be a good idea."

By now I was pretty clear that she was not a fan of the concept, but her tone made me want to dig in. "There was that female teacher and her student we saw on the news. She went to jail but they stayed together. Even had a kid, I think. Doesn't that mean something?"

"No, all it means is that she preyed on that poor kid and he became infatuated with her. That's not a healthy relationship."

She was probably right about that not being the best example. I tried another tack.

"Okay, fine. But don't people talk about age being only a number, and don't people sometimes fall in love with someone you'd never expect? And maybe it isn't all happily ever after but it's still real? They still care about each other?"

She stared at me, her eyes searching my face. "Is there something you want to tell me?" she said slowly.

"Tell you? No."

"Because if there's a teacher at school, or maybe a friend of the family, who is pressuring you—"

It clicked. "Oh God, no. No." For some reason, my mind went not to Mr. Matthews, but to a visual of Mr. Richards using his potbelly to trap me against the circular saw.

"Are you sure? Because you won't be in trouble, but if there is, then it's *very* important that we talk about—"

"No."

"There isn't?" A sliver of hope entered her voice.

"No," I repeated firmly. "I promise."

"Oh, thank God." She leaned against the sink. "Because age really isn't just a number, Jess. Remember that, and never trust someone who says otherwise. Okay?"

I nodded, because I really wanted us to get off the subject already. Bringing it up had been a huge mistake.

"Okay," she said. Then she glanced down at her hand. "Oh, I really should put a Band-Aid on that."

"I'll get you one," I said, happy to have an excuse to get away.

As I went through the bathroom cupboard, I wondered why I'd said it. And I kept coming back to how I wasn't so clear anymore about how I felt about the idea of Mr. Matthews and Anna. Initially, I'd thought if they'd been together, that made him a creep, a predator. Yet watching him in his house had made it more difficult for me to think of him that way. I wondered if it was possible there'd been something good between them. In a way, I hoped there had been, because there would be no do-over for her, no second chance to find someone who'd get it right.

Still, maybe it was delusional to think they could've had anything good together, naïve to feel differently toward him because I'd seen him cry and talk to his cat. I wasn't sure.

I missed being sure.

THIRTY-FOUR

POLICE OFFICERS TALKING ABOUT DARE had been a main-stay of school assemblies since middle school. Once a year, a well-scrubbed officer wearing a starched uniform would come out and give us all a speech about the perils of drugs and drinking—how taking one sip of alcohol before legal drinking age, or one hit/shot/dose of any drug ever, would lead to a rapid decline into addiction, homelessness, and (for girls) pregnancy.

I wasn't really in the mood for this annual round of caution-ary tales, but it wasn't like there was anyone to appeal to, so after the announcement was made for everyone to assemble in the gym, I trudged along.

When I got there, Sarah waved me over, forcing the guy who'd just sat down next to her to move.

"Hey, did I mention that I passed my driving test?" she asked.

"Yes," I said. "Several times now."

"Wow, you really know how to make a person feel good about their achievements," she said. Then she frowned. "You doing okay?"

I followed her gaze and found that I was cradling my left arm.

"I smacked it on the doorframe coming in," I told her. "I broke it once, so it's just a little sensitive."

"You broke it fighting crime, I presume?"

"Rope swing accident. I misjudged when to jump."

"I prefer my explanation." She nodded toward the microphone set up on the floor of the gym. "So, what do you think it will be this time? One of those 'Hey, I was young once too and thought I had to drink and take drugs to be cool' guys, or one of the tough-love 'Let's look at pictures of baby-faced kids and the flaming car wrecks they died in' guys?"

"Hard to say."

She nodded thoughtfully. "I'm hoping for one without all the gruesome photos. Actually, scratch that, what I'm really hoping for is a reenactment of the time when one of the debate kids started cross-examining the guy about how bad was marijuana anyway given how a bunch of states have legalized it already."

I smiled. "I remember that. The guy got all red in the face."

Sarah dropped her voice. "Look, kid, it's illegal here, right? I don't make the laws and I'm not here to get into arguments about it. Just don't do it."

"Critical thinking at its finest."

"Yep. They should just focus on meth. I mean, with meth, it's got to be easier. One look at a photo of a meth addict, with their creepy hollow faces and their messed-up teeth, and I'm pretty much convinced to never touch the stuff."

The principal walked up to the podium and smoothed her hair behind her ear, looking calmly out at the crowd of disgruntled and fidgeting students. The drone of conversations dimmed, and then she cleared her throat and the room became silent.

"Thank you all for coming," she said. "Let's give a warm welcome to Officer Myra Heron from the Birdton Police Department."

What followed was a mixture of perfunctory applause and ironic slow clapping.

Officer Heron walked up to the front and exchanged a quick handshake with the principal. I hadn't recognized the name, but there was something familiar about her broad face, her steady forward gaze.

When she reached the podium, she spread her hands out, held the corners, and surveyed the room. It was then I placed her. She was the policewoman who'd offered me hot chocolate at the hospital. Details from that day rushed back to me, and I had to lean forward, suddenly dizzy. I pinched my arm hard, willing myself to snap out of it. *Not here*, I thought. I pinched the same spot harder and made myself look up and focus on Officer Heron.

"I attended this high school fifteen years ago," she was saying. "Sat in this room and listened to how drugs and alcohol ruined young lives. I didn't think it applied to me, and didn't really care if it did. So I ignored it. Did all the things I wasn't supposed to do."

She looked out at the room before she continued. "Until one night I got high and decided to go for a drive."

Everyone in the room stopped shifting around, stopped whispering, waiting to hear about how she plowed into a pregnant lady, or woke up hours later hanging upside-down from a tree with four broken ribs.

Then, unexpectedly, she laughed.

"Which was a terrible idea, of course, especially since I was too bombed out to actually open the garage door first, so I only got three feet before I smashed into it."

There was a smatter of laughter in response, as well as a distinct wave of disappointment that the story didn't have a juicier end.

"I was grounded for a month," she said, shaking her head and smiling. "And my parents made me pay for a new garage door and for the repairs to the car. And let me tell you, garage doors are a lot more expensive than you'd think. I'm talking *years* of babysitting money down the drain."

She stopped smiling. "That's the thing—it sucked, and it was embarrassing as hell. But now it's a funny story because in the end nothing really happened. Because the door was closed, I didn't end up hurting anyone, didn't even have the space to get up enough speed to hurt myself beyond some minor whiplash. If it had been open, though, who knows what would've happened? What I might have done to a neighbor or a friend, what I might have done to myself? That's the thing. You never know. In mere seconds, your life can change forever."

There were over three hundred students and teachers in the room, including kids whose substance abuse had long passed from open secret to running joke—any number of people at whom that message could have, should have, been directed.

Instead, for what felt like an eternity, she looked right at me.

"DID YOU SEE THAT?" I asked Sarah quietly as we streamed out of the gym after the assembly finally finished.

"What, you mean those slides she showed at the end?" she

said. "Yeah, but I wish I hadn't. Those were grim. Also, is it just me or did she spend a really long time talking about not letting anyone come near your drink when you're at a party? I mean, a *really* long time on that?"

I shook my head. "No, before that. I meant how she looked at me."

"Looked at you when?"

"Right after her whole banging-up-the-garage-door story."

She shrugged. "No, sorry, I didn't notice. She probably wasn't really looking at you, though. She was probably just looking out around the room. I've heard there's a technique people use to make everyone feel like they're being looked at so they pay attention or whatever."

"No, she was definitely looking at me."

"Fine, she looked at you. So what? Unless you've been secretly getting wasted and plowing into garage doors, I don't think you've got anything to worry about."

I was about to argue and then I stopped myself. Sarah was probably right; it didn't mean anything. People had to look somewhere and her gaze had simply happened to fall on me.

Still, it was like a piece of sand in my brain the rest of the day, a low-level irritant that kept resurfacing.

I CALLED THE POLICE STATION that night and asked for Officer Heron. I was told that she'd just left for a family vacation and would be out of town for the next two weeks.

"Did you want to leave her a message?" the chirpy voice on the other side of the line asked. "I can send you to her voice mail."

"No," I said after a moment had passed. "That's all right." And then I hung up.

It was probably nothing, I told myself, my phone still in my hand. Probably nothing at all. Probably. Still, I opened my phone's calendar and marked the exact date that Officer Heron would be back in the office.

This was a mistake, I told him. We need to stop.
I must have looked panicked, determined, because
he didn't argue with me—didn't try to talk
me out of it. He said he'd been thinking the
same thing, that he should never have let it
happen to begin with.
I felt so relieved.

THIRTY-FIVE

I LET SARAH TALK ME into going to the basketball game with her. "He's intense," I told her as the coach blew his whistle, forcing all the players on the court to skid to a stop.

"Yep," Sarah said. "That's part of what I love about these games. So much blood, sweat, and tears over nothing. My only regret is that Mona isn't a cheerleader anymore—I enjoyed making fun of her bopping around in formation."

"Do you know why she quit?" I asked.

"I don't know. I guess she came to her senses. That or she got sick of my awesome cheerleading impression."

I leaned forward and tried to focus on the game. As a whole, not just Nick. Although he was an important part. Even from an unbiased perspective.

As I was watching him, the coach blew his whistle again— loud and hard.

"What happened?"

"Another foul from Charlie," Sarah said. "Not even a subtle one that time. One of these guys will get fouled out soon if they don't watch themselves."

"Fouled out?"

"Too many fouls and you get benched for the rest of the game."

I shook my head. "This game is bizarre—more than half the team isn't even playing."

"The couch will sub them all in at different points." She pointed as Brian headed from the court to the bench and another guy jumped up and headed into the fray. "See, the coach is putting in someone else to be shooting guard now."

I gave her a blank look.

She laughed. "Okay, I probably wouldn't know that either if my dad didn't watch so much basketball. Here's the short version: there are five positions—point guard, shooting guard, small forward, power forward, and center." She pointed out at the court. "See, they've got Nick as point guard, and then Charlie as power forward, and then that beanstalk in the middle, Trent"—she waggled her finger toward the guy who was by far the tallest guy on the court—"they've got him as center because he could probably dunk the ball without so much as leaving the ground."

"Got it," I said. "The game now fascinates me."

"Wow, sarcasm. You're learning."

I rolled my eyes.

"Pro tip," she said. "If you want to soften Nick up, you should tell him that he's a super-awesome point guard with amazing ball-handling skills. He'll be like putty in your hands."

"I do not want him to be 'putty in my hands,'" I told her.

"Actually," she said, with a wicked grin, "I think you kind of do."

———

SARAH WAS NOT RIGHT. BUT then again, she wasn't wrong. It was confusing.

And I was still thinking about that—about Nick, about hands—the next day when Mona slid into the seat across from me in the cafeteria.

"I'm here to give you back your phone," she said.

I nodded, bracing myself for disappointing news. "Nothing you could do, right?"

"Oh no," she said, smiling. "I fixed it."

"You fixed it? Really?"

Mona started to search through her bag. "Yeah. It still looks like hell, of course. It's up to you if you want to pony up for a new screen. But it turns on now, and I'm ninety percent sure that everything will still be there—though you'll only know for sure once you put in your—I mean her—password."

She handed over the Ziploc with Anna's phone. The phone looked just like it had before, the screen a maze of spider-webs, but somehow it felt different, now that I knew it worked again, like it contained more than metal and chips. "That's amazing. Thank you."

She nodded, then blushed. "Oh," she said. "I just realized . . . wouldn't it have been turned off by now?"

I shook my head. "Family plan," I told her.

"Oh, okay. Good." She paused. "I can stay for a minute if you want me to look at it. Make sure all the data is still there."

"No thanks," I said. "I'd prefer to do it on my own."

"Right. Of course," she said, and started to stand up. Then she stopped. "If she has anything weird on her phone, maybe you could let me know?"

"Weird how?"

She paused. "I wondered if—" Then she stopped. "You know

what? Never mind. I hope it works, Jess. I hope you find whatever it is you're looking for."

AT FIRST NOTHING HAPPENED, AND I thought Mona had been wrong, that it was still broken. I almost dropped it on the floor of the bathroom—where I'd retreated for privacy—when it lit up and buzzed in my hand.

Anna's password was the month and year of our birthday. I'd told her a million times to change it, to make it something harder to guess. Now I was grateful that she hadn't.

I looked at her texts first. The last one she'd received was from Lily:

Sorry, but need to push it back by 30. And the boys may stop by first before we head out.

Anna had texted her back shortly afterward:

Okay, see you then!

That was all there was. On the surface, it kind of fit with the narrative Mom had proposed—that Anna and Lily had been planning to hang out together but expected that some boys might drop by. *The boys.* One must have been Charlie for Lily, and the other . . . Brian? Certainly, Lily wouldn't have described Mr. Matthews that way. But maybe he was the next part of the itinerary—what they were heading toward.

I kept scrolling back through her messages with Lily, hoping to find something more concrete—a name, a telling detail. Nothing.

I went to Anna's photos, thinking maybe I'd find some picture of her with the guy—their faces close together, smiling. Or even just a picture of Mr. Matthews alone. She would have wanted that, I thought, some proof, something to carry around with her. Except there was no photo like that. Close-ups of flowers and trees and ruined old barns, yes; some goofy group shots from cross-country, photos of her and Lily, and some shots of me and her, her arm stretched out to catch us both.

And then, from a few weeks before she died, there was something different. A photo of her taken in a mirror. A full-length one of her completely naked.

And she hadn't sent it to one phone number.

She'd sent it to two.

A week later, Lily disappeared while we were at the bar, leaving me alone as time ticked by.

After a while, I got nervous. I checked the bathroom, every corner of the bar. I finally went out into the parking lot. And there she was walking back, wearing a secret smile, hair mussed, arm around some guy. I pretended not to see her—just headed back into the bar.

So when he put his hand on my leg again, I didn't move away. Instead, I thought of Lily that night. And I moved closer.

If Lily could have her secrets, then I could have mine.

THIRTY-SIX

I FELT SICK TO MY stomach, knowing I'd seen something Anna would never have wanted me to see, and also deeply confused. If she'd sent the photo to one number, I'd have assumed I had my answer. But two? Two was different.

Additionally, there was something off about the photo. She wasn't smiling—wasn't looking flirty or pouty or anything I thought someone might aim for in that kind of photo. Instead, she looked almost angry. Like she resented taking it.

One of the numbers had no name attached, only the number. There were no other texts to that number.

The second one was listed as "pf5." There were other texts from this number, unfortunately all unhelpfully short and clipped:

Not today.

Meet me in the parking lot.

You're late.

I HEADED OUTSIDE TO TAKE the next step. When I reached the outermost white line of the football field and took a deep breath. Then I used Anna's phone and called the first number she'd sent the picture to.

As it rang, I couldn't help but picture it vibrating in Mr. Matthews's pocket, his fingers reaching in to picking it up. Couldn't help but wonder what his face might look like when he saw her name on his screen.

No one picked up. And when the phone finally stopped ringing, I was dumped into a generic voice mail box.

My hands were shaking so hard that I had to hit the button twice to hang up.

Then I tried calling the second number.

It rang three times before a voice came on the line. A cold, mechanical voice telling me that the number I had dialed was no longer in service. I listened to the message four times before it sank in and I slowly hung up.

I sat down in the grass, my nerves shot. I'd thought Anna's phone would provide answers. Instead, I only had more questions.

THIRTY-SEVEN

I PAGED THROUGH MY FRESHMAN yearbook after I got home, searching for someone with the initials PF. I went carefully through each grade, all the teachers, all the staff. It was strange to see how each individual looked, boiled down to a single shot. Some of my classmates had already transformed within the space of less than a year into someone almost completely different, while others had never really looked like their photograph to begin with—the image missing some essential aspect, flattening them into a pancake version of themselves.

The only one with the initials PF was Penelope Fetts, a junior with shiny dark hair and a wide gap between her front teeth. While I was trying to be open-minded, the birth control pills in Anna's locker seemed to squarely rule Penelope out.

I did a second sweep through the book, to see if I'd missed anyone. This time, I lingered for a moment when I got to the photographs of me and Anna, which were, as always, side by side. Even in black-and-white, Anna glowed with that wide, unmistakable smile, like a child who'd just been handed a warm puppy. Next to her, I looked sullen, watchful, like I was deciding what I wanted more: to vanish into thin air or to kick the photographer in the shins. Our parents had laughed when they'd seen the photos. "There it is," they'd said. "They got you both."

Neither of us appeared in any other photographs. Nick, I noticed, showed up three times—his official school picture, jumping to make a shot in a game, and then in the back row of the basketball team photo. It was only in this last photograph that he was smiling, his teeth shining a brilliant white, a hint of dimple in his left cheek.

It was distracting, that dimple. It really was.

THIRTY-EIGHT

THE BREEZE FLARED AND SKATED along the surface of my arms and neck, cooling the patches of sweat that had formed as we'd run.

"I went to the basketball game the other day," I told Nick, casting it into the air like confetti at a wedding. I planned to follow up with some astute commentary about the game—totally stolen from Sarah—into which I'd skillfully weave one or two compliments about his playing.

I was thrown off course when Nick nodded and said, "Yeah, I noticed."

"Oh. I didn't realize you'd seen me."

He smiled a little at that. "Our fan base isn't exactly so vast that it's hard to take everyone in. In fact"—he raised a finger and closed his eyes for a second before opening them again—"I believe you and Sarah were there together, four rows up near the edge, by the exit that goes out to the bathroom."

"That's pretty good," I said. Sarah and I had actually been five rows up, but I thought I'd let that slide.

"Yeah, well, I didn't expect to see you there—hadn't pegged you as a big sports fan." He paused. "You know, I thought maybe you'd come say hi once it was over."

I'd wondered about that, how it would feel to make my way over to him, navigating the crush of people who'd descended upon the court after the game—the parents, friends, girlfriends who'd surrounded the various players. It had seemed so public, so vulnerable a thing to do, though, to stroll up to him like that and publicly demand his attention.

"Sarah had to get her parents' car back," I lied. "So we left right afterward."

"Sure," he said, his voice a fraction stiffer, like it had taken on a protective coating. "I get it. Running is our thing. That's fine."

"That's not—"

I was interrupted by a sharp chirping sound. He paused and then reached into his pocket for his phone. He stared at the screen and laughed.

"What is it?" I asked, both relieved and annoyed by the interruption.

"Nothing," he said. "Just my mom. She's decided that her fight against global warming involves texting me every time I forget to turn off a light or mess up the recycling."

He flipped his phone around and showed it to me.

She'd sent a picture of what I assumed must be his room, lights on. Below she'd written:

Every time you do this, a polar bear pup dies.

"That's dramatic," I said.

"I'm getting better about the recycling. Left to my own devices, though, I'd probably end up leaving all the lights in the entire house on. So maybe I secretly hate polar bears."

"Or maybe you really like seals," I said.

He smiled. "Good point."

We could have just gone on from there, not circled back.

But I felt that I'd messed up, left behind an incorrect impression. So I tried again.

"I really am glad that I went to the game, you know. And I wanted to say hi afterward, I did."

He shook his head. "It's okay."

"No, I wanted to. . . . I particularly, uh, enjoyed watching your point guarding. And all that ball handling you did. But there were all these people, and I just . . . I don't know." None of it came out the way I wanted it to. My original version, my planned version, had been so much better. I closed my eyes and willed the blush rising in my cheeks to subside.

He was quiet. After a few painful moments, I snuck a look at him and found that he was smiling at me.

"What?" I asked.

"Nothing," he said. "I'm glad you enjoyed watching me play."

"I wasn't like *watching* you, watching you," I said. "I just noticed, in the larger context of the game." Even as I said it, I started smiling. I couldn't have explained why.

"Uh-huh," he said. "You can tell yourself that if you like. But now I know the truth, that you're a huge fan of . . . point guarding."

And I smiled wider. It made no sense, because my plans had gone totally awry, yet I was pretty sure it had all ended up where I'd hoped it would. The two of us outside in the sunshine, flirting.

We didn't talk much, him and I. Not when it was
just the two of us.
I feel so ashamed saying that. I want to tell you
that there was something beautiful there, that
we spoke of deep things together, shared our
hopes and dreams. But then it would be a love
story, and that's not what this is.

THIRTY-NINE

THE REMINDER THAT SHONE OUT at me from my phone two days later was unnecessary. Because I'd known from the second I woke up that this was the day Officer Heron would be back at work.

The night before, I'd sat outside Mr. Matthews's window and tried calling the number from Anna's phone again. His phone was in front of him on his coffee table. I couldn't see the screen, couldn't tell if it lit up, but I couldn't hear it ring, and his attention didn't waver from his television. No one else picked up either.

I'd tried calling the number a third time at lunch, dialing and then scanning the room to see if someone might answer, if I could connect a voice with a face. No luck. I tried a fourth time, calling from my own phone. Again, no one answered, and there were too many people looking at their phones to tell if any of them had received and ignored the call.

It was a relief when the last bell rang and I could finally start making my way toward the police station. The station was located near the top of a small hill, a good twenty minutes from school—or closer to ten if I jogged. Which was, of course, what I did.

Jogging is much easier when you're not wearing jeans and

loafers and carrying a heavy backpack, so I was slightly winded when I arrived. I paused to catch my breath and stared at the station. It needed a new coat of paint, and had for some time—the original color, a rich forest green, could still be seen in some of the protected crevices of the walls, but the passage of time had bleached most of it to a muted mint.

Inside, I walked up to the first person in uniform I saw, a middle-aged woman with a blond ponytail and an excess of eye shadow who was reading something on a clipboard. She moved her lips slowly as she read, and her forehead creased with effort.

"I would like to speak to Officer Heron, please," I said.

"I'll see if she's available," she said, sounding bored and barely looking up from her clipboard. She disappeared through a swinging door. As it was closing, I caught a glimpse of two officers standing up, arguing, while another one sat at a desk and consulted his watch.

I waited. The walls of the front room were decorated with a few photographs of Montana's finest scenic vistas, their edges turning sepia.

Officer Heron appeared from the back area. She blinked when she saw me.

"Jess Cutter?"

"Yes," I said. "Hi."

She paused and scanned the room behind me. "Are you here with your parents?"

"No," I said. "It's just me."

"All right," she said. "Would you like to come back and talk?"

I nodded, and she held open the door for me.

We went into a small side room with grayish-brown walls and a musty smell. In it were a small table and two chairs, all of which had a look of resignation to them, like they were tired out.

"Please sit," she said, gesturing to one of the chairs. "What can I help you with?"

Now that I was here face to face with her, I stalled.

"You gave me hot chocolate that day," I said. "It was kind of you. I didn't realize how cold I was until you did that."

She smiled. "A mixed blessing, then."

"It gave me something to do with my hands," I said. I realized, in retrospect, it had been helpful. Some small thing to concentrate on. Small like a button. I might as well ask about that too, I thought. Get it all out now. Start with something concrete.

"There was an item missing from the box of Anna's things," I said. "I wondered if you might have it here."

"Okay, what was missing?"

"A button."

Her eyebrows went up. "A button?"

"Yes," I said. "There was one missing from her dress. It should have been somewhere on the ground right next to her."

The skin between her eyebrows folded together. "I don't think we found anything like that. I can check, though. It might take a couple of minutes."

While she was gone, I played sudoku on my phone. I'd almost finished my fourth round when she came back.

"I'm sorry," she said once she'd sat down again. "I checked the report and there was no button picked up at the scene."

The scene. Otherwise known as my backyard. "Well, thanks for checking."

"Of course," she said. "Is there anything else I can help you with?"

Okay, I thought. *Now you have to do it. Now you have to ask.*

"You came to the school, to talk about DARE. I thought . . ."

I closed my eyes, trying to make myself power through it. "It seemed like you looked at me, right after you talked about how badly it could have gone, with you in the car. . . ."

I trailed off, feeling foolish, my gaze dropping to the desk. *This is when you say you have no idea what I'm talking about,* I thought.

"I'm sorry about that," she said. "I wasn't thinking. I hope you know I didn't mean anything by it."

I looked up again, frowning in confusion.

"Accidents happen all the time—without or without alcohol being involved," she continued. "It doesn't make what happened less tragic, doesn't make it anyone's fault. It wasn't even like she'd had all that much—but when you're petite, like—well, you, it can certainly have an effect."

She wasn't making any sense.

"What are you talking about? Anna hadn't had anything to drink. They were supposedly going to drink at Lily's place, but Anna never got there."

"No, they found—" She cut herself short and searched my face, looking for some kind of understanding, some sign that I knew what she was talking about.

"I'm sorry," she said finally. "I must have been confusing her with someone else."

There are lies that are subtle and hard to spot, and then there are lies that burn with the brightness of a million suns, blinding you with their sheer audacity.

"With someone else?" My disbelief was palpable.

"Look, I shouldn't have said anything." She paused. "I'm sorry. I didn't realize . . ."

I continued to stare at her. She shook her head. "Shit."

"I don't understand. Are you saying Anna was drunk?"

"I'm not saying anything. I didn't say anything." She wrapped her fingers together, squeezing them tight, as if trying to regain control of the situation. "I'm sorry, but I think you should go." She didn't look at me as she said it, not in the eyes, anyway, instead focusing on an area between my mouth and my chin.

"I don't understand," I repeated, at a loss for any other words.

"I shouldn't be talking to you about this," she said. She got up and opened the door. "You should leave now."

"She was my twin," I said desperately. "How can it be wrong for you to talk to me about her? Why can't you just tell me?"

She looked me in the eye for a moment. And there it was, that sadness again.

"I think you should talk to your parents," she said.

Once, I made an effort to really talk to him,
  thinking that if I opened up, he'd follow suit.
  I told him about how you and I had been
  obsessed with Greek myths growing up. Told
  him about how angry you'd gotten with
  Orpheus, going into the underworld to find
  his wife, to bring her back, only to lose her by
  turning to see her right before they'd reached
  the surface again. Told him that I'd always
  loved the story of Icarus, that I'd been
  fascinated with the idea of this man who'd
  soared so close to the sun, wondered if those
  few perfect moments before the wax melted
  were almost worth it, to fly like that.
After I finished I thought maybe he'd tell me a
  story about himself.
He didn't.
I don't think he'd even listened to what I said.

FORTY

AT DINNER THAT NIGHT, I was very quiet.

My parents were debating whether we had anything for dessert when I cleared my throat and made the words come out.

"Is there something I should know about Anna's death?"

Mom looked up, confused. "What do you mean?"

"About her death, about that night, is there something you haven't told me? Something the police told you?"

She looked at Dad. They exchanged a long look, as if trying to gauge whether the other one had slipped up and said something.

"Something like what?" Mom asked carefully. "Did someone say something to you?"

"Don't do that," I said. "Don't fish around to see what I already know. Just tell me."

"We told you everything important," Dad said. "We did."

"What did you *not* tell me—what did you decide I don't need to know?"

"It's not like that. It's just . . ." He looked over at Mom and this time she nodded. "They did a tox screen. They found some alcohol in her blood."

I shook my head. "That doesn't make sense."

"It wasn't that much. And there was nothing else, just alcohol," Mom said. "Really. It doesn't change anything. Not to us."

"Nothing else? What are you even talking about? She wouldn't have had anything to drink."

"The police found two empty beer bottles in her closet," Dad said softly. "She must have drunk them before heading out. We already knew about them. The tox screen just confirmed it."

"No, that's not right. That's not what happened. They must have gotten the test wrong. They must have mixed it up with someone else."

"I don't think so, sweetheart," Mom said. "But this is why we didn't tell you—we were worried you'd get upset. This doesn't change anything. Kids sneak out, have a beer, all the time, and they're fine—this was just a terrible accident. It's no one's fault."

"But you're wrong. You don't know what you're talking about." I found myself standing up, my words echoing through the room. Mom leaned forward against the table and began to cry silently. "Show me the report," I said, trying to bring my voice down a notch, to sound calmer, more reasonable. "They've got it wrong."

Dad put his arm around Mom, like he was sheltering her from me. "I'm sorry, sweetheart," he said. "I know it isn't what you wanted to hear."

"That's not what this is," I said. "They messed up. Give me the report."

"We don't have a report," Dad said. "We don't want one. The police chief himself told us the findings, and they confirm what we already suspected. That's all we need. You have to accept this. It's important that we all accept it."

I opened my mouth and then closed it again and stiffly pushed away from the table.

Dad called my name but I kept on going, up the stairs, into my room, closing the door behind me.

I clambered into the top bunk and pulled the comforter tightly around me.

They didn't understand at all, either of them. Because they thought I meant I didn't *want* it to be true, that I didn't want to face the idea that Anna might have, even in some small way, contributed to what happened to her. And maybe I didn't, but that wasn't what I meant. Because it wasn't that I didn't want her to have drunk those beers that night. It was that I *knew* she hadn't.

I knew because we'd drunk them together, five months earlier.

FORTY-ONE

BEER IS REVOLTING. WHICH HAD come as a shock. I'd really thought it wouldn't be so bad. I'd figured it would be like mustard greens or radishes—foods you won't touch when you're little and then later you find out are actually delicious. Or at least not as terrible as you'd thought.

Beer wasn't like that.

Still, between the two of us we'd made it through both bottles.

It had been an unusually warm autumn night, and our parents had gone out to the movies. We'd been bored and hot, so Anna had snuck two bottles of beer from the fridge. We'd drunk the bottles one by one, trading them back and forth. And there was something that had felt . . . cool about sitting on her bed, the warm night air flowing in through the window, trading the cold bottle between us, letting its neck dangle from our fingers.

Anna kept asking if I felt anything. I'd felt looser, maybe, my limbs less tense. When I asked her, she'd smiled and said she thought she might feel a little buzzed. We'd laughed a lot, at even sillier things than usual, but that could have just been from nervous energy, the edge of worry that our parents might suddenly show up again, their movie canceled, to find us with beer on our breaths and guilty expressions on our faces. And sometime after the second beer, we'd both fallen asleep on her bed, too warm to bother with blankets.

Early the next morning, Anna had stashed the bottles in her closet so our parents wouldn't see them. She'd said she'd sneak them down to our recycling bin once enough other bottles had accumulated that two additions wouldn't stand out.

I'd offered to do it instead, certain she'd forget about them, but she'd insisted she'd remember.

Obviously, she hadn't.

MY MOM'S SIGNATURE WAS CLEAN and smooth, each letter easily decipherable. My dad's was little more than a line with a couple of small bumps in the middle, mere upward twitches of the wrist. It was his signature I forged on the autopsy request form.

On the rest of the form, I tried my best to infuse my hand-writing with his particular style of borderline unreadable scrawl, to tick the necessary boxes with the kind of flick I'd seen him use.

While I wasn't sure if I thought, like Lauren, that the police were morons, I was pretty sure they weren't all the brightest lights in town. Also, they'd mislaid Anna's things before, so it was no major leap to think they could have misread or misinterpreted toxicology results—made incorrect assumptions. They might have glanced over the report and come to the easy conclusion, the one that matched the bottles they'd already lifted from her room.

I needed to see a copy of the autopsy report myself to

confirm whether it truly said what my parents had told me. So I'd mail in the form I'd downloaded from the county medical examiner's website and wait for a response.

In the meantime, I had to revisit all my preconceptions about Anna's death. I'd assumed, like everyone, that Anna had fallen leaving the house. If she'd had alcohol in her system that night, though, that pointed to an entirely different story. In that version, she'd had no problem at all leaving—the problem had been getting back up to her room. Which would mean that there was unaccounted-for time. Time when Anna had been out in the world, alive, while I'd been asleep. Time when she'd been with someone. Time when things had happened.

I wanted to be responsible, in at least one way.
The nurse I met with at the clinic called me
     "honey," and her eyes were kind as she pressed
     the sample box of birth control pills into my
     hands.
I must have looked sad as I stared down at the
     box, because she asked what should have been
     a simple question.
Is he nice to you, this boyfriend of yours?
I didn't know how to answer. Didn't know how
     to tell her that he wasn't exactly nice, and he
     definitely wasn't my boyfriend.

FORTY-TWO

THE FOLLOWING SATURDAY THE TRACK team had its first meet of the season.

My first race was the 100-meter. Longer distances could involve a certain amount of strategy, decisions about whether to try to take the lead at the beginning and hold on to it or save your energy for a burst at that final stretch, but the 100-meter was all about pure speed—strategy only got in the way.

I was positioned four lanes in. The girl on my left slowly cracked each of her knuckles, ignoring my pointed glare as she finished one hand and moved on to the other one. I wanted her to fall flat on her face and later develop early arthritis in all her finger joints.

Then I put thoughts of her and her hopefully unpleasant future aside and focused on taking deep, deliberate breaths. I could do this. It was running, and I was a runner. *This is running and I am a runner.*

"Ready!"

Inhale. Exhale.

"Set!"

Inhale. Exhale.

The starter pistol fired.

My feet hit the track. One, two. One, two. One-two, one-two.

My arms pumped, my legs reached forward, and everything else followed.

This is running and I am a runner.

I was only dimly aware of the other people on the track. It wasn't about them anymore. It was only about me.

One-two, one-two, one—

I hit the finish line in first place.

I came to a halt, feeling light-headed.

"Great job, Jess!" my dad yelled from the bleachers. My mom held his arm and beamed at me. I was glad they were here, that they had seen me win.

Sarah and a bunch of my teammates cheered. And Lauren looked unhappy, the ultimate sign of success.

As I headed back to the stands, Mr. Matthews grinned at me and put his hand up for a high five. I hesitated. It wasn't clear how to avoid it without being obvious, though, so I quickly slapped his hand and then beat a hasty retreat to go sit with Sarah.

"Good job," she said. "Your parents are pretty cute, getting all excited."

"Thanks," I said. "Did your parents come?"

"My dad did," she said.

"But not your mom?"

"Nope, she had lunch plans with one of her girlfriends or something." She gave a weird laugh. "It's probably just as well. The last time she came to a meet she pulled me aside afterward and told me I should be careful—she'd noticed that my thighs were getting 'bulky.'"

I looked at her thighs. They looked strong and hard. *Bulky* was not a word I would have applied to them.

"They look fine to me."

"Yeah, well, you're obviously not the thigh connoisseur she is."

I shook my head and thought back to the last time I'd seen her mom, all willowy limbs, her hair up in a perfect chignon. Beautiful and ethereal, as if she'd be blown to pieces by a strong wind. Then I thought about my mom and how she'd always told me and Anna how beautiful we were, how proud of us she was. We'd laughed and made stupid faces and said what about now? Are we beautiful now? Are you proud of us now? And she'd said yes, always.

Sarah sighed. "The pathetic thing is that sometimes I look at her and she's so damn pretty that I catch myself wondering if all the stupid stuff she does—fasting, strange green protein shakes, obsessive moisturizing—is worth it. And then I get scared she'll suck me into caring about it the way she does. That one day I'll trade my eyeliner—which she hates—for her stupid coral lipstick and twenty years later, boom, I'll be preaching the gospel of hot yoga and spending over an hour in front of the mirror each morning to achieve the 'natural' look."

"I like your eyeliner," I said. "It makes you look like a warrior."

She smiled and rolled her eyes, even though I'd meant it— the eyeliner made her look fierce and tough, like an Amazon. We sat in silence for a few moments, and then I broached a subject I'd been wondering about for the last few days.

"If you wanted to go somewhere with someone, where would you go?" I asked.

"That's super vague," she said.

"Like to drink," I said. "Or other stuff."

"Other stuff?" Sarah grinned at me, her eyebrows arched.

"This is hypothetical," I assured her. "You can bring those eyebrows back down already."

"Hypothetical my ass."

"No, really," I said. "Where do most people go? For stuff they can't or don't want to do at home."

"So, what—you're just doing a sociological study of teenage habits in Birdton, right? Just an impartial survey to map the behavior of the natives?"

"Something like that."

"Yeah, with you it's almost possible. Well, the big place is the quarry. Especially to drink, but also to, you know, make out in dark corners or have the sexy-sex."

"The quarry? That was where there was a big party, right?"

"Yeah, probably. Anyway, most people have three options: the backseat of their car, if they have one; some random place that just happens to be available when they need it; or the quarry."

"I guess privacy is kind of hard to come by around here."

She smiled. "Yeah, yet people find a way." She stood up. "All right, my heat is coming up, so I'm going to head on down—wish me luck."

"I doubt you'll need it," I told her.

"Thank you," she said, placing her hand over her heart, beauty queen style. "That just means so much." Then she pointed at my bag. "You got a message."

I followed her finger and saw a dim light shining through the thin canvas of my bag. "Thanks," I said, but she'd already headed off to the track.

It was only after I unzipped my bag that I remembered my

phone wasn't there. It was lying right beside me on the bleacher. The phone in my bag wasn't my phone at all. It was Anna's.

I pulled it out, and there was a text on the screen:

Stop calling me, little girl.

I stared at it, bewildered.

You don't know, I thought. *You don't know that Anna is dead.*

We kept going to the bar. We needed it to escape.
I didn't ask Lily what she was trying to escape.
  I should have.
I was trying to escape myself—even as I began
  to worry about what I might say if I got too
  drunk, talked too much.
Somehow I thought of the bar as a safe place.
That was a mistake.

FORTY-THREE

BIRDTON WAS NOT EXACTLY AN exciting metropolis filled with lots of newsworthy mayhem. People would get cited for drunk driving, someone might get arrested for shoplifting, and every couple of years, some guy went out hunting alone and either got lost in the woods or accidentally shot himself, usually in a painful but not lethal way, earning a new nickname in the process. That was the kind of news Birdton typically served up. Anna's death had been major news, and it would've been very hard for a resident of Birdton to have missed it.

For someone to not know that she'd died, they'd need to have been practically in a coma for the last few months, or to live outside town.

Another thing that was odd about the message was the tone. Curt, annoyed. Dismissive, even. Whoever it was had seemed utterly unworried about not having heard from her in all this time, and totally uninterested in reestablishing contact.

I had no idea how to track down someone whose only known characteristics were not living in Birdton and being an asshole.

So I decided to move on to the quarry.

THE QUARRY WAS ONLY THREE miles from school if you walked through the wooded area behind the parking lot. Which was what I did on Monday afternoon, after asking Sarah to tell Mr. Matthews I'd gone home because I wasn't feeling well.

In the woods, the trees were getting green again, and the sun filtered through their new leaves in an ever-changing pattern of light. I picked my way over dead logs and fallen branches, trying not to crush the occasional batch of emerging wildflowers.

It took me almost an hour to make it to the fence. There was a sign, its wooden post embedded deep in the earth, telling people to stay out, and ancient frayed caution tape strewn across the barbed-wire fence. Someone had clearly made an effort, a long time ago, to keep people out. Now, though, the sign and the tape functioned as little more than a tepid suggestion, particularly since not far away, a section of the fence had been cut and curled in on itself, providing an easy gateway to the heart of the quarry.

As I stepped through the wire, my foot hit a beer can, which rocked slightly and made a hollow sound. There were a lot of cans and bottles scattered around the dusty rock of the quarry, accompanied by the occasional fast-food wrapper or cigarette butt.

I slowly made my way toward the base of the quarry, staring at the ground as I walked. At first, I hoped I might find the button from Anna's dress or some other sign that she'd been here that night, but the longer I walked, the more I hoped I *wouldn't* find anything. Because it was an ugly, sad place. This wasn't somewhere you took someone you cared about, someone who wrote poems about you. This wasn't anywhere I wanted Anna to have spent her last hours.

I shouldn't have expected anything else, I told myself. It was late and dark and she went to meet someone. It shouldn't matter where they went. It shouldn't.

And then I thought back to us passing the beer between us. How it had briefly felt like we were embarking on something new together—both experiencing something more adult, more complicated than we'd known before. And I wondered if maybe I'd had it wrong, if I shouldn't have stopped her from leaving that night, if instead, I should've headed out with her, had some guy of my own waiting. And I could've simply suggested that we just go—quietly, quietly—out the back door.

Except that hadn't been on the table. Not really. She'd known I wasn't ready, that I would've wanted her to stay inside with me. So instead, she'd had Lily. Lily, who'd been ready for the same things she had, who'd usurped me as Anna's best friend, her confidante, without my even knowing it had happened. Things might be changing now, but I would always be two steps behind, running after a ghost.

I shook my head fast, trying to snap myself out of it, to keep moving. *No crying,* I thought. *Not here, among the bottles and the condom wrappers and the gray rocks.*

So I continued to hike toward the bottom, looking for a tiny button in a vast quarry, looking for a sign of something that may well not have happened. Button in a quarry, needle in a haystack. This was not, I thought, behavior that Mrs. Hayes or my parents would approve of.

By the time I reached the bottom, I had almost fallen twice, had scraped my hands from catching myself on the rocks, and had, I was fairly certain, a deep bruise forming on my left thigh. I had not, however, seen anything even vaguely useful.

Some small branches lay scattered around a large pool of water, presumably victims of a strong wind that had pulled them off the trees. Other than those, the only debris was more trash. After three meandering loops, I stood by the pool of water, trying to gear myself up to start heading back through the rocks to the trail. I stared down into the pool's muddy depths, its layers of dead leaves and rainwater. I picked up one of the branches and half-heartedly poked at the leaves, trying to push them aside so I could see how deep it was. The leaves swirled around the stick, circling it before settling. Nothing but dirt. Dirt and leaves and rocks and—

I paused, unsure of what I'd seen. I pushed the leaves aside again, using a gentler sweeping motion. There it was, a metallic glint. The rounded edge of something. I tried to carefully brush back the leaves again, but they settled back too quickly for me to get a clear look. It was too far into the pool for me to easily reach it, so I took off my shoes and socks, rolled up my sleeves and pant legs. And then I waded in, treading lightly in case there was broken glass in my path, and plunged my hand into the water where I'd seen it.

At first, all my fingers encountered were leaves and mud, and then the rock underneath them. Then they hit something firm. I reached around it, and then, even before I could see it, I knew what it was. A phone.

I pulled it out and held it in my hands. It had been a nice phone once, in a plain black case. I stood there in the pool of disgusting water, holding the dripping phone, and suddenly I began to laugh. *Good job,* I thought. *You've solved the case of the drowned phone. Here it is. The phone some drunk kid lost—probably eons ago—you've found it. Well done. Gold stars all around.*

I laughed until I was no longer sure if I was laughing or crying. Then I made myself take a series of long, slow breaths, and I tucked the still-wet phone, my treasured prize, into my pocket. *Anna, if only you could see me now,* I thought. *You wouldn't know whether to laugh or cry either.*

I backtracked out of the pool without stepping on any glass and collected my shoes and socks. I made my way to one of the larger rocks near the path back up and sat down to try to clean the mud off my feet.

Once my shoes and socks were back on, I stood up. My leg knocked against an upright bottle, which swayed and threatened to fall. When I leaned forward and steadied it, the label caught my eye. It read AMBERMOUNTAIN ALE, but the name wasn't what drew my attention. It was the pattern—a brightly colored series of intertwined geometric shapes. The exact same pattern as the coasters on Anna's bedside table. The ones I'd set aside, not giving much thought to where she might have gotten them from, not then knowing how much she'd kept from me.

I stared at the bottle.

The world, I felt, was giving me some very mixed signals.

One night, we were in the bar's parking lot, ready to go home. When Lily turned the key, the car only stuttered.

She tried it once, twice, three times. Nothing. She started to panic. I had to talk her down, make sure she didn't flood the engine. I told her it would be okay, that someone would help us.

FORTY-FOUR

ONLY ONE RESTAURANT IN BIRDTON had a liquor license, and when I called and asked if they sold AmberMountain Ale and used its coasters, they told me they weren't a "coasters kind of place." Which left me with bars.

I looked up all the ones within an hour's drive and started calling them. Only one stocked AmberMountain Ale, and they were pretty sure they had some coasters lying around. Unfortunately, that bar wasn't accessible by foot or by bus. Which meant I'd have to get someone to drive me there. Someone I trusted.

It was not a very long list.

"YOU WANT ME TO TAKE you to a bar?" Sarah asked, loud enough that I was worried the whole bus had heard her.

"Yes," I said. "And could you keep it down, please?"

She raised a single eyebrow skyward, but she did lower her voice. "I didn't think you drank. You been holding out on me, Cutter? All those books an elaborate charade—just props to hide the party girl underneath?"

"I'm not going to drink."

"You want to go to a bar but you don't want to drink. Okay, mystery wrapped in an enigma, I'm going to need a bit more than that," she said.

"No, this is me calling in a favor for going to the basketball game. I want you to take me to a bar and not ask me why I'm asking you."

"That doesn't seem like a fair trade to me, especially given how you *enjoyed* going to the basketball game," she said.

"Who knows, maybe you'll enjoy driving me to the bar," I countered.

She was not amused by that. Still, she did—eventually—agree to do it.

THE BAR WAS A GOOD half-hour drive out of town, on the side of a road in the middle of nowhere. It was long past sundown when we got there, and the parking lot was dark.

Sarah peered out her window at the bar. "God, this looks like the kind of place where when someone slumps over dead they just put a bowl of peanuts on top of them and use them as furniture." She turned to me. "You sure you don't want me to go in with you?"

"No. I mean, thanks, but no. I shouldn't be long. Probably not much more than fifteen minutes."

"I'll give you five."

"Ten."

"Fine. Ten minutes. Any longer than that, though, and I'll start honking the horn and embarrass you in front of your new biker friends."

I COULD HEAR THE MUSIC before I opened the door, but the smell of stale smoke only hit me after I walked in. The lighting was dim enough that it took my eyes a few seconds to adjust. Once they did, I could see the tall wood bar in the back, where three people, two men and one brawny woman with a large neck tattoo, were vying for the bartender's attention, raising their voices to be heard above the music. I looked around, half expecting some bouncer to swoop down and demand my ID. While some of the men seated in booths looked up, watching me, none of them moved.

I grabbed a stool at the end of the bar, assuming that the bartender, a guy in his forties with a ponytail and a ripped T-shirt, would be the best person to talk to. So I waited patiently for a lull and watched him as he took an order from one of the men, reaching down behind the counter for two beers, which he uncapped on the counter with a smooth, quick flick of his wrist. He nodded at me. "Be with you in a minute," he mouthed.

Four beers later, two bottled, two from the tap, the bartender walked over and leaned his hairy forearms on the bar.

"So," he said with a smile. "Haven't seen you in a while."

He thinks I'm Anna, I realized with a start. Which meant I'd found the right place. Anna had been here. I looked at his face. It was broad and open, and he had a large nose and curious eyes. Could it be him? I thought. Was he the reason Anna came here?

"No," I said. "I've been . . . busy."

"Fair enough," he said, with a lack of interest that inclined me to rule him back out. "You want the usual?"

I nodded. He put up his finger and walked away. A minute later he brought me a glass. "That'll be four bucks, but you can pay at the end if you like." He looked around. "Where's your friend? Parking the car or something?"

"Friend?"

He laughed. "Dark hair? Pretty? Looks like trouble? The one you always come with?"

Lily.

"Right," I said. "She's just on the phone, outside. She should be in, in a few."

"Good," he said. "I wouldn't really recommend you hanging out solo for too long." He paused. "It really has been a while—I kind of figured you guys had gotten bored with this place."

"No. We've just been busy. With school. I mean, college."

He laughed again. "Right, college."

I swirled the ice in my drink, trying to buy myself time to find a good way to phrase what I wanted to ask. "There might, uh, be someone joining us. A guy—I think maybe we brought him here before?"

He shrugged. "If you did, it wasn't during one of my shifts. Your friend's pretty friendly, but I don't remember seeing you let anyone too close." Then he smiled. "That reminds me— how was your big date?"

"Sorry?"

He shook his head in mock disappointment. "Girls. Last time you guys didn't talk about anything else, now you can't even remember it. You were all secretive about it too, kept asking her not to tell anyone about it."

"Oh. Right," I said carefully. "It was that night?"

"Nah, I don't think so. Next day or something."

The sound of a car horn sounded outside. It went on for three seconds. Sarah's warning that my time had elapsed.

I put a five-dollar bill on the bar. "I think that's my friend. I should go check on her."

"All right. Don't stay away so long next time," he said.

I threw him a half smile, trying to channel Anna.

I was almost to the door when it opened and a man walked in—a man in his late forties with pale blue eyes and skin that had been out too long in the sun. I tried to walk past him, but he saw me, and faster than I'd have thought possible, he caught me by the wrist.

"Hey, look who it is," he said.

I yanked my hand away hard. "Let go."

"Careful, now," he said, moving to block my access to the door. "It's rude to rush out just as I'm trying to say hello."

I stared at him. *No.* I thought. *Not him.* No matter how little I knew about Anna, not this guy. Not because he was ugly, which he wasn't—not exactly—but because the way he looked at me made my bones want to crawl out of my body. "Get out of my way," I said.

He narrowed his eyes. "You should be nicer," he said. "Given what I have, you should be much nicer to me than that. Nice when you see me, quiet when you don't. Don't you forget that."

"Is there a problem?" the bartender called from behind the bar. "Because otherwise, I think you should let her by."

"There's no problem," the man said, without taking his eyes off me. "No problem unless she makes one."

He stepped aside when the car horn sounded again.

"Take care, little girl," he said.

Little girl. I looked at him, with his baked skin, his cold, mean eyes. Thought of him looking at Anna's picture.

I only just made it out the door before I vomited, everything I'd eaten that day pouring out onto the gravel.

And one of the men from the bar did help us.
But after he fixed the car he kept Lily's keys tight
   in his hand. He said that if we wanted them
   back he'd need something in exchange.
A photo. A photo of me.

FORTY-FIVE

LAUREN WAS, AS SHE OFTEN was, in a bad mood. I'd snagged the changing room first, and when I emerged she'd glared at me like I'd stolen her most valued possession.

"Christ, what were you doing?" she said. "I could've changed four times in the time you were in there."

If this was meant to make me feel bad, or to make me hurry out, she had miscalculated. Because after last night, I wasn't exactly in the best mood myself. I'd spent an hour in the shower after I got home, and another hour this morning, and I still felt unclean. Taking too long in a changing room was not something I was interested in being made to feel bad about.

So I leaned against the curtain, still half inside the changing room. Tried to think if there was anything I wanted to ask her about while I had the home court advantage. And I realized there was.

"I meant to ask you about something, actually," I said.

Lauren sighed, a long, exaggerated sigh. It was not endearing. "What?"

"You said once that the police were incompetent assholes," I said. "Why?"

"I don't remember talking to you about that." She crossed

her bony arms and narrowed her eyes. "Are you, like, spying on me?"

"You have a very distinctive voice," I said. "It's pretty hard not to hear you."

The corners of her mouth twitched upward. She seemed to take "distinctive" as a compliment. "Okay, fine," she said. "Yeah, I do think that. They don't see anything other than what they want to see—they don't ask the right questions."

"Do you mean the interviews they did about Anna?"

"Among other things. And yeah, I'm sorry, but those were a mess. It was weird—they even asked if I'd seen her at the party at the quarry, when clearly I wouldn't have, since she didn't even leave the house." Then she paused and looked a little embarrassed. "Aside from, you know. Falling. Anyway, I guess I was one of the first people they interviewed. Sounds like later they figured it out."

I remembered the police officer telling us about the chief being on his way back from Boise, as though he'd been the key to getting the investigation under way. "They probably hadn't talked to Lily yet," I said, then paused. "You didn't see Lily at the quarry, did you?" I asked, wondering if I could catch Lily in a lie, prove she wasn't telling the truth about her and Anna's plans for that night.

"No, I didn't see her—thank God."

"You didn't like Lily?"

Lauren shrugged. "Usually she was all right, but she'd been a total nightmare at practice that day."

"Why?"

"I don't know. She did that sometimes. Got all pissy or whatever."

That was less than helpful, so I tried to get back on track.

"So, the police asked you if you'd seen Anna that night and that's what makes them incompetent assholes?"

"Yeah, well, that and other stuff."

"Like what?"

Lauren paused for a moment. "They just have their own agenda, okay? Just look out more for each other and their friends than anyone else."

"What do you mean?"

"I meant what I said—they're assholes. And now I'm done playing twenty damn questions, Jess—move already so I can get changed."

Slowly, deliberately, I moved aside.

WHEN I GOT HOME, MY mom's car was in the driveway and the door was unlocked. I wandered into the kitchen and then through the living room, expecting to see her camped out with a book, waiting to tell me about how a bunch of people had canceled their appointments at the last minute. She wasn't there.

I headed up the stairs to find my door open and Mom sitting on my bed, a basket full of laundry at her feet. Next to the basket was Anna's box, and she was holding Anna's cardigan.

"Mom?"

She looked up, startled, the cardigan falling out of her hands and into her lap.

"What are you doing in my room?"

"We had some cleanings canceled," she said. "I was going to do laundry and I thought you might have some socks under your bed. And I found this." She gestured to the box.

I said nothing. She had come into my room without permission, I thought reflexively. She should never have found the box.

"How long have you had it?" she asked.

"A while."

"How long?"

"A couple of weeks. A policeman brought it over."

"Were you ever going to tell us about it?"

I shrugged. I hadn't planned on telling them. Not really.

She waited, her eyes searching my face. I didn't know what else to say.

"I know that you . . ." She looked down at the box. "I know that your relationship with Anna was special, but we miss her too. We lost her too. And I don't—"

Her voice cracked and she stopped. She got up quickly, leaving an impression in the quilt. She brushed past me as she left the room, her eyes never reaching my face.

I straightened the quilt and returned the cardigan to the box before I went after her. I found her sitting on the couch, rigid against the cushions.

"I'm sorry," I said to her back. "It wasn't personal."

She inhaled slowly and then breathed out.

"It is personal. It's very personal. And right now, I need to sit here by myself for a while."

"I—"

"Jess, please leave me alone." Her back looked small, even frail. She had lost weight. I hadn't noticed. I had spent so much time noticing things and yet I'd missed it. "Please."

"All right, I'll go."

I thought that would be the moment when she'd relent and

tell me it was okay, that she knew I hadn't meant anything by it.

That was what she always did. Always had done.

Instead, she remained motionless on the couch, staring straight ahead. She didn't so much as glance back as I left the room.

FORTY-SIX

WHEN I WAS LITTLE, I liked the sensation of running my hand over a wire mesh fence. Liked the feel of the cold metal, the bump of it against my fingertips, the bumps coming faster and harder as I began to run, dragging my hand across it.

Once, I cut myself pretty badly on a raw edge. Anna helped me clean it, and neither of us said a word to our parents about it. We'd handled the situation, we thought. No need to bring them into it. No need for me to get a lecture about being more careful in the future.

The bandage gave it away. Mom had promptly dragged me to the doctor and he'd given me a tetanus booster, which hurt.

That night, she and Dad sat me and Anna down and gave us a lecture about the importance of not keeping things from them. We'd both nodded seriously and sworn we would never do such a thing again. But we knew: the real take-home message was that we should be more careful in the future not to get caught.

That was my initial reaction to Mom's discovery of the box. That I should have hidden it better. Yet I couldn't stop thinking about her on the couch, unable to talk to or even to look at me. And I felt like maybe I hadn't hidden it to protect Anna. Maybe I'd hidden it to protect myself.

It wasn't Lily's fault that the man asked for my
  photo, not hers.
It wasn't her fault, yet it felt incredibly unfair
  that I alone was paying the price.
So I took a photo of myself in the bathroom of the
  bar that night—angry, refusing to smile—
  and sent it to the man.
And then, before I went back out to the parking
  lot, I sent it again. To a different number.

FORTY-SEVEN

I DON'T LIKE IT WHEN people hover. Which was exactly what Mona was doing as I sat in the computer lab, trying to print out my English paper. When I'd come in ten minutes before, we'd nodded at each other and I thought that would be it. But then she'd gotten up, and I could feel her behind me. Hovering.

Reluctantly, I turned around in my chair to face her.

"Hey, Jess," she said. "I wanted to . . ." She paused briefly and then started again. "I wanted to ask if you ended up finding anything."

Finding anything. I'd been looking for so many things, yet hopefully no one, Mona included, knew about any of them.

"Finding anything?"

"On the phone?"

"Oh." I thought of the selfie. There was no way I was telling her about that. "No, not really. I mean, it was really helpful, though. Thanks." Then I thought of the phone from the quarry. "Nothing you can do about a phone that's been submerged in water, I suppose?"

"In water? Probably not. You could try putting it in a bag of rice to dry it out and see if that helps. But it's probably a brick at this point." She smiled. "Did it fall into the bath or something? Don't tell her I told you, but that totally happened to Lauren."

"Something like that." A few seconds in a clean bathtub. Untold amount of time spent in muddy quarry water. To-may-to, to-mah-to.

Mona smiled again. When she smiled, it was hard for me to believe I'd seen her so sad and broken on the roof. *What happened to you?* I wondered. *Why do you keep asking about Anna's phone?* The question slipped out before I had time to think about it further, to weigh the pros and cons of asking. "What did you think I might find?"

"Oh. I . . ." She paused and looked away, so that all I could see was her hair and the curve of her cheek. "I've been trying to understand something." She looked back at me after a moment, a blush spreading across her face. "I know she didn't . . . I know it was an accident, what happened to her. But when I first heard, I thought . . . I thought maybe she and I had something in common."

I stared at her. It took a second for the implications to register.

"You thought she jumped?"

"It was stupid. The police were pretty vague about it at first, and I . . . It was just me projecting, I guess. I'd—I'd been having a hard time. I am having a hard time. And she'd started hanging out with people who . . . I thought . . . I don't know."

I could see her hand around her arm, clutching it tight.

"What happened to you, Mona?"

"I don't know," she said. "I mean, I do know, but I don't. I . . ."

I sat, waiting for her to keep going, but she didn't say anything else.

"I'm sorry," I said. "I don't understand."

She took a deep breath. "There was a party last spring. Me and Brian had been having stupid little fights all week—whose friends to hang out with, what movie to watch, if we should even go to the party or do something different. Nothing big, nothing I thought was all that important. Then, at the party, Brian wanted to leave early, and I wasn't ready to go. We had another fight about that, I think. I don't remember, really."

She stopped.

"You mean you don't remember what you fought about?"

"No, I mean I don't remember *anything*. That's the problem. There's this vague memory of us fighting—me being upset, him being upset—and then after that . . ." She closed her eyes. "After that, there's me waking up alone in the middle of the football field, my shirt wide-open." She paused. "They took a photo of me like that. Took it using my own phone and left it for me. Like a reminder. Like a warning."

" 'They'? You mean Brian?"

Mona shook her head. "I don't know. I think it must have been—I don't know who else I would've gotten into a car with—but it's all a big blank. I tried asking a couple of people if they saw us leaving together, but they'd all been busy getting hammered. I don't even know what happened between me being at the party and being left in that field. It's just a big gap."

"I'm so sorry. That's . . ." I didn't know how to express what that was. "Did you report it?"

Mona laughed, low and hoarse. "I went to the police that very morning, sure that they'd want to get to the bottom of it, that they'd believe me. Instead, they acted like I was insane, or worse, just a stupid drunk whore making up stories. They kept asking me if I was sure, if maybe I'd just had too much to drink and gotten confused walking home—took off my shirt for attention or because I was making out with my boyfriend. If maybe I was just trying to get Brian in trouble because we'd had a fight. I probably shouldn't have expected anything else. After all, Brian's dad is the police chief's best friend. No one wanted to know; no one wanted to look into it."

She looked away. A long silence followed. Someone else would have known how to fill it. Someone else might have been able to say something that might make her feel a tiny fraction better.

"I don't know if I really wanted to jump, you know," she said eventually. "I just want it not to have happened. Just want whole minutes to pass by when I can feel like everything is still simple, when I can pretend I'm still who I thought I was before: a cheerleader in love with a guy who'd never hurt me."

"You were in love with him?"

She finally turned back to look at me. "Yeah, I really was," she said. "And the messed-up thing is, part of me still is. I can't even ask him about it, because I'm afraid I'd believe anything he told me, and then we'd be right back together."

"Like magnets," I said quietly, a distant echo.

"Yes," she said. "Like magnets."

Texting him that photo was a mistake. I knew that as soon as I hit the send button. The stupid thing was, I liked how I looked in it. Tough, like the kind of girl who knew what she was doing. A girl, I thought, so different from my former self.

And even as I regretted it, I thought I understood what I'd risked. Thought I understood the worst-case scenario.

FORTY-EIGHT

ON SUNDAY, I SET OFF earlier than usual for my run with Nick, circling the park three times before he showed. When he did, I didn't even slow down, just nodded at him and made him scramble to keep up.

Ever since I'd talked to Mona, all I wanted was to run. Run and run and run and not stop until things made sense again. Mona had been drugged and assaulted, and she clearly wondered if Anna had experienced a similar trauma, and a similar despair in its wake. While I very much hoped she was wrong, I had to wonder if there might be some connection between them after all. Had to wonder if Brian had Anna's number in his phone not because they were lab partners, not because they were friends either, but because they were something altogether different. It would fit, I thought. Fit with Lily's text: *And the boys may stop by first.* Charlie and Brian, a logical duo. One for Lily, one for Anna.

Nick slowed down a few times, but I ignored him until he finally shook his head and stopped outright. Only then did I stop.

We sat together in silence for a few minutes, sucking in the warm air.

"One of these days, you're going to lead us all the way into the next town," he said.

"It's hardly a bad thing to get out of Birdton every once in a while."

"True," he said. "When I graduate, I'm never coming back. I'll go to any college that takes me as long they give me a scholarship and it's nowhere near this place. I'll be done with here forever."

I stretched my arms above my head and then let them flop back down. "I'm going to head to the East Coast for college. Somewhere where no one knows anything about me." *Where no one knows that I was once a twin. Where the worst thing that ever happened to me isn't common knowledge.*

"Why the East Coast?"

"I don't know—it sounds nice. In my head, it's all redbrick buildings, libraries, and perfect windswept beaches." I hadn't considered it closely before, but I was pretty sure my vision came half from *The Great Gatsby* and half from some admissions brochures that had come in the mail.

"Sounds nice," he said. "Preppy but nice."

"Yeah," I said. It was tempting to stay on the topic forever, discussing this perfect future away from Birdton—a beautiful blank slate. I needed to ask him, though. Needed to find out if he knew anything that might help me.

"You didn't go to the party at the quarry, did you?" I asked. "The one back in November?"

"Yeah, I went," he said. "Not my usual scene, but I went for a couple hours. I wish I'd just stayed home."

"Something happened?"

"Nah, I just don't really enjoy wandering around in the dark. I was already not in the best mood anyway—Brian made a big deal out of wanting me to go, even had the nerve to tell me to look nice for once, when he practically lives in the same shirt all the time. Then, after all that, he forgot to pick me up—I had to borrow my parents' car and drive over myself. I couldn't even find him for ages."

"He wasn't there?"

"Oh, I found him eventually. He was wandering around at the bottom of the quarry, throwing rocks into the pool of water, drunk off his head. Not exactly the best company."

"Was he looking for something down there?"

"Something?"

"I don't know," I said. "A phone, maybe?"

"He didn't say anything about a phone," Nick replied. "Maybe that was what he was doing, but he wasn't exactly being efficient about it if he was."

I tried to think of a slick transition to asking about Brian and Anna. When none sprang to mind, I went for a less subtle approach. "Was his, uh, girlfriend with him?"

"His girlfriend?" He frowned. "I don't think Brian's dated anyone since Mona."

"Oh, I thought I'd heard something about him hanging out with someone—maybe some girl on the cross-country team."

Nick shrugged. "I never heard anything about that. He took it real hard when Mona broke up with him. I think he's still pretty hung up on her even now."

I kept my face as neutral as possible, trying not to see an image of Mona unconscious in the middle of a football field, her shirt ripped open. Because I didn't want to see that. Didn't want to hear the guy I like championing the guy who in all likelihood had done that to her. Had taken her away from herself. Didn't want to hear about how sad he was to have lost her. Some people didn't deserve my pity. Some people didn't deserve second chances. And I really hoped Anna hadn't given him one.

Nick propped himself up on his elbows. "What's with all the questions?"

"Nothing."

"Nothing? Nice try there, Ace Detective."

I looked up at the sky and noticed a plane flying above us, almost lost behind a cloud. "I found a phone in the quarry the other day. I wanted to try to give it back."

He shrugged. "That's a nice thought, but I doubt it would have been from that night. Even if it was, they'll have replaced it months ago. No one is going to wait around for their phone to turn up for that long." Then he paused. "Wait, why were you at the quarry? Were you, uh, hanging out with someone?"

I looked at him blankly for a second and then I remembered Sarah's comment about why people went to the quarry, the reason I'd first gone to look it over to begin with. And I almost smiled at the idea that he seemed to think I might have other guys in my life.

"No," I said. "I was just, you know, by myself. Taking it in."

Taking it in. I had no idea what I might mean by that. And apparently neither did he.

"Is everything okay, Jess?"

He looked so sincere, so sweetly concerned, that for a moment, I considered telling him the truth. Not just about the quarry and the phone—everything. Telling him about Anna and the alcohol and my suspicions about Mr. Matthews and now Brian. I was afraid, though, that going down that road, that telling him any part at all, could lead to my unspooling in front of him until there was nothing left. That said out loud, it wouldn't sound at all like the straightforward, logical process I liked to think of it as, but like evidence of how desperate and sad and deeply, deeply messed up I was. *You think I'm strange already,* I thought. *I don't think I can handle your knowing how far it really goes.*

I forced a smile onto my face. "I'm fine. I was just curious about the quarry because I'd never gone there." Then I stared out at the sky. The plane had disappeared, only a faint trail of white left in its wake.

FORTY-NINE

I DIDN'T SEE IT AT first. It was buried among the other mail—obscured by an athletic clothing catalog and a water bill. An envelope from the Montana medical examiner's office, addressed to my dad. Who was fortunately not around to intercept it.

I deposited the other mail on the kitchen table and then retreated to my room, holding the envelope close to me like someone might suddenly appear in the empty house and snatch it away.

I'd thought I'd rip the envelope open once I finally received it, tear it apart so fast I'd risk harming the autopsy report inside. But that was before it was in my hands. Before I'd thought about what it might do to me—reading the description written by someone who'd cut into Anna, another written by someone else who'd tested the contents of her insides. It had been hard enough thinking about someone touching her clothes.

Still, here it was. Answers, contained within a thin envelope. I had to move forward with it.

I delicately ripped the envelope along the side, tipped out the sheet of paper within, and braced myself.

It was difficult to read the autopsy report, seeing it laid out in black-and-white. Her injuries, the clinical description of them, of her—*Caucasian female, 5′2″, brown hair, brown eyes.* Her birthday, my birthday. A paint-by-number version of her.

I read it all, unsure where the toxicology results would be listed. Where the part about the alcohol would be. I read carefully, in case they used different language than I expected, in case it was reduced to a simple check in a box.

I am a good reader, a close reader. I don't miss things—not facts, not details.

But that didn't matter this time. Because the toxicology information simply wasn't there.

THE WOMAN WHO PICKED UP the phone at the toxicology center was less than excited to take my call.

"We cannot provide any information to you over the phone. You'd need to officially request the report," she said, with pauses between her words that indicated she was probably working over a piece of gum. "There's a form online for that."

"I did request the report. I have it right in front of me," I said. "I just had some questions about it."

She sighed. "If you already have the report, then all the information you need should be there."

"Yes," I said. "It should be. But I think there may have been a mistake."

"That's very unlikely," she said. "We have a state-of-the-art facility here."

"I'm sure you do, but my issue isn't with the results, but with the fact that none are listed."

Her sigh was louder the second time. "You know," she said,

"I'm going to transfer you to Dr. Travers. I'm sure she'll be able to answer any questions you have."

Before I could reply, music came on. A few minutes later, it switched off, and a brisk, slightly clipped voice came on the line.

"This is Dr. Travers. I understand you have a question about one of our reports?"

"Yes, I do—"

"Could you please provide the name of the tested party?"

"Anna Cutter."

"One moment, I'll bring it up in our system."

I could hear the faint sound of her typing and then a pause.

"Can you please confirm the spelling of the last name?"

"Yes, it's *C-U-T-T-E-R*."

The keyboard keys clicked again in the background.

"It's not coming up. When would this have been submitted?"

I thought back. "Early December, probably."

"Okay, it's possible, then, that we just don't have that uploaded into the system yet."

I shook my head, forgetting for a moment that she couldn't see me. Because my parents had told me about it weeks ago, and they'd sat on it for a while before that. "Oh, this would have been processed at least a month ago."

"Well, that's just not possible," she said.

"Why not?"

"Because we've been backed up. We only just started tackling toxicology reports from December last week. It's not like the TV shows, you know. It takes a long time to process these kinds of reports."

"They told us, though," I said. "They told my—me that they had the results."

"You must have misunderstood them," she said. "Or perhaps they misspoke."

She sounded confident, like that must have been what happened. And it wasn't like it hadn't happened before, my misunderstanding something. But I didn't think that was what happened here. This time I'd been paying very close attention.

He didn't text me back after I sent the photo, and when I next saw him, he didn't mention it. A foolish part of me hoped that meant he'd deleted it, or that it had gotten lost along the way— vanished into the ether.

FIFTY

"I NEED YOU TO EXPLAIN something to me," I said.

The police chief looked up from his paperwork, pen poised over the form he'd been working on. He looked at me and then at the officer behind me. Then he slowly put down his pen, setting it beside the framed picture on his desk.

"What's going on?" he asked, addressing his question not to me but to the officer.

"I'm sorry," the officer said. "She demanded to see you, and then when I asked her to wait, she just marched on in."

Demanded was a strong word, I thought. I would have said that I asked politely but firmly. *Marched*, however, was probably accurate.

"It has to do with my sister's case," I said to the police chief, ignoring the officer. "You're in charge of that, right? You called my parents about the tox screen?"

The police chief nodded. "I did, that's true." He addressed the officer. "It's all right. I'll talk with her."

"I'm so sorry," the officer said again. "She really did just barrel past me. I couldn't stop her."

The police chief raised his eyebrows. "I think you have

about a hundred pounds on her," he said. "So I'm not sure she's exactly the unstoppable force you seem to think she is."

"Yes, sir," the officer said, his face reddening. "Would you like your door open or closed?"

"Closed is fine," the police chief said.

After his door was closed, he turned to me. "Officer Heron mentioned that you came by a few weeks ago. She was worried she'd upset you."

"This isn't about that."

He tilted his head. "I thought you said this was about your sister and the tox screen. Didn't your conversation with Officer Heron focus on the alcohol she'd had?"

"Yes, but this is something different."

"Okay," he said, leaning back in his chair and crossing his arms over his chest. "So why don't you tell me what it's about, then?"

"There wasn't a tox screen for Anna."

"What do you mean?"

"I requested Anna's autopsy report and there was no toxicology information. I called and they don't have anything on file."

"You requested your sister's autopsy report?"

The question had an odd weight to it. It fell heavily between us, reminding me that I'd had to forge my dad's signature to make the request.

"I meant, my dad requested it. Because I asked him to." I hurried along, trying to move past the whole forgery issue. "Anyway, the point is that there wasn't any toxicology information. But my parents told me you said the tests had shown alcohol. Could you have been looking at the wrong report? Did they send you the report for someone else, maybe? Or did my parents get confused—were you basing this all on the bottles in her room?"

I forced myself to stop at that point, to wait and let him reply.

And at first, he didn't say anything. He only looked at me. Then he took a deep breath and leaned forward against the edge of his desk, settling his forearms in front of him like a judge proclaiming a sentence. "Do your parents know you're here?"

"I don't see why that matters," I said. "I want you to check your file for Anna. I want you to make sure the toxicology report is there, and that it's for her."

"It was an accident," he said slowly. "A horrible, tragic accident. I understand, of course I understand, why you're so upset, why you're looking for some kind of loophole or mystery to solve here. But there's nothing you can do, nothing I can do, that will change what happened. I'm not sure what you're doing is healthy."

"I'm not trying to change what happened, I'm trying to *understand* what happened. Because if she did have alcohol in her system, then I think she went out that night. That she was with someone."

He looked at me, his face flat. "Okay," he said. "So what, then she fell coming back in?"

"Yeah," I said. "Maybe. I don't know. Maybe she even fell somewhere else."

"Somewhere else?"

"I don't know."

He shook his head. "I'm sorry, but I really don't think that's what happened. And even if she fell coming back inside the house, that doesn't change anything. I don't think your parents know you're here, and I don't think your dad requested the autopsy report either. I think maybe I should call your parents and ask them to take you home."

He reached for the phone on his desk.

"Don't," I said quickly, remembering their faces across the dinner table, staring at me in horror as I tried, and failed, to explain to them about the bottles. Remembering Mrs. Hayes and her notes. "Please. They—I don't want to upset them."

He paused, his hand hovering above the phone. Then he moved it back to rest on his desk again.

"All right," he said. "I don't want to make things harder for you or your parents. I know it's been hard enough for you all."

"Thank you," I said. I paused and thought of the autopsy report, of the blank space. Of the call with the toxicology center. "Is there any way you could check about the report?

He stared at me for a long, long moment. I wondered if he was deliberately counting to ten before speaking.

"Look," he said. "I have a meeting that's starting soon, but if you really think something went wrong, then yes, I can check later today, and if I find that anything went awry, then I'll let you, and your parents, know."

"Thank you," I said. "And if you don't find anything?"

"Then there will be nothing to say," he said. "And maybe you should take that as a sign that you need to find a different way to grieve for your sister. Need to stop forging letters and hiding things from your parents. All parents want is to protect their children, you know. So maybe you should let them for a while." His eyes briefly settled on the framed picture. Then he looked at his watch, pushed his chair back, and stood up. "I need to go to my meeting, Jess."

And with that, we were done. And as I walked out of the police station, I started to wonder if he was right—if what I'd been doing made any rational sense at all. If it was crazy that a part of my brain kept coming back to the fact that he hadn't exactly answered my questions.

FIFTY-ONE

CROUCHED BENEATH MR. MATTHEWS'S WINDOW, I was starting to wish I hadn't come. It was becoming harder and harder to remember what I thought I'd find, watching him like this. To believe that peering into his window, listening to him talk to his cat, would actually accomplish anything.

It had been two days since I'd gone to the police station and talked to the chief. I'd heard nothing from him since, and while I'd held out hope at first that maybe he'd just gotten busy, I was steadily reaching the realization that the call wasn't going to come. I felt foolish now for going. Felt foolish for being here, underneath Mr. Matthews's window.

To make matters worse, my left leg had begun cramping up. The best way to get the cramp to pass would be to get up and move around. Still, unobservant as Mr. Matthews was, I thought my prancing around his backyard might draw his attention. So I stayed put, quietly massaging my calf muscles.

Mr. Matthews had been a little off this evening. For one thing, he'd let his tea brew for too long. He hadn't set the alarm, so it had been steeping for at least ten minutes. He hadn't gotten anything to eat either, just sat there with his tea steeping, cradling his phone, as if willing it to ring or gathering his strength to make a call. I'd seen him make calls twice before. They'd been polite, restrained conversations, one about a delayed package and the other about rescheduling a doctor's appointment, and neither of them involved this kind of indecision.

Finally, he began to dial.

He hesitated for a few seconds before pressing the final number.

Nothing happened for a long time. Then he twitched and tightened his grip on the phone.

"Don't hang up," he said. "Please don't hang up."

I straightened and leaned closer to the window, momentarily forgetting the throbbing pain in my calf.

He opened his mouth and his shoulders fell. "I know. I know. I wanted—" The words came out crowded together, apologetic.

I strained to hear the other side of the line, but it was too quiet to make out.

"No, I don't think anyone knows anything."

He turned his mouth closer to the phone and turned, making it difficult to hear everything he said.

"—promised not to tell—"

He began to shake his head vigorously.

"How can you say that? You know it wasn't like that."

"Of course I lied about that night."

"Of course the school wouldn't have liked it—I know that. They don't like anything that doesn't fit into their narrow-minded understanding of how life should be."

His free hand froze beside his head, palm up, as if beseeching an invisible audience.

"Why don't you understand why I feel like this? I can't talk to anyone, can't explain. . . ."

He slumped down on the couch, his voice low, his eyes closed. "Don't. I cared about that girl. You know that. But—"

I stayed stock-still, not breathing.

Then, right before he hung up the phone and put his head in his hands, before he sat motionless, devastated, it came— what I had both wanted and not wanted for so very long:

"Anna's death changed everything."

I started to feel guilty. Started to miss how things
    had been before. So I told him that maybe we
    should slow down. Think about an exit plan.
    Find a way so that no one got hurt, no one
    had to know.
He waited for me to finish my speech, outline all
    my reasons, before he pulled out his phone,
    and brought up the photo.

FIFTY-TWO

I'D THOUGHT WHEN I FINALLY learned who Anna had been going to see that I'd confront them about it, right then and there. But instead, I staggered home, dazed. It was hard to believe I'd finally gotten what I'd been waiting for—real confirmation. I'd begun to think it might not happen, that I'd never know. That maybe Mr. Matthews had simply been her coach, her English teacher, and nothing more.

I barely knew what to do with what I had now.

Which was basically a full confession. More than enough to make him talk to me, to convince him that I knew. The only thing I didn't know was who he'd called. Which hardly mattered. Nothing mattered except that he had been the one. Anna's one.

I'd thought there'd be a measure of relief when I learned the truth. To finally know who to talk to, to finally know that all this skulking around had served a purpose. I'd thought I'd come to terms with the possibility of it being Mr. Matthews, that I'd gotten to a place where I could handle it. Instead, I felt ill, unable to rid myself of the thought of them together, touching. Of him touching someone who looked almost exactly like me.

Images of skin on skin, with pressure and heat.

Not like butterflies.

Not like butterflies at all.

FIFTY-THREE

I DIDN'T EVEN PRETEND TO pay attention in any of my classes the next day. I didn't pretend to take notes, didn't look toward the front of the room.

I waited until the end of the day to confront Mr. Matthews, hoping to catch him alone, before track. When I arrived at his classroom, though, a girl was still there talking to him. She looked annoyed and Mr. Matthews looked frustrated. They both kept pointing to the same piece of paper.

I stayed outside until the girl left, her expression dark. Then I went in, closing the door quietly behind me.

He was walking around to the back of his desk, shaking his head.

"Mr. Matthews?"

His head jerked up, his face irritated, and then he saw me. For once he looked relieved to see me—he probably expected it to be that girl again, coming back for round two.

"Oh, hi," he said, sinking into his chair. "I'm sorry—I didn't hear you come in. I guess I'm a bit off-balance—it's amazing how hard people will fight for the grade they want, even if it isn't the grade they deserve. Makes you wish they put that same amount of energy and passion into writing the paper to begin with."

I stood rooted in front of his desk. He turned a little pink.

"Sorry, I shouldn't have said that—it wasn't very professional. What I can help you with?"

I took a deep breath and cleared my throat. His casual chatting had thrown me off. I'd expected to be able to get right to the point.

Another breath. I could do this.

"I know it was you Anna was going to see that night."

He stared at me blankly, like he didn't know what I meant. It was almost convincing.

I continued. "I know you were involved with her."

His eyes widened and he straightened up in his chair. "Wait," he said. "What?"

I shook my head. I couldn't backtrack—I needed to get through this, and I'd begun to shake. "I want to know if she was with you that night. I want to know if—"

"Involved? Are you serious?"

I nodded forcefully. "I don't want to get you in any trouble. I don't care about that." I clamped my hand on my arm to try to stop the shaking.

He began to stammer. "Jesus Christ, I would never— I can't believe you'd actually think—"

"Stop it," I said. "Stop. I know you were. I know. I heard you."

"What are you talking about? You heard what?"

"I heard you say it. At your house. On the phone. How you didn't want anyone to know, how they wouldn't understand—"

He was shaking his head, standing up behind his desk. I kept going.

"—how her death changed everything. I heard it. I know."

"Oh, Jesus. It's not . . ." He didn't seem to know what to say. The effort of even those few words seemed to push the air out of him, force him back into his chair. He looked dazed.

"I just want to know," I said. "I want you to admit it. I need to know the truth. I need you to tell me what happened that night. Did she come over? Did she get drunk? What happened?"

He held his head in his hands and didn't respond.

I hadn't expected this. I'd expected denial, maybe anger, but not this retreat. I began to get desperate.

"Please. Tell me." My voice was getting louder. I needed him to say something. To look at me and tell me something. Anything.

He shook his head, his eyes focused on the papers on his desk.

"Did you love her?" I didn't know I was going to ask that. But once I had, it seemed like the only real question there was. The only thing that could give any meaning to what had happened.

"Jess—"

The second time I almost screamed it. "Did you love her?"

He looked up. In his eyes, I saw horror and sadness. Also pity.

You have no right to pity me, I thought. *No right. I'm fine. You're the one who— You're the one . . .*

I tried to say something else, anything else, to regain control. What came out was a huge, broken sob.

And then I fled.

He'd looked at it, the photo. It's funny, he said,
but you nailed her expression here—that
frown, like she's angry and on the verge
of explaining why. People might think
something was really wrong with her, sending
a photo like this to a guy she's never even
talked to. The school, your parents, they might
be really concerned.

It took a minute for me to understand what he
was saying. Then it registered like ice water
down my spine.

I'd tell them it was me, I said. I would.

That's exactly what they'd expect you to say, he
said.

Then he put his hand on the back of my neck, like
a clamp.

FIFTY-FOUR

BACK IN FOURTH GRADE, THERE was a long stretch of time when I had the same boring dream every night. In the dream, I sat in the living room with Anna, Mom, and Dad, and we were all reading books and eating apples. That was all there was to it. The only thing that changed was the color of the apples. Sometimes they were red, other times a yellowish green.

Anna still slept in the top bunk back then, and every morning she'd ask what I'd dreamed about. I'd tell her that it was the same dream as before. Then I'd ask what she'd dreamed about, and she'd tell me how her dreams had been filled with strange elongated animals, multicolored icebergs, and other surreal things. And I was jealous. Jealous of how she had the interesting dreams while I was stuck on this same dull dream of our family hanging out together in the living room doing absolutely nothing special.

Now I wanted that dream back. Needed it back. To know that when I went to sleep, I would return to that place. To the security, the normalcy of that moment. Of the luxury of not paying attention to each other, knowing that at any moment I could look up and see Anna there. That I'd look at her and feel like she was someone I still knew.

Because I had messed it all up. I had learned nothing from Mr. Matthews. Nothing about Anna, nothing about that night, nothing about how he'd felt about her. I wanted to bang my head against a wall, kick a tree—anything that made me feel something other than this ever-expanding hole of regret.

I'd spent so long trying to understand what had happened, and now I'd looked back at the wrong moment, looked back and lost what I'd been searching for all along. Mr. Matthews was never going to say anything to me, was always going to be on his guard around me. I'd lost the last fragments of Anna left for me to find.

FIFTY-FIVE

I WENT THROUGH THE NEXT day in a fog. As if on autopilot, I found myself walking toward the locker room after class. As soon as I got within a few yards, I stopped. I stood, my feet frozen in place, staring at the locker room door. I hadn't gone to track the day before, and I couldn't go today either. Couldn't face Mr. Matthews. Couldn't bear to see him.

"Hey, you okay?"

I turned to see Nick standing nearby, looking concerned.

"I'm fine," I said.

He looked at me closely. "I'm not sure that's true."

"I just . . . I'm just not sure if I can take track today."

"Sick or sad?"

I didn't know what he meant.

"Sorry?"

"Those are the two reasons why I don't want to do things I usually enjoy, and I know you love track. Tell me which one it is so I can help."

Sick or sad. I looked at him: at the planes of his face, at the way a fold had formed between his eyebrows that made me believe he really cared about my answer.

"What would you do if I said sick?" I asked.

"I'd buy you an orange soda from the vending machine to get you some vitamin C and then leave you be because that's all I can do about sick." He smiled. "Plus, you might get *me* sick, and I don't half-ass being sick, so that's me laid up in bed for a week, minimum."

I smiled back, a little. "What would you do if I said sad?"

I expected this answer to be as flippant as the first, but the concerned fold reappeared. "If you said sad, I'd buy you whatever you wanted from the vending machine and then I'd stay by your side until you told me to leave you alone. Track and basketball practice be damned."

He looked at me full in the face and waited for my response.

It would be easy to say I was sick. So easy to leave it at that. Sick was straightforward. Medical. Simple.

Sad, however, was complicated and messy. Too messy to get someone else involved in. But I was sad. And angry and frustrated and humiliated and a billion other things I had neither the inclination nor the strength to delve into. But at the base of it all, I was sad. So sad I ached from it.

And besides, I'd never liked orange soda.

"Sad," I told him. "And also hungry."

STANDING IN FRONT OF THE vending machine, I had a hard time deciding whether I wanted a Snickers or a Twix. Nick ended up getting both, claiming he'd eat whichever one I didn't want, and then he got himself a can of diet soda.

"I thought you went for Big Gulps," I said, watching as he fished it out of the machine.

"Desperate times call for desperate measures," he said.

"Besides, I'm trying not to indulge too much before the big game next week. You know, not too much sugar."

Then we both looked at the candy bars in his hand.

"This is an important exception," he said.

AT THE PARKING LOT, WE looked out at the cars. "Where to?" he asked. "I drove today, so I can take you anywhere you'd like."

A beautiful boy was asking me where I wanted to go. The right answer, I knew, would be somewhere fun or interesting. Even romantic, if such a place existed in Birdton. I knew that was what I should suggest.

Then a breeze brushed my face and I heard the faint sound of a far-off generator roaring to life. The sound of wind and metal.

And I knew somewhere romantic, somewhere fun, wasn't what I needed today. Today I needed to go somewhere else, somewhere I hadn't been in a long time. Somewhere I didn't want to go alone.

"I think I know where," I said.

I WASN'T SURE I'D REMEMBER how to get there. But soon enough there were signs. Little wooden ones, not big glossy ones. WINDMILL MUSEUM, they said. Which made it sound very different from what it was, raising the expectation that there would, for example, be an actual museum.

"Is that where we're headed?" Nick asked. "The Windmill Museum?"

I nodded.

"Sounds cool," he said. "I've never gone."

"I went once," I said. "A couple years ago."

The last leg of the trip was up a dirt road, and the car bumped along over the uneven ground. And then there it was, looming in front of us. A beautiful old windmill. There was no other building, no "museum," only an old wooden box where you could contribute to the preservation of the windmill. And then there were stairs that went almost to the top and a small platform where you could sit.

"That's great," he said. "It's . . ." He took one hand off the wheel and made a gesture up and down; then he was quiet.

"Yes," I said. "It really is."

He parked the car in the patch of dirt that served as the parking lot and we got out of the car and stood together, looking up at the windmill. The paint was starting to peel, and in patches the wood was visible underneath, yet the structure itself conveyed the same sense of solidity it must have when it was built more than a hundred years earlier.

"Do you want to go up?" he asked.

"Yes."

I went first, climbing the steps slowly, then lowered myself to the platform, my knees up and my back against the heavy wood. Nick sat beside me. We looked out over the surrounding fields. The sun was still high above the horizon, and there were farms in all directions and mountains in the far distance.

"I came here once with my family. Anna loved the view," I said. "And I loved the sound the blades made, like we might become airborne at any second. We didn't even want to come and then the two of us ended up sitting here for over an hour until our parents made us come down."

I turned around and searched along the wood behind me. At first I couldn't find them, and then there they were: Our initials. Mine and hers, next to each other, tiny but unmistakable. I turned back, keeping my hand pressed over the spot.

"We meant to come back. It's one of those places you always mean to come back to, you know? It's not that far. We could have gotten our parents to take us anytime, and we never did. It seems so stupid that we didn't."

My throat started to close up.

"You thought you had plenty of time," Nick said quietly.

"We should have. We should have had so much more time."

He nodded and said nothing.

Which was perfect, actually. Saying nothing was the perfect thing to say.

I closed my eyes and imagined Anna sitting next to me, smiling, even as our parents paced impatiently below. Imagined the air warmer, the end of a long, hot summer. Imagined us when we'd spent every moment together, when it hadn't mattered if we'd worn the same things or not, when there hadn't been a question of Anna having to either hold herself back or cut me loose.

I knew that our relationship hadn't been as simple, as easy as I'd once thought; I knew that even now I was probably glossing over things, making that memory more sun-soaked than it had actually been. I was okay with that. Because I had to believe it hadn't all been me pushing her away or her striding off. That there had been times when we really were on the same page.

Eventually, the silence was broken by the distinct sound of my stomach rumbling. I coughed.

"I think I'm ready for my candy bar."

"Of course," Nick said, digging through his jacket pocket. He pulled out the two bars and presented them to me with a flourish. "Take your pick."

I took the Snickers. It had melted slightly and the chocolate was soft. He unwrapped the Twix and we ate side by side, the sound of the windmill at our back.

IN THE CAR ON THE way back into town, the space between us felt like a living, breathing thing. Not a tense creature, all curled up with claws, but an inviting presence that my thoughts kept returning to. I found myself wishing we didn't have to go back, wishing I could ask him to turn around and keep driving—to drive and drive and drive until the sun went down and the world was quiet.

But then I realized, for the first time in quite a while, that maybe there were things in Birdton for me. That I could stop chasing after Anna, stop following her shadow to dead ends, and instead concentrate on my own life and what to do next.

So when we got to my house and he stopped the car to drop me off, I didn't get out immediately, didn't reach for my seat belt.

"I'm planning to go to the game next week," I told him.

His eyebrows flicked up and he smiled. "That right?"

"Yes." Then I tiptoed out on the ledge. "So maybe we should hang out afterward. Get some food, or dessert. Something like that."

"Sounds like a plan," he said. Then he paused. "Sounds like a date, even."

I smiled. Because it did. Because that was how I'd wanted it to sound.

And I only hesitated for a moment before I leaned over and kissed him.

And he kissed me back.

The kiss felt nothing like what I'd imagined, and yet it was exactly right. It lasted for a couple of seconds; it lasted for forever. And throughout, my whole body was in my mouth and my mind was at peace in a way it hadn't been in a long, long time.

I felt like I'd fallen into a deep well with slick,
wet walls. There was no way out, no air.
I dreamt I was drowning, and when I woke the
water was still pouring in.
I never thought any of this could hurt you.
Never thought anything I did could be used
against you.

FIFTY-SIX

I STOOD IN THE DARK kitchen making a turkey sandwich, humming quietly under my breath. I'd been humming a lot since the kiss with Nick, and the cool linoleum felt good underneath my bare feet, in harmony with the act of making a covert sandwich.

After I finished, I bagged up the sandwich and hid it in the usual place behind an oversized jar of homemade pickles.

As I closed the fridge door, my dad appeared in the doorway, wearing his plaid pajamas. The top button of his shirt hung loosely by a single thread.

"Honey, what are you doing?"

I was tempted to lie, out of loyalty to Mom. I was tired of lying, though, so I told him the truth.

"Making my lunch for tomorrow."

He blinked, and scratched his neck.

"I thought Mom did that for you?"

"Sometimes she forgets parts."

He started to smile. "Ah, yes. I myself have received a lettuce sandwich or two, and once a pita with mayo. Only mayo." He mock-shivered in revulsion.

I smiled back. Dad's hatred of mayonnaise was legendary in this house.

"I haven't had the heart to tell her either. She really wants to take care of us, so it feels only fair to try to let her."

"She's been doing better recently," I said. "Mostly the sandwiches are okay now."

"I think you're right. But I still worry about her."

I made myself sag against the counter, relaxing the pressure on my left knee. In reality, there was nothing wrong with it, but I'd told my parents that I'd been getting sharp pains, used that as my excuse to continue to skip track practice. I missed running, but I couldn't go back. I had that much self-preservation, at least.

"If it makes you feel better," I said, "Mom never made great sandwiches. Anna and I tolerated it for as long as we could, but after she made us hot dog sandwiches, we told her we were old enough to start making our own lunches."

He made a pained face. "Hot dog sandwiches? That sounds terrible."

"They were truly atrocious."

We stood there, basking in the normalcy of the moment. Just a father and daughter making fun of Mom's cooking. It felt like how we were supposed to be together. Felt like family.

"I'm sorry about hiding the box of Anna's stuff from you guys," I told him. "I am. I want to say that to Mom, but I don't know how."

"I know, sweetheart. And your mom knows that as well. It's just that we miss her, too. The two of you were always so close that we felt shut out sometimes. And it feels like you're still shutting us out, and she worries that's how it will always be."

"Oh." I'd thought it was all about the box. Or rather, all about Anna. "I'm sorry," I repeated.

"It's okay. We're all still a mess, really. It's going to take us some time to figure out how to move forward. How to handle the fact that she's not coming back."

I nodded and then looked away, staring at the moon through the kitchen window.

The furnace kicked on and we were surrounded by white noise, its static forming a cloud around us.

Dad stretched his arms and yawned. "Well, I'm going to head back to bed—go to sleep soon, honey."

"All right, Dad."

He waved. I waved back.

FIFTY-SEVEN

MOVING FORWARD. CONCENTRATING ON MY own life. That was what I wanted to do. I needed closure, though. And since I wasn't going to get that from Mr. Matthews himself, I wanted something else. And I decided that what could suffice were Anna's English papers—the version with Mr. Matthews's ink on those pages, his words. They were, I knew now, probably as close as I was going to get to hearing what she had meant to him, and it was important to me to have them. Then I could move on.

The door to his classroom was unlocked, just as it had been before. When I got to his desk, I looked out at all the empty chairs and wondered where she'd sat. *Did you sit in the very front?* I wondered. *Or did you sit toward the back, wanting him to search for you through a sea of faces? Would I have seen what was between the two of you if I'd been in class with you? I might not have. I was so very good at not seeing things back then.*

I turned my attention back to the desk and opened the drawer. The thin file at the back was still there. Only the two from Anna remained. Maybe he planned to give them to us, in time. Or maybe he had no intention of letting them go—maybe they were important to him, all he had left. I began to take out the whole folder and then I stopped, remembering him crying on his couch, how he'd underlined in his note. I released the folder back into the drawer and instead took only one paper, the one with the long note.

Then I heard voices outside the door and the rattle of the doorknob turning. I dove under the desk even as I tried to tell myself I wasn't really doing anything wrong, that I had a perfect right to what I was taking.

"She left her notes for biology at home," a man said. "I found them when I went home for lunch. She's been studying for weeks—you should see the crib sheet she made."

"I'm sure she'll appreciate you bringing them to her," Mr. Matthews replied.

"You know how Sarah gets when she's nervous about a meet—she's been even worse about this test." I sneaked a quick look from beneath the desk and saw that the man talking was Mr. Hinter, Sarah's dad.

There was the gentle sound of the door swinging closed, the soft snap of the latch.

Then there was silence for a long time. Long enough that I wondered if they'd left the room again, gone back into the hall, leaving me crouched under the desk for no good reason. I shifted forward and peered out again. They were both still in the room, simply standing there, looking at each other.

"Why are you here?" Mr. Matthews asked quietly.

"I told you," Mr. Hinter replied. "To bring Sarah her notes."

"That's why you came to school," Mr. Matthews said. "I want to know why you're here."

"You're my daughter's coach. I'm allowed to talk to you."

"Your daughter's coach? Really? That's what I am now?"

Mr. Hinter took a step forward. "I'm sorry. I didn't mean it like that. I didn't mean . . . Christ. I don't know what you want me to say, Ben. You called me, remember? Tell me what you want me to say."

"I don't want to have to tell you. That's the point." Mr. Matthews took a deep breath. "I thought we had plans. I thought that was what you wanted."

"We did. It was. I'm sorry," Mr. Hinter said.

"I thought we were going to leave this place together. Have a life—" His hands stretched out toward Mr. Hinter and stayed there for a moment before he let them fall back to his side.

"I know. But I can't. I just can't." Mr. Hinter's voice cracked. "I was living in a fantasy land—I wasn't thinking. I don't want to be one of those fathers who leave their families—who only see their daughter a few times a year."

"It wouldn't be like that."

"Yes, it would. You know it would. And I couldn't handle that. It took that poor girl's death to wake me up, to make me see it." He looked down. "You see someone else lose their kid and suddenly you get it. What it would mean to not have them in your life anymore. How fragile it all is."

"It's nothing like that. It's not the same."

Mr. Hinters shook his head. "Look, when you're a parent—"

"Don't. Just don't. I don't want to hear it. Not again."

"I'm sorry." He raised his hand as if to touch Mr. Matthews's arm. Mr. Matthews took a step back and shook his head.

"I shouldn't have called."

"I shouldn't have come here."

Then they stood there, rooted to the spot, staring at each other. The man who I thought had been in love with my sister and the father of my friend, husband of the most beautiful woman in town, the silence between them so loud it threatened to shatter everything in the room.

After that, I started to skip practice. I was so tired of pretending. Of lying.

And with him? It was not good. Let's leave it at that.

I was in the well. The walls were slick. The water was dark.

I hope you never know what that feels like. I hope you never start having the kind of thoughts I had. About how much easier it would be . . . Never mind. I shouldn't tell you that.

FIFTY-EIGHT

MY KNEE MADE A MIRACULOUS recovery. I told my parents that evening that all the sharp pains had disappeared. So I would be going on a long run.

They weren't huge fans of the idea.

"You don't want to stress it, sweetheart," Mom said. "I'm glad it feels better, but you don't want to push it too hard and end up injuring it again."

Dad nodded. "It's easy to get excited when you're finally feeling better, but you should be careful."

"I'll be fine," I said.

They looked skeptical.

I promised that I would mostly walk, and only gently, experimentally jog.

As soon as I was out of view of the house, I began running. It felt like rust was falling off my limbs, like they'd been waiting for me to use them properly again.

I wasn't sure if I should tell Sarah about what I'd heard. On the one hand, he was her father—maybe that meant she had a right to know. On the other hand, whatever Mr. Matthews and her father had been to each other, whatever they still meant to each other, the relationship had obviously ended. There was no action to be taken, no change for her to brace for—no obvious anything for her to do with the information. Maybe the truth doesn't always set you free.

As I ran along the uneven pavement, I kept seeing the two men standing together. And I felt so foolish. Because I couldn't have been more wrong about Mr. Matthews and Anna. All the arrows that I thought pointed toward him were noise, not signal, all representing something different entirely. And I felt like the pervert for having seriously considered the idea of him and Anna in the first place.

But I was sad and confused for all the obvious reasons, all the logical fallout.

I was also sad for another reason. Sad that I would never again have an excuse to sit outside Mr. Matthews's window and watch him wait for his tea, his cat curled up beside him. No reason to immerse myself in someone else's quiet life for an hour, feeling connected without being asked for anything in return.

SARAH SAT BESIDE ME ON the bus, her eyes partway closed as she listened to her music.

I'd decided not to tell her. I'd wondered about it all the previous night, and in the end, I'd decided it was simply not my secret to tell.

Still, now that I knew for sure that Mr. Matthews and Anna hadn't been involved, I wondered if Sarah might be able to shed light on part of the puzzle—why Lauren might have thought they were.

I tapped the back of the seat in front of her, my signal to get her to take off her headphones, something she seemed to tolerate, if not necessarily appreciate.

"When you were in cross-country, did Mr. Matthews ever give Anna special treatment?" I asked her.

She blinked, cradling her headphones in her arms. "Special treatment?"

"Yeah, someone said something about him treating her differently from the other girls."

Sarah shrugged. "Not really." She began to lift her headphones back up, and then she paused. "Well, actually I guess he did, a little."

"How so?"

"I don't know, Anna started pretty strong in cross-country, but after a while she began struggling."

"Struggling?"

"She seemed tired, and once in a while she missed practice. A lot of people miss the occasional one, so that's not all that unusual, but I don't know, he wasn't as hard on Anna as everyone else. I mean, he likes me plenty, but if my times started to dip, he wouldn't sugarcoat it—he'd tell me to cut it out and get back in gear. Tough love all the way."

"Is that what he did for Lauren too? Tough love?"

"Oh Lord, Lauren. Was she the one spouting off about 'special treatment'?"

I nodded.

"Yeah, well—he and Lauren never hit it off, and it didn't exactly help when he reamed her out once when he found out she'd been skipping practice to serve on the prom committee. He apologized later, said he'd been too harsh, but Lauren is hardly the forgive and forget type, so she probably wasn't pleased to see Anna get off so lightly. Probably thought it was a sign of favoritism or whatever."

"God," I said. "She made it sound—" I took a deep breath. "Whatever. Even for Lauren, that's petty."

"Yeah, it is." Then she paused. "I don't know if she was totally wrong about the favoritism, though. I think he was having a bad week when he yelled at Lauren, but I think he did have a soft spot for Anna. Sometimes they'd sit together and talk about books or poetry or whatever. And not even stuff he assigned in class. I think they just really liked each other."

Mr. Matthews and Anna. Talking. Poetry. So easy to twist into something it wasn't. So much easier to think there had been something inappropriate, something romantic, between them than to think that, in their own way, they'd been friends.

I WENT TO PRACTICE THAT afternoon. Mr. Matthews looked surprised when I rejoined the team, but he didn't say anything. I was briefly hopeful that he would let the whole thing go, pretend I'd never accused him of having a relationship with Anna, that I'd never mentioned listening in on his call. It would be so great to never, ever talk about any of it.

That hope lasted until the end of practice.

"Hey, Jess," he called out as I began to walk off the field. "Can I talk to you for a minute?"

I looked longingly toward the rest of the team as they left. "I'm in a bit of hurry, so maybe—"

"Jess," he said. He stood looking at me, his arms wrapped tightly around his chest. He looked deeply uncomfortable but filled with resolve. "I'm glad your knee is feeling better, but we really need to talk about what happened." He looked around and then pointed to the bleachers. "So let's sit down."

There wasn't a question mark at the end of that. So, reluctantly, I nodded.

We trudged over to the bleachers. I noticed that he waited for me to sit down first and that when he sat, he left a notably large space between us. I couldn't blame him.

"So," he said. "I think you have some pretty confused ideas about me and your sister."

"Not anymore," I said.

"Oh. Good." His shoulders relaxed a fraction. "You understand now there was absolutely nothing like that between us?"

"Yes. I was . . . confused."

"All right," he said.

I wondered if we could leave it at that. I really hoped we could. I hoped he'd get up and walk away and that would be it.

But then he took a deep breath, and I knew it wasn't going to play out like that.

"I'm really glad you understand that there wasn't anything between me and Anna. And I could let it go at that if you hadn't referenced a phone call you had no right to listen to. A phone call that there is no way you could've overheard by accident."

He took another deep breath and I braced myself for him to raise his voice, to yell. Instead, his voice grew quieter, more distant.

"I'm not going to ask whether that was the only time you eavesdropped on my conversations, because I don't think I want to know the answer. And while I can understand how what I said might have sounded strange—taken wildly out of context—I'm not going to explain that conversation to you either. Because that's not something you need to know, not something I should have to tell you about. What goes on in my own home is private, and what you did, for however long you did it, was a huge violation."

I looked down at my hands. "I'm sorry. I really am." And I was. Because I hadn't really thought about what it meant to do that to someone. Hadn't really thought of him as a person, not in the fullest sense. Just a candidate, a possible answer to my question.

"Good. I'm glad you understand that." Then he turned and looked at me, relief but also puzzlement on his face. "What I still don't get is why you'd ever have thought there was something there. Why you'd even think to spy on me in the first place?"

I could've told him about all the things that had seemed so important at the time. How with so little to go on, I'd been grasping at straws and trying to turn them into a raft.

I didn't want to tell him, though. Didn't want to embarrass him by telling him about Lauren's comment, and definitely didn't want to say anything that might reveal how long I'd watched him for. So I shrugged. "I don't know. It doesn't make much sense now."

"There had to be some—" He caught himself and stopped. He sighed. "Look, I don't mean to put you through the wringer with this. What you did really shook me, really upset me very deeply, but I know you've been through a lot. And grief can make people do strange things."

So many strange things. So many hours of watching him.

And I thought of him with his cat, helping it down from the

bookcase, thought of how I'd left Anna's paper for him. And without meaning to, I found myself smiling.

"What is it?" he asked.

"I was thinking about the strangest part."

He raised his eyebrows and waited for me to explain. I paused, unsure whether to say it. And then I went ahead, because if there was anyone who was already justified in thinking I was unhinged, it was him. "There were moments when I almost thought that, if things were different, you wouldn't have been the worst choice for her."

His eyes widened. I flushed and wished I'd kept my mouth shut, until I noticed the tiniest trace of a smile forming at the side of his mouth. "And by different, you mean if I hadn't been twice her age and her teacher?"

"Yes," I said. *And gay,* I added silently. That also put a wrinkle in things. "I thought you might have made her happy, made her feel special."

"Oh," he said. For a second, I thought I could see another version of my mom's lecture on inappropriate relationships coming. Then he nodded. "Well, I always thought she seemed like a very special person."

"She was."

He looked at me. And for the first time, it felt like he really saw me. Not the girl with the dead twin. Not the crazy girl who'd accused him of sleeping with her sister. Me.

"She was lucky to have you," he said. "I know you meant a lot to her. I know you were her best friend."

Best friend. I shook my head, even though it hurt to do it. "She was always *my* best friend, but I wasn't hers—not by the end. By the end it was Lily."

"I don't think so," he said. "I don't think by the end the two of them were that close."

His voice was strained, like it was hard for him to say it. I didn't correct him. I knew he was trying to be kind. Sometimes it's good to let people try to make you feel better.

*Sometimes I thought of you on that rope swing.
About those few seconds when you'd soared
before crashing down. For those seconds, it
had looked like you were flying, and I'd felt
like both of us had wings. And then you'd
been on the ground, unmoving.*

That had been the worst moment of my life.

I think it still is, despite everything else.

*Everything else I can bear, I'd tell myself when
I looked at him. At those eyes, with those
lashes—beautiful eyes in a face that had
become so very ugly to me. Everything else I
can get through.*

FIFTY-NINE

ON SUNDAY, I WOKE WITH a low buzz deep in my stomach.

Because I was going to see Nick.

I started to put on my running clothes. Then I stopped, deciding I wanted to look nicer than that. Not too nice, not fancy, but nicer than normal. I put on a short-sleeved top with a slight pattern and left my hair down rather than pulling it back into a ponytail. Brushed it twice too.

Then I went downstairs for breakfast.

I downed a bowl of cereal, a banana, and an orange and followed that up with some scrambled eggs and sausage links. I checked the cupboard to see if there were any granola bars. No such luck.

Mom sat at the kitchen table watching me, nursing a grapefruit and a piece of whole-wheat toast.

"All that running you do must be catching up with you," she said. "I can pick up some granola bars tomorrow if you like—maybe the ones with almonds?"

"Thanks, that would be great," I said.

She smiled. She looked younger in that moment, smiling, her hair back in a loose ponytail, and it reminded me of something I'd meant to ask her about months earlier.

"Were you popular in high school?"

She blinked. "Popular? I guess that depends on your definition."

Which pretty much answered the question. Because if you weren't popular, you knew it. It was only the people who were popular who seemed to have trouble knowing how to classify themselves. Still, I clarified. "Lots of friends, homecoming queen, that sort of thing."

Her cheeks turned pink. "I suppose so. I wasn't homecoming queen, but I was on the court, if that counts." She hesitated. "I think I may still have pictures of it, if you'd like to see them sometime."

I started to say no. Her face had opened up, though, for a second, just a sliver, and as I formed my predictable response, I could see it start to close again.

I adjusted accordingly. "That would be nice."

She blinked. And then she smiled. A bigger, more genuine smile than before. "I'll bring down some albums sometime. I should have them in the attic. We could go through them together."

"I'd like that," I said.

When I left the house, it was much earlier than when I normally met Nick, but I couldn't wait, couldn't sit around until the usual time. So I decided to surprise him at his house. New chapter, I thought. It was right to start it off somewhere else. Somewhere fresh.

It was a long walk, and I took it slow. Walked carefully along the uneven sidewalk, the parts that were cracked and crumbled. Everything was green now; even the trees that had been stubbornly denying the presence of spring were displaying new growth. Anna might've written a poem about these trees,

I thought. And though I felt a pang, there was also a certain pleasure in thinking that I had, for a second, seen the world through her eyes.

I knew roughly where Nick's house was, but I'd had to look up his exact address in the phone book. It turned out he lived in a tall, slim gray house. The windows had deep sills and tidy white shutters. There was a tall tree a few yards to one side of it that practically begged for a tree house to be built on its long, sturdy branches. Tulips were planted along the edges of the house, their heavy heads bowing their stems.

I paused halfway down the front path, steeling myself to go knock on the door. I hoped Nick would be the one to answer. That he'd open the door and smile at me like he knew precisely why I was there and what I wanted to say.

I looked down at my shirt, belatedly concerned I might have spilled something on myself during breakfast.

No crumbs, no juice.

I was buying time, I thought. I needed to move forward.

I started to look back up toward the front door. In the process, something caught the corner of my eye, something small by the tulips at the side of the house.

Something small and white with a light sheen.

I left the path and walked over to the white speck, bent over to inspect it more closely.

It was a button. A pearl button.

And through its center was a single piece of thread. Purple thread.

Anna.

Anna, here. Here at Nick's house.

And suddenly all I knew was that I knew nothing. Nothing at all.

I was running even before I knew my feet had begun to move. Running with no coherent thoughts, just one long, loud scream inside my brain. And no matter how fast I ran, I could not escape it.

SIXTY

ANNA.
   Nick.
   Anna and Nick.
   Anna's button.
   Nick's house.
   Anna's button at Nick's house.
   Nick was the boy. Nick was the destination.
   Nick was a *liar*.

I thought I was completely alone. I thought if
*   anyone found out about him and me they*
*   would despise me. That I'd be the one they'd*
*   blame.*
And then one day someone told me they knew—
*   a friend of his, another guy on the team.*
*   I braced myself for him to call me a slut, a*
*   whore, but instead he said he wanted to try to*
*   help me.*
And he had an idea for how.

SIXTY-ONE

WHEN MY MOM KNOCKED ON my door the next morning, I pulled my blankets tighter around me.

"Sweetheart," she called from the other side. "You have to go to school. You can't stay in your room all day. If you're sick, we should take you to the doctor, but you can't just stay in there."

I could hear her leaning against the door and imagined her with her hand cupped to the door, listening for signs of life.

"I don't need a doctor," I said.

"Then you need to either tell me what's wrong or you need to go to school."

"I'm getting up," I said. "I'm getting dressed, okay?" And I slowly made myself throw back the blankets and stand up. Because I really didn't want to talk to her. Didn't want to talk to anyone except Lily, who I'd left several long rambling messages about buttons and lying and how she needed to tell me what happened and how I knew everything. She hadn't returned any of my calls.

I got dressed. And I walked to school so I wouldn't have to deal with talking to Sarah on the bus. I ate my lunch in the bathroom and moved between classes like a ninja, avoiding anyone who might try to interact with me, including the cheer-leaders handing out flyers about the big basketball game.

I did a good job avoiding people. Maybe I wasn't a ninja, I thought; maybe I was a ghost—maybe I'd been wrong to think I'd been anything else all this time.

In English class, I sat right behind Tom—drawer of the macabre—and watched as he sketched a guy being cut in half with a machete. *If you are going to go apeshit, do it now,* I thought. *Grab your weapon from your bag and I'll tackle you so hard you won't have time to aim. Or maybe you'll shoot me and we'll both be done with all this.*

Nothing happened, of course. His backpack stayed on the floor next to him, probably filled with nothing more than me-chanical pencils and textbooks. He kept on drawing in his note-book, going over one area harder and harder until it was shiny and slick with graphite. He might not be violent, but he cer-tainly was angry.

And I envied him that. Anger seemed like such a nice clean emotion. I craved its purity, its lack of complication. All I wanted to be was angry. Just angry.

I wished I were one of Tom's samurai.

I wished I had a sword and honor and a code.

I wished I knew what the hell I should do.

Because I doubted Lily was going to call me back. And I had no idea how to talk to Nick about it, no idea what I wanted to ask him or accuse him of. All I knew was that he'd lied to me from the second he'd first talked to me in the hallway, telling me his sob sorry about Anna, the girl he'd always liked and never gotten up the nerve to talk to. And I'd believed him. I'd believed every word he'd said.

SIXTY-TWO

IT ONLY TOOK UNTIL WEDNESDAY evening before Sarah and my mom ganged up on me.

It wasn't clear who instigated the attack, which they both pretended was uncoordinated, but at six o'clock on the dot that evening, Sarah appeared at the front door, claiming we'd had plans for me to go over to her house for dinner. I told her this was very much not the case, only to have my mom, who'd started removing all the sharp knives from the utensil drawer the day before, emerge behind me and proceed to all but push me through the front door.

"Go have fun, sweetheart," she said. "It'll be good for you to get out of the house for a while—get some fresh air, hang out with your friend."

Her face was so hopeful, like she really believed this was what I needed. *This isn't something fresh air and friendship can fix,* I wanted to tell her. *If it was, I'd go over to Sarah's house every night. Eat mung beans and celery and let her mom tell me all about Pilates and the best colors for my complexion. But what I need right now is to be by myself.*

That was too much to try to get out, though; too much like peeling my skin off in front of them both. Instead, I kept it simple. "No, it won't," I said. "Really, I just want to stay home. Please."

Mom hesitated, and I thought could see a crack in her resolve—a tiny hairline crack that I could leverage until it broke open.

"Please," I repeated.

She looked at me and took a step to the left, as if to allow me to retreat into the house.

Sarah shook her head. "Nope," she said. "Nice try. We're doing this. My mom even made a side dish that contains carbs especially in your honor. This is happening."

I looked at my mom beseechingly, but the rupture in her resolve had disappeared. "Sarah's right," she said. "You should go."

AFTER WE LEFT THE DRIVEWAY, Sarah nodded toward a paper bag on the floor of the car between us.

"There's a burger and fries in there for you if you want it," she said. "Well, there's two of each, actually—one for each of us. If you don't want yours, though, then I'm happy to eat all of it myself."

I stared at the bag, confused by this twist. "I thought we were eating at your house?"

"We are, but I figured you might be pissed about being hijacked from your self-imposed exile, so this is my peace offering. Plus, you know what my mom's food is like—I don't know if I have the strength to deal with you if you're both angry *and* hungry."

"I'm not angry," I said, slumping against the window,

watching the houses pass. They all looked the same to me; only the paint was different.

"No? What are you, then?"

What was I? It felt like the million-dollar question. I settled by giving a ten-cent answer, directed at the window. "I'm tired and I'm confused. All I want is to be left alone."

"You've *been* alone for the last three days. You've had three days of not talking to anyone—of ignoring me, freaking out your family. So we've officially tried that and it hasn't worked. Anyway, nobody gets to be left alone forever." She paused, and her tone softened. "Look, tell me what's wrong. If you talk to me, then we can skip dinner and do anything you like—go to a movie, get milk shakes, go to the basketball game—"

I flinched involuntarily. "I *don't* want to go to the basketball game."

In the reflection of the window, I could see her glance at me. "Is this about Nick?" she asked. "Did something happen?"

"Yes. No. I don't know." I closed my eyes. "Let's just have dinner."

"Fine," she said.

We drove in silence after that. I breathed in the smell of the hot, salty fries, trying to remember when I'd last eaten. Eating seemed like an activity that went with another version of me, one from a long time ago. I wanted to be that version of me again. I wanted to want to eat the burger and fries she'd brought me. Instead, I handed the bag to Sarah at the next stop sign.

I DON'T KNOW WHAT SARAH told her parents, but when we got to her house, her mom eyed me with pity, as if I were a doomed baby bird that had fallen out of its nest, and she took my jacket and placed it on the coatrack with such care that it could've been made from spiderwebs. Sarah's dad, on the other hand, practically had to be physically restrained from hugging me.

"She's not a hugger, Dad," Sarah told him. I nodded and looked away. I didn't know how to meet his gaze, didn't know how to fuse this man with the one who'd stood across from Mr. Matthews, brokenhearted but resolute.

The dinner, as advertised, did include a small bowl of pasta salad in addition to the other, more fiber- and protein-intensive dishes.

"You look nice," her mom said to me after we all sat down and began loading up our plates.

After three days of not eating and only one shower, this seemed doubtful, but I thanked her anyway. It was, I knew, a well-intentioned remark.

"Did you do something new with your hair?" she tried again. "It's shorter, maybe?"

"I did get a haircut," I told her. And I had. Three months earlier.

"That must be it," she said. "Well, it looks lovely." Then, to my relief, she turned to Sarah. "Which reminds me—you're going to need a trim soon. You're starting to get split ends."

"I like split ends," Sarah said without missing a beat. "Love them. Why do you think I haven't been cutting my hair?"

Sarah's mom sighed and poured herself some more water. A round of contemplative chewing commenced. I fiddled with the food on my plate, taking a few cursory bites before putting down my fork and focusing on the art on the wall in front of me. Someone in the family was clearly a huge fan of desolate farmscapes, preferably ones with sad-looking horses in the foreground.

Sarah's mom caught me looking at them. "My uncle painted those," she told me.

"They're very nice," I said politely.

"He used to have a ranch up north. He loved his horses very much."

Perhaps sensing that my enthusiasm for conversing about horses was limited, Sarah's dad intervened and addressed the table at large. "Speaking of horses, did you hear someone tried to burn down that old barn again? The one on the Kilmans' property?"

I hadn't heard, but it wasn't surprising. The Kilmans had both moved to an assisted-living facility several years earlier, and ever since, their property, which their children appeared to have no interest in either living in or selling, had been an easy target.

"Tried?" Sarah asked, raising an eyebrow. "How is it possible they didn't succeed? It's pure wood and it hasn't rained in ages. It should have gone up like kindling."

"I guess their neighbors saw it and were able to get the fire department out before it got too far."

"They should just tear it down," Sarah decreed with a wave of her fork. "It's falling apart anyway."

"Maybe it's sentimental for them," her mom said. "I think Mrs. Kilman's grandfather built it. Besides, they shouldn't have to tear it down just because our town has too many men who like to play with fire."

"Or women," Sarah said. "It could have been a woman, you know."

"In theory, but I bet it's a man. It usually is. There's something very male about fire. Fire and any kind of property damage, really. Woman don't do that kind of thing."

"That's sexist," Sarah said.

"It's not sexist. I'm saying it's a *good* thing."

"Good things can be sexist, Mom," Sarah informed her.

Her mom ignored her. "I mean, property damage is just so pointless. Burning things, smashing windows, breaking things, scrawling graffiti on walls—it's always men doing it."

"Not *always*," Sarah said.

"That's true," Sarah's dad chimed in. "Especially graffiti. Just back in the fall, a girl at your school did that."

Sarah frowned. "I don't remember hearing about that." She turned to me. "Do you?"

I shook my head.

"Well, I don't think she was quite caught in the act," Sarah's father said, "but the teacher who mentioned it was pretty sure." Then he paused and laughed. "I mean, usually there might be other interesting reasons why a girl would be in the boys' bathroom, but apparently she was alone and the ink was still wet when she came out."

Wet ink. Boys' bathroom. A clicking noise started in my brain.

"Wow," Sarah's mom said with a laugh. "I swear, I let you go to one PTA meeting in my stead and you get all the dish. So what happened—did the girl get off scot-free? Or did the teacher report her?"

"Report her?" He paused. "I don't know," he said, turning his attention back to his food, his shoulders suddenly hunched under his shirt. "That was the last— I don't know what happened after that."

The clicking continued, getting louder and louder.

Girl.

Ink. Bathroom.

"Jess?" I wasn't sure who said it or even if it was the first time. I blinked and found that I was frozen, my water glass halfway to my mouth. The three of them were staring at me, looking worried.

"Are you okay?" Sarah asked.

Slowly, deliberately, I put down my glass.

"I'm sorry," I said, pushing back from the table. "I don't feel good."

"Is there anything we can get you?" Sarah's mom asked. "Maybe some Advil? Or maybe you need to lie down?"

"No," I said. "I think I need to go home. I think I need to go home right now."

*Nick is a good guy and he likes you, he said. I'll
delete the photo. You can leave the rest
behind you.
It felt like a path. A way to get back into the light,
a way back to resembling the person I used
to be.
A way back to you.*

SIXTY-THREE

WHEN WE GOT BACK TO my house, I let Sarah explain to my parents why I was back early as I brushed past them, their faces anxious and concerned. I heard her suggest something about food poisoning or maybe a migraine as I jogged up the stairs. "I'm not sure," I heard her say. "She seemed fine, until suddenly she wasn't."

"There's migraine medicine in the bathroom if you need it, sweetheart," Mom called up the stairs. I paused and nodded down at her before I kept going. A migraine was as good an excuse as anything. Plus, a migraine meant being left alone.

When I reached the top of the stairs, I didn't head to the bathroom, didn't head for my room either. Instead, I went to Anna's room.

I pulled her backpack onto the bed and went through her notebooks until I found the right one.

I flipped through it until I came across what I was looking for. The notes between Anna and Lily.

I stared at Lily's handwriting. Particularly the phrase she'd written in all capitals: *SO CUTE.*

I looked at the letters carefully. I thought I was right, but it had been a while, and I needed to be sure. Sure that this wasn't another wrong direction. Another misinterpretation of the facts.

I tucked Anna's notebook under my arm.

I turned off the light.

Closed the door.

And opened the window.

Don't think about it, I told myself as I put one foot and then the other over the ledge. *This isn't what happened. This isn't where it happened.*

And so I let go.

And I hit the ground running.

AS I ENTERED THE SCHOOL's lit but empty hallway, I heard cheers from the gym, followed by the herdlike sound of feet pounding back and forth.

This time I didn't knock before entering the bathroom. This time I didn't care if I startled some guy into hastily buttoning his fly, didn't care if someone saw me enter.

It was empty, though, and that did make it easier, not having to deal with someone asking me questions, asking me to explain. Running here, I'd worried that Mrs. Hayes might have arranged to have another layer or two of paint applied after our conversation, rendering the graffiti invisible. Fortunately, that had not happened. It was still there, obvious when you knew where to look.

ANNA CUTTER IS A WHORE.

This time, it felt different. Seeing it. The whole room, in fact, felt different, although nothing had changed—the same musty air, the same red brick that this time I left along the side of the wall. It felt different because this time I didn't feel like I was alone. This time, in my mind, Mr. Matthews stood beside me, his arms folded. I saw him reach out and lightly touch the ink, still drying. And then I heard him say it again: *I don't think by the end the two of them were that close.*

I'd thought those words were nothing more than an attempt to make me feel better, but when I compared the writing to the letters in the notebook, I knew he'd been right. By the end, they weren't close at all.

Because now I knew who Anna had sent the second selfie to.

And I suspected that I also knew why someone might have two flasks, why there'd been no toxicology report.

Because, like the police chief said, parents protect their children.

So on my way out, I stooped down and picked up the brick.

*I'm buttoning my dress now. Dabbing on some
     lavender perfume. It's overkill, maybe, but it
     feels right somehow, treating this like a first
     date. A new beginning.*

*Lily should be arriving soon. She'll drop me off
     before she heads to the party at the quarry.*

*I wonder if I should tell her. Not tonight, but
     soon.*

*I don't know. Maybe it's too late for me to try to
     be a good friend.*

SIXTY-FOUR

THE BRICK WENT THROUGH THE car window more easily than I expected.

I braced myself for an alarm to start blaring, for someone to rush over and ask what the hell I was doing.

No alarm went off. There were no footsteps. Perhaps, for once, things would go my way.

I extracted the brick and set it down on the asphalt. Then, belatedly, I wrapped my sleeve around my hand as I reached back inside to unlock the door, grazing the glass. Blood began to seep from my knuckles.

I found the first flask almost immediately, nestled inside the glove box. The second proved much harder to locate. It took me a good few minutes before I managed to find it, shoved elbow-deep beneath the front seat. I set it beside the other one on the hood of the car. They were almost identical, distinguished only by a large red dot on the side of the one from beneath the seat. I uncapped them both and put them, one at a time, up to my nose. One of them smelled like alcohol. The other, the flask with the red dot, smelled like nothing at all. Mixed with a drink, there would have been no way for Anna to detect it.

Nick was her destination, I thought, but this happened before she got there.

I recapped both flasks, holding them tightly in the crook of my arm.

"What are you doing?"

I swung around, hoping it might be anyone other than who it sounded like. But my luck had run out. Because there he was. Charlie. Staring at his shattered car window.

I didn't really know what to say, so I looked around the parking lot. It was dark and quiet and we appeared to be very much alone.

"Aren't you supposed to be on the court?" I asked.

"I got fouled out," he said. "Asshole coach had it in for me. Then I checked my phone and found an alert about someone breaking into my car. Thought I should check it out. Definitely didn't expect to find you." His tone was curiously neutral, and I noticed that his posture was looser than normal, almost like he was swaying. He may not have been drunk, exactly, but he certainly wasn't sober.

"I thought you didn't drink before games."

"The game is over. Over for me, anyway. So I helped myself to some of Trent's water bottle o' vodka—made sitting on the bench a little easier." He took a step closer, and the hoodie he'd pulled over his basketball jersey swung open. Right in the center of his jersey was a huge number five. Another piece slotted in.

"Power forward, number five," I said. "PF5."

His eyebrows flicked up before he managed to pull them down again.

"I don't know what you're talking about," he said.

"It's how you entered your number in Anna's phone."

He frowned. "I thought her phone was broken. That's what my da—" Then he stopped short. But not short enough.

"That's what your dad told you?" I filled in.

He looked at me for a moment, then shrugged with exaggerated nonchalance. "It's a small town, and people talk, Jess. I'm sure I'm not the only person who heard about the dead girl's crushed phone."

The dead girl.

"You were sleeping with her," I said. "The least you could do is use her name."

He began to shake his head, but I cut him off.

"Don't deny it. I know you guys were together."

"How?" he asked. Not like he was admitting it—more like he was testing me, preparing to disprove my claim.

All the threads, all the things that got me here felt too convoluted, too tenuous. So I decided to make it simple, to say what I wished had been the truth.

"She had a diary. She wrote it all down. Everything."

I thought he might challenge me. Instead, to my surprise, he laughed. "You know, I wondered about that. She seemed like she might be the diary type."

"So you admit it, then?"

"Fine, we hooked up a couple times. She came on to me, and I went along with it. It was no big deal. I was planning on breaking it off anyway—wasn't worth the hassle."

It all came out so easily, his casting himself in the role of the beleaguered love interest, more than ready to pull the plug. I thought back to the bartender, of how he'd described Anna urging Lily not to tell anyone about her plans, her "date."

"If she was so into you, and you couldn't care less about her, then why was it a secret that Anna was going to see Nick that night? Why would it matter if you knew?" I felt myself tensing with anger. "Why would you even want to be with someone who so obviously didn't want to be with you?"

I must have hit home with that, because his face tightened, as though a screw had turned, rearranging his features so they were hard, ugly.

"Why? Because it wasn't *her* call," he said. "*She* didn't get to be the one to end things."

"Why not?"

"Because I made that very clear. Because I *told* her. But then she goes slinking around, trying to get together with someone else? Dragging my best friend into it?"

His best friend. "Brian?"

"Oh, Lily told me all about that. How Brian was trying to help pair off Nick and Anna. God, Lily actually thought the four of us would hang out or some shit. That's why I showed her the photo. So she could see what her friend was really like."

I blinked, confused. I'd assumed Lily had found out about him and Anna by accident. "Why did you do that? Why would you have wanted Lily to know you were having sex with Anna?"

He laughed at that, low and mean. "I didn't. I told her Anna had been embarrassing herself, throwing herself at me. That I hadn't wanted to say anything before, what with them being friends and all, but that the four of us hanging out wasn't going to happen. Said it seemed like a shame for Nick to get involved with someone like Anna. That maybe it would be good for him—Mr. Straight-Edge—to realize she wasn't as sweet as he thought. Lily agreed. She was so angry I think she would've have agreed with anything I said." He paused, his face tightening again. "Of course, it turned out she wanted everyone, or at least all the boys, to know right away."

I put my arm out to steady myself against the car, trying to put it all together.

"So you drugged Anna to humiliate her in front of Nick? Because you were jealous?"

"Jealous?" His face flushed, and his voice rose. "No, I wasn't jealous; I didn't care about her. She just needed to understand she couldn't get away with going behind my back, acting like none of it had happened."

It hurt to keep on going, but I knew this might be my only chance, so I pressed forward.

"So you were going to, what, just leave her at Nick's house? Drugged? That was the plan?"

"Pretty much. He was supposed to come out and find her all messed up. And if he tried to help her and people thought he had something to do with it, that wasn't exactly any skin off my back. Or if he decided to help himself instead, if he wasn't as nice as she thought—well, it didn't matter to me how it played out." He paused. "Of course, we'll never know *what* he would've done, because when we got to his house, his light was on but he wasn't picking up his phone."

Nick was already gone by then, I thought, already driving to the party. He just hadn't turned off his light.

Charlie shook his head. "I thought maybe I'd have to call it quits—head on to the party and leave her to sleep it off in the car. And then I saw her look at his window with the light on and then to the tree across from it. The window was way too far away for her to make it, but she was high as a kite, so maybe I nudged her a little. Told her she should climb the tree, try to get to his window. Told her she could make it if she wanted to. Told her it was time she took a bit of a risk, time she tried to fly. And she smiled at me like I'd found the perfect answer, and then she opened the car door."

He paused, deliberate, thoughtful—as if he was still working something out. "Lily could have stopped her, I think. Brian couldn't have reached her in time, but for Lily, sitting right next to her, it should've been easy. I even saw her start to reach for Anna's arm. But then she hesitated. And then we all just watched as she got out of the car, as she ran to the tree. Watched as she fell."

His voice took on almost a dreamy quality. "Her fingers did graze the sill, you know. For a moment, I thought she might make it—thought maybe she could fly after all." Then he shrugged, his voice returning to its normal state. "So there it is: the truth about that night. You're the only one who wanted it, and now you have it. And that's that."

That's that. Like there would be no consequences. Like he'd return to the gym and watch the rest of the game from the bench, and I'd simply go home and never say a word.

"No, I'm going to tell everyone," I said. "You drugged her, you told her to jump. You're responsible."

He shook his head like he felt sorry for me. "You really think the truth matters, don't you? But it doesn't. All that matters is what people believe happened, not what actually did. That's the beauty of it—me versus you? I'll always win."

"What are you talking about?"

"Everyone knows you're messed up. Even before Anna died, you creeped people out. And you've just kept picking at this, while everyone else wants to let the wound heal and move on."

"But the tox screen—"

"It could be passed off as an administrative mistake—a miscommunication, at most. Those happen all the time."

"But I'll tell them everything you told me—"

He shook his head. "And I'll tell them that I made the mistake of being nice to you once and you developed some big crush on me—got upset when I kept turning you down, started making up weird stories. Maybe I'll show them that picture you sent me."

"What?" I'd never sent him a picture. Only Anna had. . . . *Oh.* I shook my head. "It's not even me."

"That doesn't really matter," he said, like I was a small child denying some fundamental truth. "Nothing matters other than the fact that I have it and it looks just like you."

"No, but—" I forced myself to breathe, to calm down. Then I thought about the phone in the quarry and how he'd said he didn't have Lily's number because he'd gotten a new phone—one without his old contacts. So I gambled a little. "You couldn't. You lost your phone that night."

"That didn't matter. I'd backed it up weeks earlier. I mean, a picture like that? I'm not stupid. Come on, Jess. Think about it. Think about how it looks. The photo. You smashing my car window—making wild accusations? Claiming I drugged your sister? And what good would it do for anyone to hear the truth anyway? Hear about her slutting around with her friend's boyfriend? What good would it do your parents to think about her like that?"

"Shut up, Charlie. Just shut up."

The words were low and steady, and they did not come from my mouth.

I turned.

And there was Mona. Her face was pale and tense, and her eyes were fixed on Charlie.

"Mona." He paused and collected himself. "Hey, I don't know what you heard, but Jess is pretty confused—"

"Shut up," she repeated. "I heard more than enough."

She took a long deep breath and then let it out slowly. There was a ragged edge to it, like the air had cut into her throat as it left her body.

"It was you, wasn't it?" she asked, still staring at him.

And at first I didn't understand. Because if she'd listened, she knew what he'd done.

"I don't know what you're talking about," Charlie told her. Except there was something about the way he was looking at her that made me think that, unlike me, he did know.

"I should have realized a long time ago," she said. "But I thought it was wishful thinking to believe it might have been anyone other than Brian." She shook her head. "You offered me a ride, didn't you? Probably minutes after you handed me a drink. My boyfriend's best friend. I wanted you to like me. I wanted to go home. Of course I said yes."

Charlie's eyes flickered between me and Mona, like he was trying to assess how to turn this around. It was too late, though, because I saw it like a mirage forming in the air between us: Charlie carrying Mona onto the football field, her head swung back, her eyes at half-mast. His words to Brian played themselves back to me: *I barely saw you when you guys were together. You're better off without her.*

I felt sick, a sharp nausea building inside me, and my fingers loosened on the flasks.

Mona looked away from Charlie and turned to me. Her body was shaking but her voice remained steady.

"Come on, Jess," she said. "Let's go. We'll tell everyone everything—everything he did to Anna, everything he did to me. If it's all out there, then the police will have to do something this time. They'll have to test his flasks, find the drugs. There's two of us who know now, and we have proof. We can do this together."

Something deep inside me unknotted when she said that. I didn't trust myself to respond out loud, so I nodded and took a step toward her.

It was then that Charlie lunged at me, grasping at the flasks.

He was fast, and I was slow to react, only twisting to the side at the last minute. He collided with the left side of my body, knocking me to the asphalt so hard it forced a gasp from the back of my throat.

I managed to keep one of the flasks held tight against my chest, but the other one, the one with the red dot, the one he stored deep under the seat of his car, escaped from my grasp. I watch it bounce and then spin away.

At first, it looked like the cap had held tight, but then a puddle began to form underneath it.

Charlie reached over me to grab it, so I pulled back and elbowed him in the mouth. He reared away, clutching his mouth and screaming in pain, and I stretched and grabbed hold of the flask.

Mona was yelling, and I could see her pulling at Charlie. He was much bigger than her, though, and I knew she wouldn't be able to hold him for long. *We won't be able to prove it,* I thought in a panic. *They won't have to listen. Not if there's nothing for them to test, not if he gets to the flask and dumps it all out. He'll lie, and he'll get away with it. That's what he does.*

I had to save it.

So as he began to reach forward again, I kicked out at him to buy myself a few more seconds, to get him to rear back for just enough time.

Just enough time for me to tilt back my head, swing the flask back, and down every last drop.

Just enough time to make my body the proof, my body the vessel.

Lily texted me just now. The plans have changed—Charlie is insisting that he and Brian have a drink with us, but she'll drop me off at Nick's after. That's not what I want, but I can hold out a little longer—a short delay shouldn't change anything.

SIXTY-FIVE

SOMETIMES TIME MOVES LIKE A movie, a continuous shot. Other times, it moves like a slideshow, a series of distinct separate moments.

And after I drank from the flask, each moment was a freeze-frame, something I was watching from outside myself, sharper and more real than reality had ever been before.

Charlie, his face contorted and purple with rage, his foot raised to kick me in the ribs.

Mona's mouth open in a scream as she punched out at Charlie.

Charlie shoving her away.

The blow from Charlie's foot that connected with my face, the blood rushing into my mouth.

I watched it all, tasted the blood, felt the impact. It felt so very far away. Like it was receding into the distance, like it would all soon disappear. Like *I* would soon disappear. And I closed my eyes and curled up tight, readying myself to go.

It was okay, I thought, even as I began to slip away.

I'd been so tired, and maybe now I'd have a chance to rest.

And the last thing I registered, before everything went still, was that in the far distance there was a sound not unlike sirens.

*I'm starting to get nervous. Or maybe I'm
excited. I'm not sure.*

*All I really know is that in the morning, I'll be
another person again. Even if it doesn't work
out with Nick, the photo will be gone and I'll
be different again. I'll be out of the well.*

In the morning, it will all be in the past.

SIXTY-SIX

WE'RE LYING TOGETHER ON THE bottom bunk. Her hair is in my face, but I don't mind. Her hair is the same as mine, after all. The exact same.

"The apples were red this time," I tell her. "Red with flecks of yellow and green."

"And what were you reading?"

I like how she always asks, always acts like these details interest her. So little varies, there's not much to report otherwise.

I close my eyes, try to think back. It's a blank. "I don't remember. You were reading Shakespeare, though."

"Which play?"

I close my eyes again. This I can see. Her sitting across from me, the cover of what she was reading—a girl on a balcony, a boy waiting for her below. *Romeo and Juliet.*

"Next time you should make it a happier one, a comedy."

I smile and shake my head, my cheek pressing against the warm pillow. "I can't control it. If I could, then I'd dream something more interesting to begin with."

"Maybe you could control the details, though. If you tried. If you tried hard enough."

She sounds sad. I don't understand why.

"I'll try," I say, because I don't want her to sound sad anymore. "It may not work, but I'll try."

"Okay." She pauses. "Did you really have to drink all of it?"

I don't know what she means. "I didn't drink anything. It was just apples. Just books and apples and us all in the living room. Same as always."

"Jess."

"Same as always. I promise." I try to laugh, try to show her that it's okay. That she doesn't need to be sad anymore. The laugh doesn't come out right. It sounds more like a sob.

"Jess."

I shake my head. The pillow feels colder this time. "Come on, tell me about your dreams. They'll be better than mine."

"I can't. I'm sorry."

"Please," I say.

"No, I have to get up now." And she begins to sit up, to move away.

"I'll come with you." I start to move, to follow her, but she shakes her head.

"No. You have to stay."

"I don't want to stay here by myself. I want to come with you."

"I'm so sorry, Jess," she tells me, her voice so quiet that I have to hold my breath to hear her. "But I can't let you do that."

I know you probably won't have heard any of this. That you're probably fast asleep.
That's okay.
In the morning, I'll tell you everything.

SIXTY-SEVEN

EVEN WITHOUT OPENING MY EYES, I knew it was light outside. *I must have overslept,* I thought with a jolt. *I must have slept through my alarm.* I struggled to wake up fully, to get moving, but I found it surprisingly hard to surface. Things were off, somehow.

I tried to concentrate, to pinpoint what was different. The first thing I noticed was the throbbing pain in my hand. The second thing I noticed was that I had my arm wrapped around something large and warm. This was confusing, so without opening my eyes, I used my undamaged hand to poke it.

The thing jerked away. "Ow," it said. "That hurt."

I opened my eyes. "Sarah?"

"The one and only," she said. She sat up and stretched. "Oh, yes. God, it feels good to move. You were latched on like a damn spider monkey."

"Why are you sleeping in my bed?" I asked her. My voice came out rough and gravelly.

"We're not in your bed, Jess."

This made no sense, so I raised myself up on my elbows as best I could and glanced around.

Huh. She was right. This was most definitely not my bed, or even my bedroom.

"Where am I?"

"You're in the hospital. You've been coming in and out of consciousness for a while now. You talked to your parents an hour or two ago—well, mumbled to them a little. They went to get some coffee, now that you're out of the woods, but they'll be back soon."

"Okay," I said. I don't remember that, talking to them, but I believe her.

She tilted her head. "Do you remember anything? About what happened?"

I closed my eyes. There was a lot of gray, and my thoughts had a hard time coming together. I remembered asphalt and pain and . . . "Charlie? The flask?"

"Yeah," she said. "That's right."

More started to come back, yet . . . I stared at her. "I thought it was Mona there, not you."

"It was. She called me from the ambulance—had me call your parents. We all thought you were still in your room." She paused. "Migraine, my ass."

"I needed to check something," I said. "It was important." I paused. "Do you know if they tested me? Did they find the drugs?"

"Yeah, they did. Although from what I heard, they barely needed to—they'd never seen someone that far under before. They had to pump your stomach."

I considered this. Now that she mentioned it, my stomach and my throat both hurt as well. A lot.

"What about Charlie? Do they believe him?"

"Jess, half of the people attending the game came out to the parking lot after Mona started yelling—they all saw Charlie beating the crap out of you. His credibility is pretty shot right now."

"Okay," I said. "Okay." I paused. "Is Mona here?"

"No, she was for a while, but she needed to go home. Also . . ."

She stopped.

"What?"

"She came here in the ambulance with you. She told me that you were talking for a while on the way here. Do you remember that?"

I shook my head. It was all gray. Sarah was watching me closely. Too closely.

"What? What did I say?" I asked.

For a second Sarah paused, her face twisting a little. Then she shook her head.

"I don't know," she said. "Mona said she couldn't make out the words."

SIXTY-EIGHT

BEFORE SARAH LEFT, I ASKED her for a favor. I wasn't sure she'd be able to make it happen, yet two hours later there he was. Brian.

He stood in the doorway. His eyes went over me slowly, cataloging all my bruises, the lump that had formed on the side of my head. When his gaze settled on my arm, wrapped in gauze, only then did I shake my head.

"My arm is from when I smashed his window," I said.

"Everything else, though?"

"Everything else was him," I said. "And there's a lot more under the gown."

He looked surprised, and not in a good way.

"I wasn't offering to show you," I clarified. "I just wanted you to know."

He nodded. He took one last long look at me before he stepped into the room, pulled a chair up to the bed.

After he sat, he looked down at his hands. They were big hands, with long, calloused fingers and blunt fingernails. They were not in any way special, yet we both gazed at them for quite some time.

Then I took a deep breath.

"Did Nick know?" I asked. "About any of it?"

Brian shook his head. "No. I knew he liked her, though. And when Charlie told me about that photo Anna had sent him, laughed about how much she regretted it . . . I don't know. It didn't feel right. He'd told me the password for his phone once, so I thought it would be easy enough to get it away from him for a while and delete the photo. I thought if I did that, and paired off Anna and Nick, then Charlie would back off—that he wouldn't mess with her if she was with someone else on the team. That maybe he'd be pissed for a while, but he'd get over it and then everyone could just be cool again. It seemed like a good plan."

A good plan. In theory, perhaps it had been.

"Why didn't you stop it? When it started to go off the rails? When you saw that she was drugged?"

"I thought she'd taken the drugs herself," he said. "I was annoyed about that at the time, that she'd do that, when I was trying to do her a favor. Honestly, it didn't even occur to me that Charlie had anything to do with it. I mean, we practically grew up together. I thought . . . I knew he was an asshole, but I thought I knew what that meant."

"Why didn't you call the police, though? When she fell?"

Brian looked away. "I should've. I know that. I was in shock, I think, and so was Lily, but Charlie—he was so calm. He said we should take her back home, put her under her window. He said he'd call his dad, explain what happened. That his dad would take the investigation over as soon as he got back to town—make sure none of it came back to us."

"So you laid her out in our yard and then went to the party?"

I did not work hard to keep the incredulity and anger out of my voice.

"That's where people expected us to be," he said. "Charlie said that's what we needed to do. So we went." He paused and shook his head. "I know how it all sounds. It sounds crazy. It was crazy. But in a way, that made it easier—it felt so surreal, what had happened, what we'd done, that it was easy to start pretending that it had happened just the way everyone thought it had—her falling out her window."

Nick's description of Brian wandering around at the bottom of the quarry came back to me. How Charlie hadn't had Lily's phone number because he'd had to get a new phone. "You tossed his phone into the water at the quarry," I said.

He blinked, surprised. Then he nodded. "I pocketed it while we were on the way to Nick's house. But it turned out he'd changed the password. And when he began to freak out about where it was, I pretended to search for it. Figured water would destroy it."

The phone, yes. The photo, no. Not that it mattered. Not anymore. It was just another thing that hadn't worked out the way it was supposed to. And I couldn't let myself go down that path—the path of how things should have happened. There were too many branches, too many ways to think about how things could have gone, how Anna could have been saved. It was a labyrinth.

I leaned back against the pillow and closed my eyes.

"I'm so sorry," he said quietly. There was a long break, and then his voice got even quieter. "And Mona . . . I heard that he . . ."

I nodded without opening my eyes.

What he said next, he said in less than a whisper. "I asked

him to give her a ride home. Before I left the party, after our fight. I wanted to make sure she had a ride."

Then he began to sob, the sounds reverberating through his chest like they were going to tear him apart.

Someone else might have tried to comfort him, but I kept my eyes closed. I didn't have any room in me to try to take on his sorrow, his rage. He had kept the truth—the part he knew—hidden. Hadn't told me or anyone what had happened. He didn't deserve anything from me right now.

But I did believe him.

Believed that he was sorry.

Believed that he'd thought he'd known his best friend.

SIXTY-NINE

IN THE END, I TOLD my parents the truth.

Most of it.

I told them about Anna and Charlie. About how both Lily and Charlie had, in their own way, been angry with her, and how Charlie had drugged her. Told her to fly.

I told them about Nick too. That she was going to see him, that his house was where it happened. That he knew nothing about it, though, and I wanted it to stay that way if possible. Because I didn't know what you could do with that, knowing that someone died trying to get to you. Some things only hurt to learn about, and they don't change anything.

I didn't tell them about the bar, the birth control, or the photo. She wouldn't have wanted them to know any of that— and they didn't need to have what happened between her and Charlie spelled out in bold type or to know exactly how lost and trapped she'd felt. I didn't think it was like the box, hiding stuff they had a right to see, hiding it because I wanted to keep it for my own. This was different. This was something I was doing for them. And for Anna.

———

I'D THOUGHT FINDING OUT WHO Anna was going to see that night, finding out what happened, would give me a way to understand what had happened between the two of us—how a chasm had opened without my realizing it. Instead, what I found was Charlie and Nick. Charlie, who only saw her as someone to control—and Nick, who'd wanted to know her but never really had the chance.

She'd put on the dress, put on the perfume, for Nick. The birth control had been for Charlie. And her poem . . . I didn't know. Maybe she'd thought she loved Charlie at one point, or maybe it had simply been a poem about no one in particular—just some pretty words on a page.

All I knew for certain was that there should've been a different ending to that night. And now I knew how it actually should've gone.

I could imagine it; I could see it clearly:

Anna in her purple dress, all the buttons attached, getting out of the car—arriving exactly when Nick was expecting Brian to show up. She is clear-eyed and calm. She stands outside Nick's house and looks up, up to his window. She finds a stone and throws it gently. And then she waits. Waits beneath his window, sure that soon he'll open it and smile down at her, surprised but happy. That he'll mouth for her to wait right there, that he'll be right down.

That was how I pictured it. That was how it would have been.

SEVENTY

AT SCHOOL, MANY DIFFERENT STORIES circulated. Some of the ones about what happened in the parking lot were so far off they were almost funny—like the one where Charlie pulled a gun on me and Mona swooped in like an avenging angel and karate-chopped him on the neck. The ones about what happened the night Anna died tended to be more somber and murky. Most of them centered on Charlie, although I did hear one that mentioned Lily's role in it all, including how she'd finally broken down when the police called and confirmed everything.

Even that version didn't include the aftermath, how after Lily talked to the police she'd fallen apart completely—crying and shaking until her dad checked her into some kind of treatment center in Tampa. She'd texted me from there, a long, rambling text alternating between asking for my forgiveness and telling me that it wasn't really her fault, that she hadn't understood what was happening. I'd deleted the text and blocked her number.

There were so many stories about what had happened, but so far I hadn't heard Nick mentioned in any of them. I really hoped it could stay that way.

Nick.

I'd been avoiding him. I knew I needed to talk to him, needed to say something about why I wasn't showing up for our runs anymore, why we'd never go on that date. I knew I couldn't avoid him forever—in a school of three hundred students that simply wasn't possible—and I kept telling myself I was holding off on talking to him until I could get it right. Deep down, though, I knew I was just a coward.

When it finally happened, I was in the stairwell, late for practice. I turned the corner to go down the final flight and saw Nick heading up toward me. My first impulse was to run right back up, to stay squarely in the flight end of the continuum. It took everything I had to make myself stay put.

When he saw me, he slowed down but kept on coming until he was two steps below me.

"Hey," he said.

"Hey," I replied. It was a start.

"I tried to visit you at the hospital," he said. "I guess you were sleeping, though."

I nodded, despite knowing that in all likelihood I'd been awake. After Brian left, I'd told the nurse not to let anyone but family in. There wasn't anyone else I could handle seeing, including—especially—him.

"How are you?" he asked.

"I'm okay," I said. White lies, they serve a purpose sometimes.

"Okay, good." He stood there looking at me. "I think you've been avoiding me," he said. "You haven't really been subtle about it. And I get that all the stuff with Charlie must be a huge amount to process, but you don't seem to be avoiding other people, only me. And I'd really like to know why."

He looked at me with serious eyes.

I said nothing. I didn't know how to begin.

"We can just be friends, if that's what you want," he said. "There's no pressure to be anything else, if that's not something you want to deal with at the moment."

"Is that what you want? To be just friends?" I shouldn't have asked that; it wasn't fair given what I'd already decided, but selfishly I wanted to hear the answer.

"No," he said. "It's not."

For a second, my heart held still, trapped in an alternate world in which that made all the difference. A world in which I didn't know that he'd already been spoken for—that I was nothing more than an accidental interloper in a relationship that should have been, would have been, Anna's. A world in which I could look at his face without imagining her broken body lying beneath his window. And then my heart started again, started beating back in the real world.

"We can't be anything," I said. "I'm sorry."

He frowned. "Why not?"

I struggled to come up with a version I could tell him. So much was off-limits. "You liked Anna," I said. "I thought it didn't matter, but I was wrong."

"Why does that matter?" he asked. "I did like Anna, I did, but I didn't even know her that well."

"I think she's what connected us," I said. "I think she's the reason you talked to me in the first place."

"That's not true," he said.

"Okay, then tell me you would've stopped in the hallway no matter who I was," I said. "Tell me it didn't matter for one moment that I have her face. Tell me you never once thought I was your second chance."

His body tensed, like he was wrestling with the request; then he sagged against the banister. "You guys were twins. Of course I noticed. Of course I wanted . . ." He shook his head. "That doesn't mean I don't like you, doesn't mean that what I feel for you doesn't count."

You're not wrong, I thought. *But you're not right either. Because I don't think you would ever have fallen for me if you hadn't already fallen for her.*

"I'm sorry," I said.

"Me too," he said. "I think we could've been kind of amazing."

He looked at me and I saw it: all the time we'd had together, all the future moments we could share. *Maybe I could push it all down,* I thought. *Maybe he'd never find out that he was the one she was going to see. Maybe I could make myself believe it doesn't matter.*

But then I saw Anna, and how she glowed that night, thinking of him. How she smiled like she had a secret. A good one. Finally, a good one.

So I said nothing.

And when he pushed himself off the banister and kept on going up the stairs, I didn't call out and stop him, didn't reach for his arm as he brushed past.

I just watched him go.

SEVENTY-ONE

A FEW DAYS LATER, I went to Anna's room and retrieved her poems from the bookcase. I sat on her bed and started reading through them again.

Last time, I'd read them quickly, searching for clues. Hadn't balanced each word on my tongue, hadn't paid attention to how they fit together to tell a story, to make a larger image. How the poem about a flower wasn't just about a flower but about how she'd seen the flower, about her memory of it and what it had meant to her. Mr. Matthews might have been worried about her, might have liked her as a person, but in terms of her writing I suspected he'd simply been stating the truth: she was becoming a wonderful writer, and he was so glad to have her in his class.

The love poem I left to the side, unsure whether I could cope with reading through it again, knowing that I might now see Charlie in every line.

I'd gone through most of the stack before I heard a soft knock on the side of the door, and then Mom slowly pushed it open.

"Hey," she said. "I wanted to let you know we'll be eating in about half an hour."

"Thanks," I said. "I'll come down and help set the table in a few minutes."

"That would be great." Her gaze settled on the pile of poems beside me. "What are you reading?"

"Poems," I said. "Of Anna's."

"Can I look?" she asked. The question came out casual, nonchalant, but there were traces of something else there, something echoed in the creases that had appeared at the corner of her eyes and her mouth.

I hesitated briefly, not wanting to let them go. Then I remembered the box, and I nodded.

She sat down beside me. I watched her read through two of the nature ones. Saw her smile and occasionally silently mouth some of the phrases. I had expected to feel a sense of loss watching her absorb Anna's words, but it wasn't like that. It made me feel lighter inside, like there was less pressure.

Still, when she picked up the love poem, I felt myself start to reach forward, wanting to take it from her. I stopped myself, though. *It's okay.* I thought. *You don't know that it's about him.*

She read the poem twice. I could tell by the way her eyes tracked down the page.

"It's lovely," she said. Her hand held it lightly, as if that piece of paper were more fragile than the others.

"I guess. It's a little sappy." It was hard watching her hold it, and I wanted her to move on from it, to put it back down, so my words were sharper than I intended.

She furrowed her brow and looked at me quizzically.

"Sappy?"

I shrugged. "You know what I mean. Just a generic love poem."

She shook her head slowly. "Sweetheart—I don't think it's

a love poem." She paused. "Or, I suppose it is a love poem, in a sense, but not a romantic one."

It sounded like a riddle. "I don't know what you mean."

She got up from the bed and flattened out the page for me.

"Read it again," she said. "Take your time. Take as much time as you need." And then she left the room, closing the door behind her, the latch clicking shut.

I picked up the poem, steeling myself for the possibility of seeing Charlie through Anna's eyes while also knowing how it all ended.

I read through the poem slowly, hesitantly, waiting for the trapdoor to open underneath me.

I read it again.

And again.

It took a while for me to understand.

Because I had assumed it was about a boy. Because that fit with what I was searching for. Because it fit with the dress.

But I had been wrong. Just like I had been wrong about so many things.

Because it wasn't about Charlie. Or even Nick. Wasn't about a boy at all.

It was about me.

It was about us.

> *I want to tell you everything*
> *Want to talk deep through the night—*
> *Sometimes I feel you already know*
> *All the things I hold inside.*
>
> *It's hard being away from you*
> *And it's hard being too close by*

You want so much, you are so sure—
I feel so far behind.

And I can't forget you lying there
Stretched out beneath the sky—
How my heart only started to beat again
When you opened up your eyes.

SEVENTY-TWO

SARAH AND I HAVE STARTED running together. We do shorter runs than Nick and I did, and we take a different path. Sometimes she gets sick of maintaining a steady pace and she sprints off like a jackrabbit and then waits for me to catch up. I tell her it's good practice for when she's in cross-country again. Or, rather, when we do cross-country together in the fall. I think I'm going to be good at it. I think I'm going to be better than her. I haven't mentioned that to her. Not yet.

A couple of times, Mona has run with us. When she does, Sarah sucks it up and runs alongside us the whole way.

We don't talk much on these runs, even when it's the three of us. We don't talk about Charlie, or that night. Don't talk about all the other drugs the police found when they searched his room, or what we'll say when we're called up to testify against him. Don't talk about how his father resigned, the official word being that he wanted to "spend more time with his family" and the unofficial word being that he was forced to resign after it came out that he hadn't submitted Anna's samples for testing, that he'd lied to cover up for his son. Maybe there will be a time when we'll want to talk about some of it. Maybe there won't.

It's different, but we don't talk about Brian either. Don't talk about how he and Mona sit across from each other at lunch sometimes, at the far edge of the cafeteria. Sarah and I try not to pay too much attention to the two of them together, try not to notice how most of the time they don't talk and they definitely don't touch. It's private, whatever there is between the two of them, and delicate. But it looks a little like hope, like a new beginning.

I think Anna would have liked that.

I think she'd have liked how Mom brought down a photo album from the attic the other day, and we looked through it together, looked at old pictures of her. At the photo of her on the homecoming court, her hair stiff with hair spray, and a huge, huge smile on her face. Anna's smile. I'm not sure why I never noticed that before.

Sometimes I tell Anna about these things—all the things she's missing. All the things I think she'd want to know about.

Sometimes I almost think she can hear me.

Sometimes I almost think I can hear her respond.

ACKNOWLEDGMENTS

For a brief period of time, I harbored pleasant delusions about the kind of writer I'd be, picturing myself as the confident yet mellow sort who'd calmly go through the process without much fuss. Instead, it turns out that I'm a grumpy and angsty writer—not mellow at all, and far from a joy to be around. So, many thanks to everyone who put up with me while I wrote this book. I can't promise I'll be any better in the future, but I'll try.

I would also like to thank the coffee shops and bakeries of Chicago, where I spent many hours typing away, fueled by tea, cookies, and the occasional iced coffee. Bourgeois Pig, The Perfect Cup, La Colombe, The Grind, and Floriole, you guys all really know what you're doing.

Moving on to my family, who are even better than sugar or caffeine (and I do not say that lightly). My parents are amazingly supportive and kind and just delightful through and through, and my sister is brilliant and wonderful and a huge source of inspiration. Mom, Dad, and Emma: I love the three of you so very, very much. Thank you for reading various drafts of this book, sometimes on ridiculously short notice, and for being such fantastic people I'm so proud to be related to.

Many thanks also to my nonfamilial beta readers and fellow writers, Jennifer Solheim and Stephanie Scott. You read my book when it was still figuring itself out, and you gave me such helpful feedback—I will appreciate that forever. Thanks as well to my other writer friends who provided great moral support throughout the process: Kristin Hamley, Jen Minarik, Rachel Leon, and Claudine Guertin.

I also owe a huge debt of gratitude to my teachers at Story-Studio: Rebecca Makkai, Molly Backes, and Abby Geni. You are all incredible teachers and you each, in your own way, inspired me to keep chugging away at this thing.

Enormous thanks to my agent, Bridget Smith. You are the best. Your taste is impeccable, your notes are excellent, and you write wonderfully soothing responses to panicked emails. I could not ask for a better agent.

To my editor, Wendy Loggia: I am still amazed and terrified by the potential you saw in this book and the trust you placed in me to get it where it needed to be. Thank you so much.

Kevin, you read the first chapter when those few pages were all that existed, and you said you thought it could be—should be—a novel. It was the perfect thing to say. You are, and will always be, my favorite husband, my favorite reader, and my favorite person.

ABOUT THE AUTHOR

Amelia Brunskill was born under sunny Australian skies but now lives in Chicago with her husband and her dog, Max the corgi. She is a librarian who drinks excessive amounts of tea and does not always return her books on time. *The Window* is her first novel.